HOT ROCKS

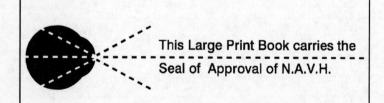

This Large Print Book carries the
Seal of Approval of N.A.V.H.

BETH BOWMAN, PRIVATE INVESTIGATOR

HOT ROCKS

RANDY RAWLS

THORNDIKE PRESS
A part of Gale, Cengage Learning

Detroit • New York • San Francisco • New Haven, Conn • Waterville, Maine • London

GALE
CENGAGE Learning®

LIBRARY OF CONGRESS CATALOGING-IN-PUBLICATION DATA

Rawls, Randy, 1938–
  Hot rocks : Beth Bowman, P.I. / by Randy Rawls.
    pages ; cm. — (Thorndike Press large print mystery)
    ISBN 978-1-4104-5651-9 (hardcover) — ISBN 1-4104-5651-X (hardcover) 1.
Private investigators—Florida—Fiction. 2. Diamonds—Fiction. 3.
Murder—Investigation—Fiction. 4. Large type books. I. Title.
PS3618.A967H68 2013
813'.6—dc23   2012046599

Published in 2013 by arrangement with Midnight Ink, an imprint of
Llewellyn Publications, Woodbury, MN 55125-2989 USA.

Hot Rocks is dedicated to my daughter,
Theresa (Tracy) Eilers, and my son,
David Rawls. I love you guys.
And to my honey, Ronnie Bender.

ACKNOWLEDGMENTS

When I decided to write a female PI story, I was sure I wanted to write a story featuring a female who was a PI, not a male PI in a skirt. And I didn't want to write a female who had to have a man to pull her through difficulties. I told the people in my two critique groups of my wishes, and the five women involved assured me they would keep me on track. They did, scuffing me up when necessary. I acknowledge those women: Ann Meier, Gregg Brickman, Stephanie Levine, Sylvia Dickey Smith, and Vicki Landis. They did all they could to make Beth Bowman a woman first and a crime-solver second. If at any time Beth appears otherwise, the fault is mine for not listening closely enough.

And, of course, Terri Bischoff, who had faith in me and accepted *Hot Rocks* for Midnight Ink.

ONE

I had no problem spotting Hector Garcia as he left the office building on University Drive in Coral Springs. Six-two, two-twenty, navy suit with red and white club tie, gray hair in a buzz cut, carrying a tan, stressed-leather briefcase. Maria Garcia had described her husband right down to his black wingtips. I didn't need the snapshot she provided, but I checked it anyway. As I watched the man walk to his red Lexus, I mentally congratulated her. Since she had also given me a rundown on his car, including the license number, I had attached a GPS transmitter inside his right rear wheel well.

In times gone by, conducting surveillance with a full team was problem enough. Doing it alone often led to losing the subject or being compromised, especially in a vehicular situation. However, modern technology with its miniaturizations solved that.

With the transmitter in place and my receiver beeping peacefully on the seat beside me, Mr. Garcia was mine to pursue until I tired of the game. His wife had paid me a nice advance to catch him with his latest dalliance, therefore, I did not intend to let him out of my sight. According to her, his bank account was fat enough to accommodate my fees. Moreover, she intended to empty it during the divorce.

I sat behind the wheel of my white Toyota Camry and watched him cross the parking lot. I picked the Camry because it was the most common car in the most common color on South Florida streets — or so it seemed. Everywhere I looked, a look-alike cruised past. Plus, it was a good vehicle for a single woman — not likely to draw the attention of carjackers.

Garcia put his briefcase in the trunk, got into his car, and backed out. The game was on.

I followed, careful to keep several cars behind him as we headed north on University. He drove at a reasonable speed, which made him slower than most of the traffic. South Florida drivers are not known for their patience. I sat in the middle lane, knowing I could squeeze left or right should he decide to turn. Another advantage of

10

conducting surveillance in South Florida is the layout of the major streets. North-south and east-west. Very few diagonals. And traffic lights galore. Even if he spotted me, he was unlikely to leave me behind. If he tried, he'd end up broadsided in an intersection. Even emergency vehicles with lights blazing and sirens blasting treated intersections with respect, often coming almost to a full stop before entering.

He took a right turn and worked his way to Route 441, then continued north into Coral Lakes. I had to admire his road manners. He even knew what that little lever on his steering column was for — something most ignored. Not the windshield wiper, the turn signal.

He blinked a right turn, then pulled into the entryway of Hotel Severn, a nice upscale place known for its live bands on Friday nights and piano bar on other nights. It was a place where older singles hung out to make friends — or whatever.

I followed him in, then drove past as he pulled into a parking space. Just my luck: the lot was almost full. I had to go around the end of the building before I spotted an empty slot. Scrambling out of my car, I yanked a tam out of my purse and slid it over my red hair. While the cap might stand out, I'd rather have it remembered than my face. I didn't have to wear the tam again. I was stuck with the face.

I rushed through the closest doorway, hoping to see Garcia in the hallway or lobby. I spotted him, entering through the front, his briefcase in his right hand. Relief flooded in that I hadn't lost him. I guessed that retrieving the case from the trunk had slowed him, making it possible for me to gain time.

I hoofed it down the hall, then turned toward the elevators, figuring that had to be his eventual destination. Garcia continued his leisurely pace across the lobby in the same direction. My hope that he'd stop at the front desk evaporated. I needed to get in front of him. I stepped it up, as if I had some place to be. I made it to the elevator bank first and punched the *Up* button.

As he got close enough that I could be sure of his destination, I opened my purse and began to fumble through the clutter, keeping my head down.

I sensed him near me, then the elevator dinged, and the door slid open. He stepped inside. I followed. He pushed the seven button, then glanced at me. "What floor?" he asked.

"Eight," I said, continuing to look in my

purse. I hoped he'd think I couldn't find my room card. There were no other passengers.

We reached the seventh floor. He stepped out and turned left.

I held the door-open button and watched his progress.

He walked straight to 727 and stopped. With no hesitation, he knocked on the door. His glances left and right were unlikely to spot me or anyone else interested in him.

There must be some prize waiting in that room, I thought. The way he acted led me to believe he'd done this many times before. That might mean I could document his visits with the hotel staff, more facts for my report.

The door opened a couple of inches then swung wide. I couldn't see inside but guessed his honey's hand was on the knob. If I could verify there was a woman waiting for him, I'd have enough for my first day's work. It was the first thing Ms. Garcia would ask. And, if I could get a name, that would be even better.

As Garcia entered the room, I left the elevator and traced his steps, stopping along the wall beside 727. I resumed my fumble-in-purse routine, noticing that the door had not clicked closed. I squinted in concentration, hoping to hear some terms of endearment that included names.

"You sonofabitch, I ought to kill you for that."

The venom-filled words came from inside the room, jolting me. Not at all what I expected. There was a smacking sound, followed by "You're dead, you bastard." Same voice.

Uh-oh, I thought. My meal ticket and his honey were in the midst of a nasty disagreement, and it sounded like he was about to beat me out of my fee. Ms. Garcia wouldn't need me if he ended up on the end of murder charges. If I hoped to collect, I had to keep him from killing her. I pushed on the door, it swung open, and I took two quick steps.

I heard a shuffle, then something slammed into the back of my head. A bright flash of stars filled the room as I stumbled forward. My knees buckled and I fell. *Ambush. I've been ambushed like the rawest rookie,* I thought before the floor smacked me in the face.

TWO

I opened my eyes, then closed them fast against the brilliance. What happened to the room? I didn't remember that much brightness. With great care, I slitted my lids, allowing just enough light to look around. What I saw was not reassuring.

A man lay in a pool of blood a few feet away, and it didn't look like he'd move any time before a doctor pronounced him dead. My instincts told me to check his carotid artery. I pushed up, then settled back. My head pounded with pain. The back of it felt like it was ripping off. After a moment I tried again, and this time made it to my knees. I crawled to the body. Even though I could see the answer in his destroyed face, I checked for a pulse. There was none. But I saw more — his clothes, his size, his haircut. It was Garcia. We had both walked into an ambush. I hung my head. I should have sensed it and protected him.

15

I pulled myself up, using a nearby chair, shuffled to the phone, and dialed 9 for an outside line, then 9-1-1.

"Emergency operator."

As succinctly as I could, I explained the situation. She countered by telling me assistance was on the way. I settled onto a love seat and closed my eyes, wishing the day could start all over again.

A few minutes later, police and paramedics filled the room, closely followed by two homicide detectives. The detectives took control and sealed the area while the EMTs checked the body. Their conclusion appeared to be the same as mine.

"How 'bout you, ma'am?" asked one of the medics. "Are you okay?"

"Other than a pounding headache, I suppose so. Someone slugged me from behind. Do you have any aspirin?"

"Let me take a look. My name's Tommy. Sit here." He pointed toward a straight-backed chair at a small table.

With effort, I rose and followed his instructions. After I plopped onto the chair of his choice, he fingered his way through my hair.

"I've seen worse, but you need to get it checked. I recommend you go to the hospital. We can transport you."

"Hold on there. Not so fast," the shorter of the detectives said. "We have a homicide scene here, and you want to carry off a witness." He turned his attention to me. "Are you Ms. Bowman, the lady who called it in?"

"Yes."

"And I understand you're a private investigator?"

"Yes. I told the 9-1-1 operator that."

"Just what we need. A damn skirt PI," the second detective said. "Must be my lucky day."

"I'm Detective Bannon," number one said. "My partner is Detective Sargent. Please excuse his manners — or lack thereof. What happened here?"

I rubbed my eyes, willing away the pain. Didn't work. "I was hired to follow the man on the floor. As you can see, it did not end well."

"I'm sure he'd say that's an understatement . . . if he could talk. But that doesn't tell me what happened."

"Obvious, ain't it?" Sargent said. "She followed him all right. Tracked him to this room, then killed him."

"Let's not jump to conclusions, Major," Bannon said. "But we do need more info."

"This your gun?" Sargent said, showing a

17

plastic evidence bag holding a small revolver. "Looks like something a skirt PI would carry."

I glanced at it. "No. Mine's in my purse. That's where I keep it."

Sargent grinned. "Nope. If that's your fancy purse laying over there, no gun in it. Wanna try again?" He held the bag out.

I took a closer look. "I don't know. Mine is similar. Where'd you find it?"

"Oh, just laying on the floor. Maybe like you dropped it after you hit yourself in the head."

"I didn't," I said.

"Really?" Sargent said, a smirk taking over his face. "These your credentials?" He held out a small case with BB engraved in the leather.

"Yeah, I suppose."

He opened it. "Under the PI license, there's a permit to carry. Says someone named Elizabeth A. Bowman registered a Beretta Tomcat .32 automatic. Looks like that's what we have in this bag. What would you call it?"

"I wouldn't call it anything until I examined it."

"Ms. Bowman," Bannon said, waving Sargent off. "I still need to know what happened here."

"I told you."

"No, you didn't," he said. "Other than a general comment that you were hired to follow the victim, I know nothing about the circumstances." He hesitated and ran the back of his fingers along his cheek. "And we have a weapon that could be yours. It appears to have been fired recently."

"Sorry. My head is pounding. Bear with me a moment, and I'll tell you everything I know. First, though, I'm going to get off this hard chair." I stood and, on unsteady legs, returned to the love seat.

Bannon sat on the side of the bed, and Sargent pulled the straight-backed chair out, spun it around, and sat backwards on it. Both stared at me.

I took the opportunity to gather my thoughts and try to force the pain down. I stared around the room, taking my first good look at it. Typical mid-range hotel room. Queen-sized bed, TV cabinet with drawers, a wardrobe, pint-sized refrigerator, microwave, and a love seat — the one I occupied. And the table with the chair I'd sat on. The accommodations probably weren't up to having a phone in the bathroom, but they weren't bad.

"Ms. Bowman. We're waiting," Bannon said.

19

I took a deep breath. "I was hired by his wife," I nodded toward the body, "because she suspected him of messing around on her. I followed him to this room. After he came in, I listened at the door. He'd left it open a bit. Next thing, I heard someone yell, threatening to kill somebody. I pushed the door open, stepped in, and that's the last I remember. From the way my head feels, someone must have slugged me. When I woke up, I saw the man on the floor and called 9-1-1."

"Did you hear males, females, or both?" Bannon asked.

I thought about it. "There was only one voice. Don't know about the sex. Could have been a man with a high-pitched voice or a woman with a low one. It was pretty neutral, but loud."

"What else?"

"That's it. That's all I remember."

"What do you mean, that's it?" Sargent said. "Who was in here with the victim? You came charging in. Who'd you see? Where did he or she go?"

"I . . . I don't know. When I came in, I saw no one, or no one that I remember. Then the lights went out."

"Oh yeah," Sargent said. "That's weak, lady, damn weak."

All I could do was stare at him. It had seemed a simple case — follow a husband, get proof he was boinking his honey, report to his wife, and be ready to testify in court, if necessary. Piece of cake. I'd had tougher cases that didn't end with someone smashing me on the head. Yeah, subjects had accosted me before, but it was usually a bluff. A couple of times when it wasn't, a well-placed knee resolved the situation.

Men tended to lose interest after I drove their gonads back to where they came from. And the tough broads were a lot less so after the same kind of treatment. Now I had a nasty cop tying me into a murder.

I glanced at the pistol that Sargent still held. If it was the murder weapon and registered to me, someone took it from my purse after I was out. Then he used it to kill Garcia and left it on the floor to be found. That same someone had played me for a patsy, had set me up to take the fall. Cozy, very cozy. Not a pleasant thought, not a situation I would choose to be in.

Tommy, the EMT, gave me a worried look. "Ma'am, I really think you should go to the hospital. We're going to have to roll pretty soon. The guy on the floor belongs to the medical examiner. Nothing we can do for him."

"No, I'm okay," I said. "Just give me some aspirin. I'll be fine."

Tommy and his partner exchanged looks. Tommy leaned toward me and whispered as he fingered my hair again, "If we take you to the hospital, it'll get you out of here. That cop's out to trip you up."

I considered what he said, recognizing the sense it made. Clearly, Sargent had his own agenda, and tagging me was high on it. Garcia dead, a gun on the floor that could be mine, and me alone in the room. Didn't take a Mensa candidate to figure the detectives would have a primary interest in me. "Okay, let's go for a ride," I said.

Tommy looked relieved. "Good decision. Can't ever tell about these things." He stood. "We're transporting her to the hospital. That knock on her head needs attention."

Bannon frowned but didn't object.

Sargent grinned, a nasty sight. "Enjoy it while you can, Ms. Bowman. You'll see me again soon. Might even have some news for you." He shook the evidence bag.

THREE

The EMTs loaded me onto a stretcher and wheeled me into the ambulance, Tommy hovering alongside all the while. His partner took the wheel, and we lurched into the street with the siren blasting.

Tommy had fitted me with a collar, which made turning my head difficult. The throbbing persisted, but I wanted to believe it felt better.

"I appreciate your getting me away from the police," I said. "Now you can drop me anyplace along the way."

"Ma'am, if you insist, I have to do what you want," he said. "But I was serious. Doc needs to examine that bump. I'd let him decide when you should be released."

"Dammit . . ." I paused, taking a deep breath as my outburst produced a fresh stab of pain, then reconsidered where I'd almost told him to park his opinion. "Whatever. I hurt too much to argue."

"Glad to hear it because I hate losing arguments with patients. Now my wife . . . well, that's a different situation." He grinned. "Sometimes she lets me think I won."

"Is it possible to turn off the siren? I don't think I'm critical, and it's not helping."

"Larry. The lady says you're not helping her headache. Can you close it down except for intersections? She's in no danger."

From the driver's seat, I heard laughter as the keening ceased. "Passengers can sure be picky. Some complain if I give them the first-class siren treatment, while others are insulted if I don't. However, contrary to what she might think, the damn thing drives me nuts, too."

"Tell him I am picky. So picky, I'd prefer a taxi."

They responded with laughter.

The ambulance reached the hospital with a squeal of tires, and they rolled me inside.

"Head trauma," Tommy called when we cleared the door.

A medical team rushed in and, before I could protest, pushed me into a curtained area and transferred me to a bed. Gentle but firm hands were all around, each doing something different, each in a professional manner. They undressed me, helped me

24

into a hospital gown that covered my chest and little else, then did a quick inventory of my possessions and whisked them away.

In what seemed like record time, I'd had my temperature and blood pressure taken, been weighed and had my height measured, been asked innumerable questions, and at least forty-two people had examined the lump on my head. Well, maybe not that many, but some took more than one look. I was sure I'd felt that many fingers. None of the nametags read *Doctor.*

A man in a white lab coat bustled into the area, blowing through the curtain like an applause-starved actor. "Hello. I'm Dr. Rasmussen, your neurologist. I'm all yours until we release you from bondage. What have we here?"

I wanted to make a sarcastic comment about his use of *we* but didn't. He'd probably heard them all. Besides, he and his line of banter were cute.

One of the nurses said, "Head trauma. Possible concussion. All vitals are normal."

Inwardly, I grimaced. *Never thought of this kind of headache as normal. Maybe I don't want to know what's abnormal.*

As he plugged his stethoscope into his ears and applied the frozen disk to my chest, I looked him over. White jacket over navy slacks. He had the right kind of name tag, or the kind I'd been looking for. It read *Dr. Rasmussen.* Also, he was handsome, wore no wedding band, and was the right age.

"Deep breath," Dr. Rasmussen said before lowering the stethoscope and fingering the lump.

Forty-third set of fingers. Still didn't feel normal.

"Yep, we do have a boo-boo. Interesting."

"To whom?" I said. "From my side, it simply hurts like hell. Break out the pain juice."

He looked at the chart. "Oh, I'm sorry. It's way too early for pain medications." He waggled his eyebrows. "There are tests to be run."

I stared at him, wondering if he was really a doctor. Doctors were supposed to be solemn people of age who said, "Hmm" a lot.

He shined an itty-bitty flashlight into first one eye, then the other. "Hmm," he said.

One test passed.

"Eyes of blue. My favorite color. And now that you know one of my secrets, it's time for us to exchange names. I'm Dr. David Rasmussen."

He gave me the eyebrows again. "That's supposed to generate a response — preferably your name."

If he was a doctor, I should cooperate. If he was a hatchet murderer, I'd *better* cooperate. "Elizabeth Angeline Bowman. Some call me Beth. Some call me Angie. Take your pick."

"Much better." He eyed me. "For now, we'll go with Ms. Bowman. After you've gotten to know me better, I think I'll choose Beth. But the fun is yet to come. Let's get on with the examination."

I groaned. "I'm okay. No need to pad the bill. Just give me some aspirin and my clothes. Then turn your back, and I'll be out of here."

"Your clothes? Not yet. You're wearing the latest in hospital attire. And, if I may add, you look just adorable in that outfit. It *is* your color."

I did a quick check to see what body parts were most exposed, then shoved the bottom of the impossible getup under my legs. Doctor or not, I didn't choose to play peek-a-boo with him.

Ignoring my security-mindedness, he said, "Back in the hall, a couple of guys badged me and asked when you'll be released. Really nice representatives of law and order. Why are they interested in you?"

I shrugged. "They could be delivering a

27

parking ticket, or maybe they like hospital doughnuts."

"Hmm."

There he went again.

"Nurse, make a note. Patient's sense of humor seems uninjured — sarcastic, but healthy. As for you, Ms. Bowman," he returned his attention to me. "Do you feel well enough to talk to the detectives this evening?"

Talk to the cops? Oh, yeah. That was way high on my list. With Sargent's attitude, the evening could end with my being charged with homicide of a homicide cop. My patience with his suggestions was at low tide.

Maybe the doctor was a way to postpone my problem. "Do I get a choice? If so, I prefer you continue to squeeze the lump on my head. Or maybe amputate a couple of toes — anesthetic not required."

He nodded, then said to the nurse. "Tell the policemen I'm recommending she stay overnight for observation. They can return in the morning. We'll see if she's in any condition to talk then."

"Yes, doctor," the nurse said, turning toward the door.

"Just a moment," he said, then looked at me and said in a serious voice, "Of course,

I can only recommend that you share our hospitality. I'd like to run some tests and keep you under surveillance, but I suspect you'll be brushing your hair without pain in a few short days. It's your call."

I gave it a quick thought — talk to Sargent while still bleary and anything I said could be twisted against me, or get a night's rest in the hospital. Not a tough decision. "I'd love to share your accommodations."

"Good," the doctor said as he switched his attention to the nurse again. "Arrange for this lovely lady to have one of our best suites. Perhaps something with a sauna and tanning salon. Hold all her phone calls." He paused. "Unless it's the president. Patch that one through to the physician of record — Dr. David Rasmussen." He grinned at me. "So Ms. Bowman, I'm sure you'll have a nice evening filled with trips to some of our most prestigious testing facilities and nurses taking your vitals every time you fall asleep. Just let one of them know what color Jell-O you want for dinner. Green is the chef's favorite color. I'll see you in the morning."

He wheeled toward the door, then turned back. "Just curious, how'd you crack your cranium? Let me see. Lump on your head. Detectives waiting for you. Do I deserve an explanation?"

"See me in the morning." I softened it with a smile. "Maybe the plainclothes will let you sit in."

The eyebrows again. "I may just do that. Now, enjoy our hospitality, although I promise you won't get much sleep."

He was right. Interruptions every hour on the hour.

The following morning after being needled, probed, pinched, scanned, and escorted along the halls with my butt hanging out of the hospital *gown,* allegedly covered by a hospital *robe,* Dr. Rasmussen pronounced me fit to face the world. I felt fortunate that in the past, many horny males had told me I had a nice ass. Of course, it could have been the beer talking when they said it, but I didn't care. When you're forced into exposure, hope for the best.

At the same time, the doctor warned me the two detectives waited in the hospital lobby. He added in his serious voice, which I had decided he seldom used, "I'm not thrilled with their being here. While the tests don't show anything abnormal, I can't be sure your mental faculties aren't temporarily affected. I may live to regret it, but there are a couple of choices. I can guide you to a phone, and you can call a lawyer. Or I can slip you out the back entrance through the emergency room and tell them you're not up to questioning yet. However, the most that will do is buy you a bit of time. I'm certain they'll catch on and track you down. Of course, if you're an ax murderer or some such, I might not want to do either." He grinned. "Are you?"

In spite of my night of troubled, pained, and interrupted sleep, I had to smile. "No. I promise I haven't killed anyone in . . . oh . . ." I pretended to think. ". . . fifteen days now. Thanks for the offer, but I may as well get it over with. Like you said, they'll find me sooner or later."

"Great. That kills . . . oops, bad choice of words . . . two birds with one stone. We'll wheel you to the lobby on the ground level and turn you over to the police. I'll let them know they're responsible for giving you a ride home. Look on the bright side. Saves taxi fare."

I groaned. "Did anyone ever say you have a strange bedside manner?"

"Yes, someone said it once, but I figure she was envious of my witty patter." He waggled his eyebrows.

When I chuckled, he added, "Much better. As much as I'd like to stay and chat with you, I really must run. You'd never guess it, but there are sick people in this hospital who think I should spend time with them. However, in case I forgot to tell you, this ends our professional relationship. I recommend you schedule an appointment with Dr. Levitson, a neurologist that I know and respect. He doesn't have my sense of humor, but he passed all his medical courses." He handed me a business card with Levitson's information.

He tore out of the room, leaving my head spinning — both figuratively and literally, but relieved to have permission to escape the hospital.

His head reappeared in the doorway — yes, only his head. "Is it okay if I give you a call? I always take a personal interest in pretty ladies with lumps on their heads."

Before I could speak, the head disappeared.

Grinning so wide it stretched the skin on the bump, I pulled on yesterday's clothes. The grin went away. Clean panties would have been nice. A hospital administrator returned my possessions, minus my gun. It was not on the hospital inventory. That bothered me. Could it be in Sargent's evidence bag? Or maybe I left it home yesterday. The crack on my head might be affecting my memory. Worrying its absence, I signed the receipt.

FOUR

True to his word, Dr. Rasmussen had me delivered to the main waiting room. I preferred to walk, but a nurse explained that the wheelchair was a hospital requirement, then passed me off to a volunteer. The trip down in the elevator gave me an opportunity to remember yesterday's activities, conjure up an image of the dead man, and wonder what I'd gotten myself mixed up in. A simple surveillance had turned deadly. Coincidence, or did someone set me up? Was the dead man my subject? With his face blown away, I couldn't be sure. The clothes, height, and build were the same. I knew he had entered that particular room. My assumption was that he had to be my Mr. Garcia.

Bannon and Sargent sat on a couch near the main entrance flipping pages in magazines. I studied them, suspecting that neither had any idea what was on the pages they turned. They appeared to be in surveillance mode, their eyes darting around the area. Their faces wore bored expressions, but changed as my chair wheeled into the area. They rose and approached.

I looked them up and down. Nothing special. Two six-footers, or thereabouts, whose clothing, while not bargain-basement, wouldn't gain them admittance to any of the fancy parties along Miami Beach. Basic blue suits, white shirts, cheap ties, and scuffed black shoes. Everything was clean, but showing age. Probably the best they could afford on a cop's salary.

"Hello, Ms. Bowman," Bannon said. "Hope you're feeling better this morning. In case you've forgotten, or your injury precluded your remembering, I'm Detective Bannon, and this is Detective Sargent. We have a few questions if you feel up to them."

I glanced around the area. "Here? In front of my escort?"

Bannon copied my eye movements. "I'm sure the young lady will give us some space. Is there something wrong with this location?"

"In case you haven't noticed, there seem to be a lot of folks interested in us. Since you have *cop* printed on your forehead, they probably assume I poisoned my husband."

"Good point. Maybe we should go some other place."

I gave him my sincerest smile. "What are my choices?"

"Doc said you need a ride home. We can go to your place, or, the most popular of all, downtown."

I chuckled. "Yeah, I'll bet. Do I get Mirandized?"

Bannon looked quizzical. "I don't think it's necessary — unless you want to confess you killed him."

"I'll pass on that . . . since I didn't." I looked at Sargent. "Are you still in the *bad cop* role?"

"Excuse me?"

"You know. *Good cop-bad cop.* Detective Bannon seems to have taken on the nice guy role so that only leaves the naughty for you. But when you fire it up, remember I don't impress easily. Hell, I've probably played as much bad cop as you."

Bannon laughed. "You watch too much TV. We're only gathering a few details to get things started." He spoke to the hospital volunteer. "If you'll trust us with Ms. Bowman and the chair, we'll return it and take her home."

During the trip to my place with Sargent

driving and Bannon riding shotgun, I began to get nervous. The back seats of police cars, even plain ones driven by detectives, are, at best, unpleasant. I didn't want to think about what some of the stains on the seat represented. And, although it was a four-door car, there were no inside handles on my doors. Guilt or innocence has little to do with such transport. No one is immune to the odor of nervousness that permeates the interior. I added to it.

By the time I unlocked my front door, the nervousness had stepped up to anxiety. After settling Bannon and Sargent in the living room, I went into the kitchen to make coffee. That turned into a competition between sloshing the water out of the carafe and dumping coffee grounds onto the counter. I told myself that the medications they pumped into me at the hospital caused the severe shake in my hands. However, deep inside, I knew it was because of the questions the detectives would ask and my decisions on how to answer them.

I prided myself on maintaining the confidentiality of my clients — unless and until called to testify, or released from my vow. I'd been a PI long enough to know the next case depended on not just my investigative prowess, but on protecting the client. No wife wanted her husband to know she hired a PI to follow him — unless and until there was a big alimony payoff in her future. And husbands felt the same way. So with each job, I took on two tasks — get the information, and deliver it without revealing the customer. Sometimes, the second was the more difficult.

This time, though, it wasn't just the client. It was my reputation, perhaps my freedom. The police would expect full particulars as to why I was in the hotel room and how I arrived there. I wrestled with the situation, wondering how little I could get away with telling them.

I felt strange, like my whole life had changed, like I was not the woman who woke up in my bed the previous morning. Too many things had happened. A dead body. A concussion — thankfully mild. Two police detectives waiting in my living room. A suspicion of murder hanging over my head. The rest of my day uncertain — mine to plan as I pleased, or a trip *downtown*.

I leaned against the table and examined the kitchen, wondering if it had changed during the last twenty-four hours. A two-door white refrigerator pushing twenty years and a stove to match. A built-in 900-watt microwave that I wanted to upgrade for more power. After all, it was my primary cooking device. The cabinets weren't great, but I had them on my list to remodel when the money became available. Then there was my pride and joy, a new dishwasher in stainless steel, a recent purchase. This one was so quiet I hardly knew it was running, while the one it replaced sounded like an out-of-control rock band. Same old kitchen, not obsolete, but not the most modern, a mixture of both. If the kitchen was the same, could I assume my life was also?

I checked the coffee and watched it drip for a moment, then opened a package of chocolate-chip cookies and spread them on a platter. Busy work, something to keep my hands moving. Their aroma reminded me I had not eaten breakfast. The rubber eggs and cardboard bacon they served at the hospital were inedible. I had drunk the lukewarm coffee and nibbled on the soggy toast that would have been fresher the previous day — not fresh, just fresher. Not exactly a gourmet meal, or a filling one, but it fit the description of hospital fare — worse than a bad fast food joint. As best I could remember, my dinner the previous night consisted of sleep-inducing drugs.

I bit a chunk out of a cookie and savored its flavor. Rearranging them to cover the plate, I walked into the living room where Bannon and Sargent sat in silence. "Coffee will be out in a moment. I need a caffeine fix before we talk."

"No problem," Bannon said. "Hmm, chocolate chip, my favorite." He picked one up and bit into it. "Thanks. Breakfast seems like yesterday."

Sargent sat with his hands clasped in his lap, scowling, not saying a word as I returned to the kitchen to watch the coffee drip.

After I poured coffee all around, Detective Bannon said, "Ms. Bowman, this is nice, but could we get to the events of yesterday? I'm sure if I tell the captain what a wonderful hostess you are, he'll be thrilled, but he'd really rather I interview you." He smiled, softening the words.

He had a nice smile, quite unlike the scowl worn by Sargent.

"Coffee's weak," said Sargent, edging up to the front of his chair. "I like mine stronger." He set the cup down. "Enough with wasting time. Give us your version of what went down in that hotel room. Start with why you were there." His scowl stayed in place.

"Easy, Major," Bannon said. "She's just out of the hospital. Cut her some slack."

40

"Like I'd forget. Not the first time the medicos have gotten in the way." Sargent leaned back. He didn't relax, maybe only unstiffened a bit.

I looked at him. "Your name is Major Sargent? Isn't that an oxymoron or dichotomy or some such?"

"Save it. I've heard them all."

I selected a cookie, took a bite, and as I chewed, turned my back to Sargent. "Okay, good cop, you ask, I'll answer. However, remember that I am a licensed private investigator, so if I was on a case, I have my client to consider. If I think your questions are out of bounds, I'll go mute. Then it will be your call as to whether I yell for an attorney. Fair enough?"

FIVE

Detective Bannon's smile was even broader than before. "There you go with those TV cop show scenarios again. I know my boundaries and promise not to step over them. Just some basic facts, okay?"

"Let 'er rip."

Sargent rolled his eyes as Bannon pulled out a notebook. "Can I start with your full name?"

I sighed. "You checked both my driver's license and PI license yesterday. But if it makes you feel more competent, I'll play the game. My parents named me Elizabeth Angeline Bowman after my grandmothers. They were very strong women, and someday, under different circumstances, I'll tell you some great stories about them." I frowned at him. "But not today. You don't seem receptive. But back to names. Some call me Beth and some call me Angie. I prefer Beth."

"Beth?" Sargent said.

"Yeah, Beth. Short for Elizabeth. Want me to write it down for you?"

"Date of birth?" Bannon said, jumping in before I could slash Sargent again.

I made a production of stirring my coffee, accepting Sargent's glare, then took a casual sip. "Next question." I hoped my expression said my age was none of his business — even though I knew he already had it.

He grinned and said, "Place of birth?"

Made me wonder if he'd forgotten to take notes yesterday. "Dallas."

"Texas? How'd you end up here?"

"Marriage, followed by divorce. Texas wasn't big enough for both of us. I left."

Detective Bannon gave me a sympathetic look. "Sorry to hear that. Divorces are always sad. Hope you didn't get hurt too bad." He made a note in his pad. "Were you a PI in Dallas?"

I stared at him, guessing that he was trying to soften me up before going to the hard questions. After sipping coffee, I took another bite of the cookie. Time to let him know I was on to his game. "I'd really like to get some rest today. We can do the soap opera side of my life at another time. Get on with what you came here to ask."

"Why were you in that room?" came Sargent's gruff voice.

I thought a moment before replying, realizing my nervousness had dissipated. Sargent's attitude seemed to fortify, rather than intimidate, as he apparently wished. Or maybe it was a chocolate lift. I took another bite, chewed, then swallowed. "Like I told you before, I heard angry voices from inside. Someone yelled, 'You sonofabitch, I ought to kill you for that,' or something similar. Being a good citizen, I pushed open the door and ran inside to intervene. That's all I remember until I woke up and saw the dead man as you found him."

"Was the door closed?" Bannon asked.

"Obviously not. If it had been closed, it would have been locked and, ergo, I couldn't have pushed it open. It wasn't standing open, but was not secured."

"You expect us to believe —"

"Be nice, Major," Bannon said. "I believe her. She looks like the type who'd try to break up a fight. Someone told me that's how Texans are."

Sargent gave both of us an incredulous look, then sulked to the back of the sofa again.

"Why were you in the building, Ms. Bowman?" Bannon asked.

I smiled and gave him a knowing wink.

"Since you're the good cop ordained to protect me from the evil Detective Major Sargent, you can call me Beth. Sargent can call me Ms. Bowman. That'll make the scenario seem more complete — you know, you soften me up, then he takes me apart." I paused, pondering how much I had to tell. I decided to start with the minimum. "Seems mighty repetitious, but here we go again. I was there because I was hired to follow a straying husband. They do that, you know. Get tired of the wifey at home and look for something not so familiar."

"So I've heard. Go ahead."

I sat straighter, decision made. "Loyal, dedicated, and wronged wife paid me to get the goods on her hubby. She said she'd had enough of his philandering and wanted out of the marriage. Having lived in her footsteps, I could identify and sympathize. But she didn't intend to leave empty-handed. She wanted to take him to the cleaners. She asked for full particulars, including pictures if I could get them. And the more *revealing* the pictures, the better — if you get my drift."

"The beast with two backs," Sargent snarled as if he didn't think my assignment proper.

"That's it," I said. "If I could catch them

in *the* act, she'd double my fee."

Bannon jotted a few notes on his pad. "All right, you were following the deceased for his wife. Did that include listening in on his conversations?"

I wasn't sure I liked the way he worded that question. "It included doing whatever was *legal* to develop a case for his wife."

Bannon appeared ready to move on. "How long were you on his tail before the shooting?"

"I picked him up in Coral Springs, then stayed with him until someone put my lights out. Thirty, forty-five minutes, tops."

"Where did he go?" Bannon asked.

"He drove straight to the hotel. It seemed to be his destination from the time he got into his car."

"Did you hear a man's voice or a woman's making the threat?"

I struggling with it, trying to re-create the scene. "We've been here before, and I still don't know. It could have been a man or a woman. The venom in the words disguised the gender."

He looked a bit skeptical, but continued. "Tell me again: when you opened the door, what did you see?"

Six

I hesitated, knowing I should have seen something. What had I seen and what should I tell him? I closed my eyes and visualized the scene — or tried to. Nothing there — nothing except an empty hotel room. An empty room? Where was the person I'd heard? Where was Garcia? There had to be at least two of them. Maybe the blow to my head was blocking what I saw.

"Ms. Bowman?" Bannon said.

"Sorry. I saw an empty room. I was re-visualizing it, and all I get is an empty room."

Sargent leaned forward, a smirk glowing. "Sure. You hear a fight going on, but when you open the door, there's no one there. Easy to believe — just like I believe in extraterrestrials. What's your client's name?"

I hesitated. It was decision time — cooperate or stall. I decided on the former. "Garcia. His first name was Hector."

"You're sticking to that?" Sargent said. "Hector Garcia. And I suppose his wife's name was Garcia, too?"

I thought about the question and the smirk on Sargent's face. Why was he being such a hard-ass? I studied Sargent, then Bannon. Something was wrong. They should have positive identity by now, so they'd know the wife's last name. What was the game? I had no choice but to play along until the rules became clear. "Yeah, her name was Garcia. She introduced herself as Garcia."

"I see," Sargent said. "And this Ms. Garcia asked you to follow her husband and catch him with his honey? Is that right?"

"Yes. We've been there already. She was fed up with his extramarital affairs. According to her, this wasn't his first. But it would be his last with her."

"I see," Sargent said, leaning back. " 'Would be his last with her' could mean she hired you to make sure it never happened again. Maybe she just hired you to eliminate a nuisance. Dick, I told you she was full of crap and wouldn't give us the truth. You're the nice guy. Explain it to her."

Bannon glared at Sargent, then, with a pained expression on his face, said, "Ms. Bowman, the facts don't seem to agree with

48

what you've told us. You see, the deceased's name was Jacobs, and he was a bachelor — never been married. Maybe you need an attorney."

I stared at Bannon, my mind playing and replaying what he'd said. "Jacobs? Bachelor? That's nuts. I met his wife. She described him, right down to his shoes. Just what are you handing out?" I stood. "I think both of you should leave now."

Bannon said, "Ms. Bowman —"

"I want you out of here — now. In case you forgot, I'm still under a physician's care. If you value your jobs, you'll leave before I get my lawyer over here to remind you of my rights as a citizen."

"I'm sorry you feel that way," Bannon said. "Let's go, Major. Ms. Bowman deserves her privacy."

Sargent stood and gave me a nasty look. "We'll be back. Bannon may be intimidated by your bullshit, but I'm not. As far as I'm concerned, we have enough to drag you screaming and kicking into the station right now. And I'd love to do just that." He stopped and smiled — not a pretty thing. "But make sure you tell your lawyer we always honor a doctor's orders. Get your rest. You're going to need it." He moved

toward the door, waving for Bannon to follow.

As the door clicked closed, I settled into
my chair, wondering what had happened. I
took on a simple case, and now it appeared
I was up that proverbial creek without a
paddle. Another way to say I was hip-deep
in shit creek.

Detective Bannon's words bounced around
in my head. *Ms. Bowman, the deceased's
name was Jacobs, and he was a bachelor.*
The following thought was the cops screwed
up again. How could they be so stupid? But
reality intruded, telling me they must have
done their homework. Otherwise, they'd
never have thrown Jacobs' name at me. If it
were simply a doubt, they'd have kept it to
themselves. It was definitely a bad moment.
I had to accept that I'd walked through a
door, not knowing I was in a house of cards.
And that selfsame house crashed into my
head, leaving mc with a minor concussion
and wading in a pool of excrement.

Time to think clearly. How had it happened? If someone set me up, and it appeared an expert had tweaked my actions,
why? I wasn't gullible. Okay, I didn't want
to believe I was gullible. I survived a stint as
a cop, a marriage to Sonny-the-Bunny, a

nasty divorce, and had rejected more guys in bars than many of my friends had ever met. Plus, damn it, I was a good investigator. I'd been in the business for years, solved many cases, and never failed a client. I could spot a phony two blocks away. Ms. Garcia was not a phony.

I stood and headed for the kitchen, my coffee cup empty. I needed more caffeine. My thinking was not as clear as I wanted it to be. I hoped it was from lack of sleep in the hospital, not the blow I absorbed.

After filling the cup, adding a packet of the pink stuff, and taking a sip, I leaned against the counter. Time to get back to figuring out what happened.

Phony. The word jumped back into my head, shoving aside the satisfaction from the coffee. A moment of discomfort followed, but I pushed it aside — no other choice. Ms. Garcia was a pro who'd put me in her purse and given me a good shaking. I should have been glad she wasn't selling Louis Vuitton shoes or my credit card would really be in trouble. Or, since I didn't wear Louis Vuitton's so-expensive articles, a more accurate parallel might be I should be glad I hadn't met her to play strip poker. Hopefully, I'd have quit before my bra and panties came off. The image of standing naked in front of another woman in a Chinese restaurant left me discombobulated. How could I have been so stupid?

I shoved the image away and considered what to do. Bannon had also said, "Maybe you need an attorney." Mulling that one over didn't take long at all. He was right. I should call my lawyer. Attorneys may be the pond scum of society, but when needed, there is no substitute. And besides, I had the best.

I dialed the office and asked Donna to let me speak with Mr. Bergstrom. Donna was his private secretary, the pit bull at his door. From nine to six, she ran his life like his wife would never dare. Part of her technique was to keep things on a formal basis. Note, I didn't ask to speak to Sly, I asked for Mr. Bergstrom. It would have been a major faux pas to use his first name, especially his nickname. She'd have given me a frozen shoulder that would have iced the line as she told me he was unavailable for the next three weeks — or longer.

I had learned early to follow Donna's rules, as Sly allowed her to enforce them. When she said it was time to meet with a client, he met. When she said it was time to go to court, he went. When she said, "Beth is on the line, and you need to talk to her," he picked up.

I said in a rush of words, "I need legal advice. Can you work me in today?"

"Good morning, Beth. I'm fine, thank you. So nice of you to ask. How are you?"

I took a deep breath, knowing Sly was jerking my leg to slow me down. "Sorry. I'm doing okay, if you consider I spent the night in the hospital with a possible concussion and the morning with two homicide detectives, who at best, think I'm a liar, and at worst, think I'm a killer."

"Interesting. So what can I do for you? You mentioned something about a meeting. What's on your mind?"

"Sly. Don't you listen?" His leg pulling was getting old in a hurry. "I'm in danger of being arrested. I need a lawyer. You're a lawyer. I need you."

"Hmm, yes. I do seem to detect a note of urgency in your voice. I'll put you on hold and see if Donna will clear some time. Five minutes enough?"

"Sly." I wanted to scream at him. Whoever said attorneys don't have a sense of humor, perverted or otherwise, hadn't met Sylvester Bergstrom. There was a click on the line, and Frank Sinatra crooned *Chicago* in my ear. He made his way from Chicago to *New York, New York,* then whined about the fog

53

in London Town. I feared he might leave his heart in San Francisco before Sly returned. Thankfully, I left Frank in the fog.

"Donna says we can do a late lunch," Sly said with no introduction. "She'll have it brought in. Be here at two."

I let my smile fill my words. "Thanks, Sly." The hum in my ear said he'd hung up. Guess he was in a hurry.

While returning my phone to its cradle, it dawned on me that the thing I wanted most was a cleansing. And I don't mean in the biblical sense. Just a simple, stinging-hot shower. Enough hot water and gel to wash away everything that happened to me in the past twenty-four hours. One day. That's all it had been. No, that wasn't right. I checked my watch. Only twenty hours since I met Ms. Garcia at three o'clock the previous afternoon. Yet, in such a short period of time, my world had spun upside down, my confidence had been shattered, and my competence placed in serious question — even in my own mind.

I showered, lathering several times, reveling in the feel of the water and the suds. Then I washed my hair, working carefully around the back of my head where a cowlick protruded over the lump. It was tender and the shampoo stung a bit, but it felt good. I realized I was flushing away my feeling of hopelessness. It swirled down the drain, replaced by my natural stubbornness. No way would Bannon or his Bluto, Detective Major Sargent, cow me again. There was a stench in this case, but it wasn't coming from me. I smelled like strawberries.

SEVEN

After blow-drying my hair, being extra careful around the lump, I dressed in jeans and a polo shirt and slipped sandals on my feet. I'd made up my mind about my next move and felt good about it. If the police wanted to play games, I was ready and had an appointment with just the attorney who would match them chess move for chess move. My boss — well, one of my bosses — Sylvester Bergstrom.

Images of my first encounters with Sly came to mind. Actually, he was one of the first people I met when I came to Florida. I had a letter of introduction from a large firm in Dallas that promised to open the inner doors of any law firm. Texas folks said when you had a letter from Jones, Staubach, and Owens, everyone paid attention. They were that prominent.

My first call to Bergstrom and Bergowitz bombed. Once the receptionist heard me say I wanted to speak with one of the senior partners about a job, she cut me off. According to her, they controlled the market and hired whomever they pleased, and that did not include walk-ins — especially call-ins. With those words, the phone clicked in my ear.

I counted to ten, then redialed the number. Same receptionist. "If you value your job, you *will* put me through to one of the partners. If you don't, my next call will be to one of the seniors at Jones, Staubach, and Owens in Dallas. Then you will be answering the phone to one of them and explaining why you're not very nice. I trust you've heard of them."

There was silence with some heavy breathing until I cut it off. "I don't have all day. Put — me — through."

She did. Next, I had Donna sparring in my ear. Before she could hang up, I squeezed in that I had a letter of introduction from Jones, Staubach, and Owens. She replied there was no free time on Mr. Bergstrom's calendar. However, if I *really* had a letter from whom I said, she was willing to take a look at it. I could fax her a copy.

I groaned, recognizing I had butted as big a hole in the stonewall as I could. I caved and followed instructions.

Less than thirty minutes later, I had a return call from Donna. She apologized — or I took it as an apology — and invited me to meet with Mr. Bergstrom the next day at ten o'clock. With a warning I'd better not be late, she hung up.

After that introduction, I faced the meeting with a feeling of trepidation. Obviously, I was no longer in people-friendly Texas. There would be no *how's the family* ice-breakers. It was put up, or shut up and get the hell out. A different world from the one I left, but I vowed to make it mine.

When I showed up a comfortable ten minutes early, I met Donna face-to-face and quickly learned who ran things. Not that she said anything overt, but ownership is easy to recognize.

She let me cool my heels, then glanced at her watch. "Come with me." She led me into an ornate office.

A man in his fifties presided over a desk that fit the room. His head was down, and he apparently studied a paper he held. The clock on the wall behind him read ten o'clock. I got the message and stopped in front of his desk.

He looked up and said in a gruff voice, "I'm Sylvester Bergstrom, senior partner. You pissed off everybody in my office. You have thirty seconds. Make them count."

"Jones, Staubach, and Owens recommend me."

"So I heard. I have a copy. What do you want?"

His abruptness didn't work. I was ready for it. "A job. I'm the best investigator you ever met. I can go to work tomorrow and dedicate full time to your firm. If you don't put me on the payroll right away, you'll miss the chance. There are other firms who will hire me, then you'll have to face me in a courtroom."

I'm not sure I heard an intake of breath, but there may have been one. Perhaps he was unaccustomed to a tough-talking woman coming into his office. He glared at me. "You're pretty sure of yourself, aren't you?"

"I see no reason to play down my talent. I'm good. Read the letter."

His eyes flashed to his desktop, and he picked up a piece of paper — my letter of intro, I assumed. The rest was, as they say, history. I contracted a large retainer from Sly starting the next day, and we have worked together since. In my mind, we have both benefited from the relationship.

Now, he was the hero I wanted riding to my rescue, the man I would have lunch with and beg to help me through this difficult situation.

Before leaving the house, I checked my living room — I hate to leave a mess — and straightened a couple of magazines. The phone rang. The caller ID caused me to frown.

My mother had tentacles into every aspect of my life. If I developed a cold sore, she knew it. And she always called at the most inopportune times. Now she was doing it again. My guess was she'd had a dream about yesterday.

"Hi, Mom. I was just thinking about you." Not entirely untrue. I did think of her when I saw the caller ID.

"And I, you, Bethy. What happened? Are you okay? Should I come out there?"

"Nothing, Mom. Afraid your radar is wrong this time. Just heading out for a meeting with Sylvester Bergstrom. You remember him, don't you? The attorney I do some low-level investigating for. Simple business as usual."

I always used the words *low-level* when talking to Mom. I wanted her to think my job consisted of sifting through paperwork. If she knew half the truth, she'd be on the phone every day. Even in civil cases, people get upset when they discover a PI digging into their life. Paparazzi get the headlines with their smashed cameras. However, they have safety in numbers and travel in packs. Picture a lone PI in the same situation. There had been some nasty confrontations, a few of which ended up in court.

"Are you sure you're okay?" Mom said. "I have a feeling something is wrong."

There it was — her suspicious tone that reduced me to the status of a three-year old. But this time, I needed to stay strong. Instead, I took the coward's way out. "I have to run. My appointment is in ten minutes, and it's across town. Everything is fine, really it is." Oops. Not too much, Beth. She'd see through it like a drunken barfly's line.

Silence took over, but I fought the urge to break it. It was Mom's play, and I was determined not to take it away.

"So, when are you coming to visit?" she said. "Dallas is still your home, you know."

"Soon, Mom, soon." Hurray. Her change of subject meant I'd won that round. "Now, I really do have to run. I'll talk to you later in the week. Bye for now." I blew her a kiss, put the phone in its cradle, and bolted for the front door. If it rang, I wanted to be able to say I never heard it.

Eight

I made it to Bergstrom and Bergowitz in record time and hit Donna's enclave at one fifty. Proving my elevated position in her world, she let me into Sly's office before the appointed time.

He rose and came around his desk, his hand extended. As we shook hands, he pulled me to him and gave me a hug. "Glad to see you. You should come by more often."

I wanted to believe he said that because he meant it, but I knew sarcasm when it came my way. "Hey, I was here a couple of weeks ago."

"Three weeks." He ushered me toward his conference table where sandwiches rested on a platter alongside chips and sodas. He went to the other side and dropped into a chair. "Forgive me, but I'm hungry. It's been a long day." He picked up a chicken salad sandwich.

I did the same and took a nervous bite, a

large one, then poured soda into a plastic glass and took a large slug of it. My hands shook and my stomach was roller-coaster heavy.

Sly leaned forward, swallowing a bite of his sandwich. "Settle down, Beth, and tell me what happened — word by word, step by step. Whatever it is has you jumping around like a cat on a hot tin roof. And your eating habits are atrocious."

I slowed my chomping and tried to chew like a lady. In an attempt to relax, I looked around. Sly was successful, no doubt about it. The office and its furnishings screamed *old money.* Nothing stood out as being ostentatious, but everything added up to good taste and expensive. Lots of dark wood and leather filled the area, a setting that calmed the most nervous person. It almost calmed me.

Sly was right with his comments though. For reasons I couldn't quite pinpoint, I was flitting all over the place. If I didn't follow his advice, no one would understand me. Not even my mom — or my ex-husband during the first months of our marriage. Later, I learned he only said that to get what he wanted. Did I mention my nickname for him was Sonny-the-Bunny?

I folded my hands together and concentrated on them. "Okay, it started with a phone call from a woman who identified herself as Maria Garcia, wife of Hector Garcia. She sounded agitated, asking if I could meet her for lunch, a latte, or whatever. I invited her to come to my office, but she refused, insisting on a public place." I looked up to make sure Sly was paying attention. He was, a bemused smile on his face — his lawyer smile. "I told her the latte idea fit me better since I'd eaten a late breakfast. She picked a Starbucks in Boca Raton. I picked three o'clock. She said she'd seen my picture on my web site and would recognize me."

"Did she say why she wanted the meeting?"

"No. I asked, but she refused to answer, saying she'd tell me when we met." I looked back at my hands, knowing Sly must be thinking that was a nutsy arrangement. How could I make him understand? "Like I said, she sounded agitated, on the verge of panic. I was afraid if I pressed too hard, I'd lose her, and she sounded like someone who needed a PI, who needed to confide in someone."

"Okay, Beth, you don't have to defend yourself to me," Sly said, his lawyer-smile never leaving his face. He sipped his soda, then leaned back in his chair. "What happened next?"

I thought through it a bit, settling myself. "I cleaned up some paperwork in the office, then headed for Boca. I intended to get a good look at the meeting place and its environs. Her tone had me edgy, not knowing what to expect. In any circumstance, I like to have a feel for the environment. I know that someday it will pay off. Anyway, I arrived about two fifteen and cruised the area. Nothing unusual. A Starbucks in the middle of a strip mall — two pizza joints, and two Chinese food places, one of them take-out. A dress shop looking for the proper time to go out of business, a picture-framing place, an ice cream parlor, and a few other store fronts that probably changed hands every six months or so. Small merchandising is a tough business. Each time I see a *going out of business* sign, I think of the dreams that have shattered. I wonder what makes them do it. What makes them invest everything they own into a restaurant or T-shirt shop or something else doomed to failure? Do you ever consider it?"

Sly smiled. "As long as there is a chance for success, there is the dream." He glanced at his watch. "Continue. I have appointments this afternoon."

I took a deep breath. "There was the inevitable shoe store specializing in average footwear at above-average prices." I shrugged. "Hey, it's a woman's world. Anyway, I parked and walked through the area, still feeling uneasy. You know, that prickly feeling on the back of your neck. Guess my intuition knew something." I paused, thinking through what I'd just said. "Wish I'd listened."

"I understand. Go on."

"About ten minutes before three, I went into the Starbucks, got a vanilla latte, and took a table by the window where I could watch the sidewalk and the entrance. There wasn't much traffic so spotting her wasn't difficult, although at first I thought I'd picked the wrong woman. She had on jeans, a pink top with a scoop neck, and white sneakers with pink trim. A harried look on her face topped it all off. She hesitated as she approached the entrance, glanced around, then continued walking. I followed her with my eyes, convinced she was my appointment. She appeared to be watching for surveillance, a bit of a frightened look on her face. She stopped in front of the frame shop and faced the window. I could tell she didn't look through it though. She used it as a mirror. After a couple of minutes, she reversed her steps, entered the Starbucks, and came straight to my table. 'That was cute,' I said. 'Are you always so cautious?'

"That earned me a glare. She said, 'Ms. Bowman, I hope you're more serious when you're on a case. This is important to me, and I don't intend to hire someone who doesn't understand that. My husband may well have brought in a PI before I decided to. He'll do anything to stop me.' "

Sly made a couple of notes. "Are those her exact words?"

"Close enough for here and now. I wouldn't swear to them on the stand, but I'd paraphrase them close to that. Basically, she admonished me for not being serious and said her husband was a threat."

"Because he might have a private detective following her?"

"Yes. That was my understanding."

"Continue." Sly had stopped eating while I spoke, but now took the opportunity to finish off his sandwich.

I sipped my cola while Sly chewed. He was a stickler for accuracy, so I had to make sure I explained everything exactly right. "Ms. Garcia wanted to change locations, saying we were too exposed in the Starbucks. We left and walked to the Chinese restaurant. She requested a booth in the back, and when she sat, insisted on the side facing the entry. Her order was a light meal. I only had tea. I asked why she was acting so spooked. She replied that she wanted it to be difficult for anyone to see her talking with me unless they entered the restaurant. And if they entered, she wanted to know."

"That didn't give you cause for pause?" Sly said.

I almost smiled at his use of his favorite phrase, wondering if he really knew it rhymed. If he did, he never let on. "Yes — and no. She had my curiosity cranked so tight I'd have probably followed her anywhere. I mean, this woman had a serious case of nerves. She was jumping around like —" I stopped, realizing I was about to repeat Sly's cliché about cats and tin roofs. "Anyway, she was being super-cautious. I didn't know if there was good reason for it or not."

When I paused to catch my breath, Sly said, "Did she finally get down to specifics?"

I figured that was his way of telling me to get to the details so I did, telling him her story about her husband's shenanigans and her desire to lose him in divorce court while keeping his money. Then, after a moment of mental outlining, I gave him the rest of the story.

His lawyer-smile wavered a bit as he scratched his cheek. "And the police say the man who died was not her husband, not married?"

Apparently, he'd understood some of what I'd stuttered at the beginning of the meeting. "Yes."

Sly looked at his notes, then doodled a couple of circles and triangles. I kept quiet, knowing it was one of his habits when weighing the points of an argument. A few cubes and cones joined the pictures. His last piece of art was a stick man. Then he steepled his fingers over his lips and looked down, a sure sign he was almost ready to speak.

After another moment of silence, he said, "Beth, I've kicked around everything you said. I just can't get worked up like you. To me, it's obvious you followed the wrong man. Unfortunately, the one you picked up walked into something that got him killed. Your intrusion was untimely enough to earn you a crack on the noggin. Since you were the only person there when the cops arrived, they had questions for you — as I would expect." He paused, locking his eyes on me. "So? What am I missing?"

NINE

"But . . . I . . ." I choked on my words, the truth of what Sly said slamming into me. I felt myself blush, as embarrassed as the first time I caught a boy staring at my budding chest. After a moment to reevaluate, I said, "You may be right. Maybe I am jumping at shadows. I only had a snapshot and the picture was none too clear. In it, he was dressed casually in shorts and a T-shirt. The man I followed wore a suit. Maybe that's it. Maybe I —"

I almost choked on my words. Snapshot. Ms. Garcia had given me a picture of her husband. The inventory list from the hospital jumped into my mind. No picture listed. I tore my purse open and dumped its contents onto Sly's conference table and pawed through the lipstick, nail polish, tissues, breath mints, and miscellaneous clutter. It wasn't there. Nothing I needed was there.

The look on my face must have been something to behold because Sly jumped to his feet and rushed to my side of the table. "Beth? Are you all right? What is it?"

Anger flooded through me. Someone, some damned asshole, had gone too far. I pointed at my pile. "Someone took it, took everything. I have no proof left." My voice was controlled, but I knew how cold it sounded. I battled the rage that threatened to overtake me.

"Slow down. Let's revisit the top. Tell me what has you so upset."

I stopped, took several deep breaths, then looked him in the eyes. "I was set up. That's the only explanation."

He pulled out the chair beside me and dropped into it. "What's missing, and why does it make you say that? Slow and easy, and don't omit anything."

I rubbed my temples while gathering my thoughts. I had to make Sly understand without sounding hysterical. I presented my case in as close to an analytical form as I could muster. "When I spoke to Ms. Garcia on the phone, I took notes on a yellow sticky. Her name, the address where we were to meet, the time. When I left the house, I put the paper in my purse — I know I did. It's not there. At the Chinese restaurant, as she told me the story of her husband's infidelity, I took notes, jotting them into my pad. She told me where I could pick up the surveillance on her husband, and I wrote that on the same page. She also gave me her card and a check for a thousand dollars, an advance on my fees. Hell, she even gave me a picture of her husband. It's missing. Everything's gone. All gone. There's nothing left in my purse to show I ever met her."

Sly stared at me a moment, emotions flickering over his face. It was the first time I'd seen a crack in his courtroom façade. "You're sure they were there?"

I stared at him, re-visualizing the scenes, not wanting to make a mistake. "I put them in my purse."

"But are you sure? Be absolutely sure. This is incredibly important."

"Dammit, yes."

"Maybe they took them at the hospital."

"Sly, that's ridiculous. The check? Perhaps. Someone could have light-fingered it, forged my name, and cashed it. But the notes, her personal card, the sticky, the picture? Why? What possible reason could anyone have for taking them? Plus, the hospital did an inventory when they checked me in. None of it is listed." I picked up a pink form from the table. "Here's a copy. You look at it."

Sly took it from my outstretched hand and examined it. "Nothing here," he said, then rose and walked to the other side of the conference table, sitting in front of his legal pad. He appeared to study his notes, a frown wrinkling his forehead, no lawyer smile crinkling his lips.

My anger was burning itself out. "There's more — and worse," I said. "My gun. It's missing, too. There was an automatic on the floor beside the dead man. The cop who was first on the scene found it and turned it over to the detectives. It may well have been mine."

His brow furrowed more than I'd ever seen before. He pursed his lips and stroked his chin, appearing deep in thought. His words came out slowly and in a no-nonsense tone. "Beth, as you know, I excel as a civil litigator. But you need a criminal defense attorney — *and a darn good one.* And that's a longer reach than I want to claim. Your yarn is so far out, even I can't stack a jury who would believe it. A couple of golf buddies owe me favors. I'll call them in and get you competent representation. Until then, be careful. Say as little to the police as you can. If one comes near you, and you feel in jeopardy, call me immediately."

He took a deep breath. "I know your investigations require you to maintain good relations with the authorities, but watch your words. The best advice I can give you is say nothing. However, I suspect that would fall on deaf ears, since you're unlikely to keep your mouth shut. But if you feel compelled to talk to any detectives, make sure you think before you speak." He stood and walked to his desk, picked up his business card holder, then came back to me. "Here." He handed me several cards. "Use these if you feel the need. Tell anyone who gets too close that I'm your attorney. I fear you could be in serious trouble."

He gave me a concerned look. "Be careful, Beth. In the meantime, I'll find someone for you."

I left Sly's office feeling as depressed as I'd ever felt. The rush of anger had drained me. There had been some low moments in my life, but that was the lowest. I had to admit my anger, or most of it was because I'd been so easy to set up, so easy to bait. Philandering husband? Yeah, right. Gullible female. Too right.

I walked to my car like an automaton, opened the door, and climbed in. I suppose the temperature was way up, it usually is in

South Florida, but I didn't notice. Only when a drop of sweat rolled in and stung my eye did I realize I was uncomfortable. After starting the engine, I pushed on the air conditioner, set it on recycle, then gripped the steering wheel. I squeezed so hard, the whiteness of my knuckles appeared to glow, the mad threatening to overwhelm me again.

Many things ripped through my brain, but the main one that concerned me, other than a frame for murder, was my lack of cognitive abilities. Why had it taken me so long to remember the check and other papers? I was off my game, and that could cost me on a case, especially this one. I hoped it was the crack on the head and not some other malady — like Alzheimer's or something worse. Next time I talked to Dr. Rasmussen, I'd have to ask.

In the meantime, my adrenalin flow continued to dissipate, and I realized my headache had returned. The lump had that wet feeling again, like it was bleeding. I touched it, then checked my fingers. No blood, but the feeling persisted. Time for me to dash home and eat a bottle of aspirin for dinner, then get some sleep. Pulling out of the parking space, I remembered the Tylenol PM I'd bought a few months earlier.

Much better idea. Two — or a dozen — of those should ease my pain and put me out for the night. Tomorrow, I'd figure out how best to find Ms. Garcia, or whatever her name was. Without a wad of her hair in my grip with her body dragging behind it, I'd never convince the cops I'd done nothing wrong.

Thanks to the miracle of modern over-the-counter medicine, I slept well and awoke feeling better in the morning. My lump was still tender, but not as much as yesterday. The important thing was my mind seemed sharper. Even without coffee, I remembered I had to find Ms. Garcia and deliver her to the police as my unimpeachable witness. Then — proof that my brain was working again — I realized I needed to move fast. The retainer I collected from Bergstrom and Bergowitz paid the basics, but extra cases provided the cash for frills that made life more enjoyable. A shortage of clients had reduced my checking account and credit cards to the point I couldn't tolerate unemployment too long. Then there was the matter of legal fees if Sly came through for me.

After I cleaned up and dressed for the day — jeans, sneakers, and a T-shirt — I sat at the kitchen table with a cup of coffee and a

76

note pad. I figured inspiration was just around the corner, rushing my way. All I had to do was show patience, and I'd get a message on how to proceed. I waited, pen poised, ready to write. Nothing. No inspiration. I was at the same place as when I went to bed last night. One idea finally popped in. Time would tell if it was a good one — go to the strip mall where I'd met Ms. Garcia and hope it was a favorite hangout of hers. Could be. She picked it.

I spent another hour reconstructing every word she and I had exchanged, concentrating on the phone call, looking for any clue, any hint beyond the obvious. If it had happened, I couldn't find it. Bottom line was, she picked the Starbucks, and I picked the time. That was it. I decided to hit Starbucks at three o'clock, the time we met. Or better yet, spend the afternoon in the strip mall, working my way from store to store.

One new thing I remembered. As I had rushed to my car to head out in hot pursuit of Ms. Garcia's *husband,* she went into the dress shop. I doubted the place had such an abundance of customers they'd forget one. Of course, with the way my luck was running, if they did, Ms. Garcia would be the forgotten one.

Too bad I wasn't in Dallas. I knew a

couple of police sketch artists I could inveigle to help me. A picture to show around was what I needed.

I doodled on my pad a moment, attempting to capture her looks. No matter how hard I tried, she came out looking like the Wicked Witch of the West — wart on nose and all. Hey, my hand went where my attitude told it to go. And I was not in a benevolent mood.

Then inspiration struck — just like in the movies. Can't say cartoons because I forgot to look for the light bulb. We lived in a world of instant communications. I grabbed my phone and, after fumbling though my old address book, dialed.

"Dallas Police Department, Jake Gibbons."

"Jake. It's Beth, Beth Bowman. You still celebrating your divorce by bedding every female in sight?"

That launched a series of raunchy give and takes that told me Jake was still my friend. That was iffy for a while after he caught Sonny-the-Bunny with his wife. But the judge gave Jake freedom, and he swore my ex did him a favor — got him out of a bad marriage without alimony.

TEN

I eased into my problem, asking if Jake could create a police sketch for me. My idea was I'd feed him the description and he'd compose, then email the picture to me. I could view and offer corrections until his talent had drawn the perfect picture of Ms. Garcia.

"Sure, Beth, but not here. I don't think the Captain would appreciate my spending Dallas dollars to help you. Look, I'm off duty in an hour. I'll call when I get home. In the meantime, jot down everything you remember. Be as specific as you can."

"I know, Jake. Been there. Remember?"

"Oh, yeah. But don't think I'm doing this pro bono. You owe me."

"What do you mean? You not getting enough?"

"Hey, easy there. You're not keeping up. I'm a happy newlywed and plan to stay that way, so get your mind out of my bedroom.

You won't get that lucky."

"Lucky? Ho, ho. Your bride must really know how to bolster your ego."

"Yes, something you might want to learn — how to please a man."

"I give up. How can I repay you?"

His chuckle told me he enjoyed the win. Fine with me as long as he did my sketch.

"Next time you're in Dallas, I know a great steakhouse with a two-pound porterhouse on the menu. You're buying — one for me and one for Julie."

"You're on and congratulations on your marriage. Is Julie her name? When did it happen?" A memory kicked in. "Julie? Not the cute redhead from records that could have any guy in the department?"

"Yep, that's her. And she only had eyes for one man — me." Minutes passed while Jake gave me a detailed description of his new wife and how happy he was. I oohed and aahed with his every word. Then we terminated the call so he could split for home and I could follow his advice. I spent the next hour recording every little thing I could remember about Ms. Garcia's appearance. This time, I omitted the wart.

True to his word, Jake called an hour later. Well, actually seventy minutes, but I was in a generous mood. We spent a half hour on the phone — me talking and him sketching and asking an occasional question. Fifteen minutes after that, I had a likeness of Ms. Garcia, or a woman who could have been a distant relative. I got Jake back on the phone, and we refined his drawing. After four attempts, I was satisfied with his work. I had a picture of Ms. Garcia that was close enough to my image of her that I trusted it. Even if it only led me to her sister, I'd have a lead. All I had to do was show it around and let someone tell me who she was and where I could find her.

After thanking Jake and inviting him and Julie to visit me in Florida, I hung up and downloaded the .jpg file. I worked on it in PhotoShop, creating three versions. One was unadorned, the second carried my name and phone number on the bottom with a message to call me if she showed up. On the third, I added a line offering a reward based on the accuracy and depth of information provided. I loaded twenty-five pound paper and instructed the printer to go for fifty copies.

By then, the clock had crawled toward two o'clock, and I was anxious to get to the mall. The sooner I started canvassing, the sooner I'd have the woman in a corner, pummeling her with questions — questions she would answer or I'd pummel her with something a lot harder. Like my fists.

I entered my closet and surveyed the left side. One of the pleasures of my house was the walk-in closet in the master bedroom. Every woman is born with the dream of a special room where she can hang every item so it can be seen without being crushed. I had such a treasure. Plenty of space and bright lighting. Even mirrored doors. It was about ten by fifteen feet. The two long sides held rods while the rear was a floor-to-ceiling shoe rack. On the left, I hung my better clothes, those I wore when my appearance was important. There was plenty of space because the inventory was quite limited. The right side held my jeans, casual slacks, blouses, and tops worthy of a hanger. Lots of those. I wish I could say the back wall overflowed with shoes, but no. Lots of casual wear and a few flats. Hardly ever worn were several pairs with higher heels, two with three-inch spikes in basic black. There were still lots of empty spaces, however. I looked forward to the pleasure of filling them one pair at a time.

From the left, I took down a navy blue pantsuit, one of my best, a Donna Karan. It wasn't too pricey, but nice enough for most any occasion, especially courtroom appearances. On behalf of my clients, I had to appear before judges often enough that I needed proper attire.

I knew we lived in a relaxed-clothing society, even more so in South Florida, but I couldn't do it. Jeans and courtrooms just didn't match for me. My upbringing, I suppose. Mom drilled into me how to dress for a formal setting.

From the shoe rack, I dragged out a pair of Anne Kleins with two-inch heels. Also purchased for appearances before judges. I never said I bought expensive brands, but I could make myself presentable when the necessity arose.

My dream closet also held shelves on both sides, above the rods. From a shoebox, tucked in the back corner, I took out my backup pistol. It was a subcompact Beretta .32 revolver — lightweight enough that it wouldn't weigh down my purse. Stopping power was limited, but it looked formidable when viewed from its business end. And it held five rounds I could fire before I threw it at the target and ran. The pistol went into my Coach bag and the pictures of Ms. Garcia into my attaché case. I was ready for the mall, the very image of a successful businesswoman.

ELEVEN

After parking my car, I surveyed the strip mall and the few patrons within view. I was overdressed, no doubt about it. My jeans, T-shirt, and sneakers would have fit in better with most of the places. However, my target was the dress shop, and I felt certain the owner would respond better to professional attire.

I walked in, exuding an air of confidence. I'd had enough wealthy female clients to know just how far upward to tilt my nose and how to look down it without coming up cross-eyed.

I stopped and scanned the area. The shop was neat, the clothing nicely arranged with hanging garments through the middle of the area. Shelving along the walls displayed more items, giving the store a significant inventory. Other than the clothing, the most significant thing were the sale signs. Apparently, everything in the shop had reduced prices. I fingered a blouse. The so-called sale price was a budget buster for me, making me wonder what the original cost might have been and what the mark-up percentage was.

A young woman stood near the rear unpacking a box, shaking the items as she pulled them out. They appeared to be simple scoop necked, single color tops. From my vantage point, there was nothing special about them, but she handled them as if they were spun from golden threads.

A well-preserved woman, perhaps in her fifties, approached me. *"Bonjour, Mademoiselle.* May I be of assistance?"

She gave assistance the French pronunciation — emphasis on the last syllable. I drew my lips into a line I hoped passed for arrogance, then gave her *the* look. "Yes. Are you the proprietress?"

I looked her over, giving her my superiority scan. She dressed the part of a successful women's shop owner. Her attire was upscale, screaming expensive, yet simple in dark green. She wore a single strand of pearls and when she fluttered her hand, a diamond glittered. Enough to show style, but not so much it looked ostentatious.

She bowed her head a bit. *"Mais oui. Je*

suis Madam Bergeron. How may I aid you?"

Her French accent had a bit of country hidden in it. I figured she was playing a role as phony as I was. With a flourish I had practiced many times, I flashed a business card, one of my good ones. "I am Elizabeth Angeline Bowman, a *confidential* private investigator." I lowered my voice on the last words and leaned into her just a bit. I've learned in the past that the snootier the woman, the more she loves to be cut in on something *confidential.* Madam Bergeron struck me as such a person.

My guess proved correct when her eyes sparkled, and she returned my lean in. "And what can I do to help you? Are you on a case now?"

"Is there some place we can talk . . . in private?"

"Oh, yes. My office."

Lots of country came through that time. I knew I'd have to not overplay my hand. If what I thought about *Madam* Bergeron were true, she knew as much — maybe more — about playing the game as I did. She hadn't risen out of her heritage without being a savvy operator. I'd have to keep that in mind.

She spun and with a conspiratorial wave,

motioned me to follow. We walked through the dressing rooms, then passed through a door she unlocked, and entered a small cubicle of an office. I scanned the wall, wondering if there was a peephole where she could keep an eye on her employees while they assisted customers with the expensive frocks. Not that I thought she was a voyeur, but much of her merchandise would fit in a small bag. A perfect way for a minimum-wage clerk to earn a few extra dollars. Seemed like a sensible precaution to me. When I turned back to her, I saw her examining me with a critical eye. Had she seen through my façade?

She smiled and offered a seat in a straight-backed chair, then took a position behind a small desk. Her raised eyebrows told me I had her attention.

The chess game was on. "For obvious reasons," I said in a whispery voice, "I cannot reveal the circumstances behind my being here. You do understand, don't you?"

"No . . . uh . . . I don't. What do you mean?"

"My client . . ." I hesitated, pretending to look for words. "I can only say she is in a position where no one must know. She swore me to secrecy. Anything I tell you must remain in this room. I'm looking for someone who may be one of your customers. Will you help me keep her secret?"

"Uh . . ."

Her expression said she had no clue I was playing on her superiority complex. She wouldn't dare let on that she had no idea what I'd said. "Well?" I asked.

"Yes, ma'am. I'll keep your secret."

Glancing around the little room, I opened my briefcase and pulled out one of Jake's sketches, one without my name, phone number, and mention of reward. "Do you know this woman?" I slid the picture across her desk.

She picked it up and examined the image as if she were studying for her citizenship test. "She . . . she looks familiar. Did you say she shops here?"

"I'm led to believe it's possible."

"Can I show it to my girl?"

I hesitated, like I was considering the question. "Yes, but no mention that I gave it to you. For her, I don't exist. I can only deal with you."

For a brief moment, I wondered why I was playing it so spooky, but gave a mental shrug when no good reason came to mind. I wrote it off as simply my dislike of phonies, even if they were no phonier than I. Plus, the deeper I got into the routine, the more fun it was. Besides, I might be able to learn more if everyone I spoke with thought they were unique. Anyway, Miss Snooty Drawers was eating it up.

"Of course," she said, rising. "You stay here. I'll find out if this woman has visited my shop." She came around the desk, then exited the office.

I relaxed, thinking I'd planted the first seed. If my Ms. Garcia had ever been near this store, I'd soon know who she was and each appearance she'd made. It felt good to have my brain on full function again. That caused me to touch, then caress the lump. Definitely smaller and no wet feeling. Yeah, I was back on my game. I took out one of the pictures and studied it, attempting to capture points I'd missed that might make it more accurate. There was something that bugged me, but I couldn't pinpoint it. I stared, searching my mind. Jake had followed my description, but there was something just below the surface that refused to pop up.

Madam Bergeron bulled her way back into the office. "My girl, Sarah, doesn't know her. However, she says the woman looks familiar, like she's seen her somewhere before. Maybe a window-shopper here in the store or some other place. No clue on a name. Sorry, that was as much as I could get. I told her to keep an eye out for her. Maybe, if I keep the picture . . ."

Madam Bergeron appeared to love a good mystery. She was ready to give her all.

"I'll do better than that," I said. I pulled copies from my case. "Here are some with my name and contact info. Maybe you could give them to your clerk, and she could ask your customers."

A look of disappointment flashed across her face causing me to think she didn't like losing her exclusivity. Then a spark showed in her eyes. "Wonderful idea. With my help, I'm sure we'll find her." *Sherlock* Bergeron was back.

As we reentered the display area, my hostess reverted to her phony French character. *"Au revoir, ma cherie.* We meet again soon, *n'est-ce pas?"*

I smiled while shaking her proffered hand and gave her a conspiratorial wink. "You can depend on it."

TWELVE

I spent the next couple of hours going from business to business with my stack of pictures. I was vague about why I needed to locate the woman, but continued to hint that it was important to a *rich* client of mine. No luck, although I thought I saw a flicker of recognition in a few eyes. Each place took one or more copies of the flyer. I promised to check back daily.

There were a couple of times my eyes betrayed me as I thought I saw her on the sidewalk in front of me. But each time when I caught up, I realized it was just someone with a similar trait. One time it was the hair and the other it was the way she walked. Perhaps I was trying too hard, willing myself to see her where she wasn't.

The last two stops were the Starbucks — a different set of teenagers on duty, so no help there — and the Chinese restaurant where Ms. Garcia and I talked. The waitress remembered my being there with the woman in the picture, but could add nothing more. It was, as far as she knew, Garcia's only visit.

Not a great day, but one that might lead to something if Ms. Garcia showed her face again. And I'd pretty much established she wasn't a regular anyplace — unless folks were lying en masse. And with forty or so mini-posters with the promise of a reward laying around, results could follow. It was still early, only four-thirty, so I went to my car and took out the book I'd been reading. With it in hand, I headed back to Starbucks for a latte. Maybe I'd get lucky and my target would walk past the window as she had two days previous.

A familiar sight caught my eye — a man standing in the median with an armload of newspapers. When cars stopped for the traffic light, he walked along the driver's side, waving a paper, making it obvious it was for sale. As I watched, most people ignored him as if he were invisible. I wondered if the drivers were invisible to him.

I spent a few minutes watching the vendor. As he peddled his newspaper, I saw that his technique was to attempt to lock eyes with the driver, while most of the drivers tried to avoid eye contact. His sales were slow. Not surprising since there were no afternoon papers published in the area, so he had to be pushing a morning edition.

He fit the profile of homeless — scruffy, several days' growth of beard, long, shaggy, greasy hair sticking out from a dirty baseball cap, unkempt clothes in layers. He was a clone of people you see panhandling on corners all over South Florida. After a moment, I stepped into the street, dodging traffic until I stood on the median. "Excuse me, sir. Do you have a minute?"

He gave me a look that asked what I was bugging him for. "What you want? I ain't botherin' nobody."

"I agree, but sales appear to be slow. Maybe I could buy you a coffee or something."

He stepped toward me. "Maybe you buy my paper. Fifty cents."

Backing off a step to lessen the smell, I fumbled out a dollar and handed it to him with my best smile. He gave me a paper with no offer of change and no smile.

The light flipped to green, and cars surged forward, the breeze from the more aggressive ones fanning my hair. "I'd really like to talk to you — preferably where there's less danger of becoming a statistic."

"Lady, you wanna talk, talk. I gotta make

enough for dinner. You think they give me these papers? Or maybe you want to give me fifty bucks for the whole bunch."

Actually, I'd heard the publisher donated papers to the homeless, but I didn't tell him that. Instead, I looked at his stack on the curb and figured he had no more than twenty. "Five dollars and you keep the papers," I said.

He gave me a *You gotta be nuts* look. "Hey, it's your money. Let's talk — cash up front."

I handed him a fin, and we crossed the street, ducking the rush-hour drivers. He stopped on the sidewalk.

"Starbucks?" I said. "It's just a few stores away."

He looked around, a frown on his face. "There's a bar down the block. I could use a beer."

"And I could use a latte. Since I'm picking up the tab, it's coffee or nothing." I had learned the best way to deal with men, no matter what their financial status, was to grab control and hold it. No way was I going to let Mr. Homeless make the decisions.

"Waste of money," he mumbled, but followed me, proving my theory correct. When we walked in, we were instant celebrities. Everyone turned to stare. That's when I remembered he wasn't as fresh smelling as he could be.

"Maybe you should find us someplace outside to sit," I said. "I'll get the coffee. Vanilla latte okay?"

He gave me a look and left. Standing in line, I thought, that was stupid. He's probably off to his bar with my money, and I'll be stuck with enough caffeine to keep Dracula awake all day.

THIRTEEN

I slipped sleeves on the two cups and walked outside, hoping my newspaper vendor was there. And he was, holding a table just like I asked him to do. I noticed we'd have no problem with eavesdroppers. There were ample empty chairs around him.

Stepping up to the table, I slid a cup of coffee toward him along with several packages of the pink stuff.

He frowned and glared at me. "Ain't they got no sugar? If I gotta drink this stuff, I need lots of sugar."

"Suffer," I said. While he stirred in three packets, I opened my attaché case and pulled out a picture. "Have you ever seen this woman?"

He picked it up and studied it. "How much reward?"

"Depends on how much you tell me. Do you know her?"

"Nah, but I see her two, three times a

week. Why?"

"Because I want to find her."

He stared at the picture, then at me. "She drives through my intersection." He stopped and resumed his glare.

"So?"

"How much reward?"

"Keep talking. The amount goes up with everything you add."

"Going up is fine, but let's see it start? Lay a ten spot on the table."

I went into my purse and took out my wallet, then selected a ten. Ripping it in half, I placed the unserial-numbered piece on the table. "That's where we start — and end unless you start telling me something." I sipped my coffee.

Homeless nibbled at his thumbnail, then fingered the half bill. "Okay. First thing, your picture ain't right. She don't wear her hair that way. Too fancy for her. Most of the time, it's just pulled back with one of them butterfly things."

"But you're sure it's her?"

He glared at me. "Said it was, didn't I? You got a problem believing me, I go back to work. You ain't got no right to insult me. I'm an honest man. I got pride, you know."

"Easy," I said, softening my voice. "No slight intended. I really need to identify her."

"That's better. Gits a bit old having people like you look down their noses at me. Treat me like a man, I'll act like one. You need me. I don't need you." His eyes locked on me and stayed that way until I nodded.

He looked at the sketch again. "Yeah, that's her. Even the do. She had it that way last Monday, and wasn't dressed like usual."

That got my attention. Had he been on the corner when I came to meet her? I didn't know. Like I said, the homeless are often invisible. "You're doing fine. The reward just went up an extra ten-spot." I took out another and tore it in half as before. "Explain how she was different?"

"Lay down the other halves or I walk."

I frowned, not wanting to give in, but I was too close to let him slip away. I complied with the two missing sections.

He grabbed them. "Most times, she's in shorts and a low-cut top. Lots of good-looking cleavage. You'd be surprised what you can see when you're looking in the car window at some of them women. Yes, ma'am. A real pleasure. Of course, not them big SUVs. Too danged high. The best is the low-slung sports cars — Corvettes, Hondas, like them." His eyes shifted to my chest. "Nice rack, real nice. You ever show much?"

My hand jumped to cover myself before I remembered I wore a blouse that buttoned high. "Knock off the bullshit," I said with a snarl, tapping the picture. "This woman. What else do you have on her?"

He grinned as if he knew he'd scored on me. "Hey, lady, I just stand there and sell papers. She ain't never bought one, just stops at the light or drives by."

"What kind of car does she have?"

"Been a long time since I had a good steak. There's a place up the street that has a good one with all the trimmin's for . . ." He eyed me. "'Bout thirty bucks."

Yeah, sure, I thought. "Go cheap. Get one for ten." I slid another bill toward him. "Talk."

He grabbed the sawbuck, folded it, and with deliberation, stuffed it in his grubby T-shirt pocket where the halves had gone. His look made me feel like a lamb in front of a ravenous wolf. He couldn't wait to take advantage of me. "White Toyota, I think."

"License number?"

"What you think? I write down all them numbers come by me? No idea. But, if that reward's big enough, I might could watch for her. I'm real good at memorizin' numbers." He went quiet.

"Anything else about the car you can remember?"

He leaned his head to the right, then to the left, the appearance of stretching his neck.

I got the message and laid a five on the table. It sat there, untouched. A game of patience that he won. With a shrug, I picked up the bill, went back into my wallet and found a ten to further enrich him. This time, he appeared happy as the bill joined the others.

"It might be an Avalon model. That's the expensive one, ain't it? How much if I keep an eye out for it?"

It was my time to examine him. If he was on the level, I could nail the bitch who set me up. Of course, he might see me as a pigeon he could con for cash. I hesitated, wondering where the truth lay. I didn't have a cheaper source. In fact, I didn't have any other source of information. What the hell. I'd bargained for a bigger pig in a poke. "You get her license number, and I'm good for a hundred bucks. But no pay until I verify the plate."

"Easy money," he said, pushing his untasted coffee aside. "Now I gotta get back on my corner. I leave it too long and some asshole will grab my spot."

FOURTEEN

My homeless recruit walked away, leaving me to wonder if he was dependable. No reason he should be except the promise of a hundred bucks. I'd have to be careful. I figured he'd feed me information. The only thing in question would be its accuracy.

I sipped my latte and kept an eye on the folks walking through the area. Not much chance I'd spot Ms. Garcia, but maybe lightning would strike. Besides, with my social life, I had nothing better to do. I could kill more time here, then find some place in the area to have dinner. Maybe in another strip mall. Mr. Homeless said there was a bar nearby. I pictured Ms. Garcia nursing a cold one, waiting for some mysterious man to show up — her accomplice in crime. Or I could walk up the street and hit the ice cream parlor. Maybe Ms. Garcia was a freak for a soft cone or a dish of rocky road. Plus, for some reason I couldn't identify, I pictured a hot fudge sundae with my name on it.

A cell phone rang. I looked at my purse, waiting for a second ring. I usually carried it there, but with the way things had gone in the last couple of days, who could say. It might be off in la-la land, or the police station with my primary revolver. The phone's soft sound echoed again from the bag, penetrating the leather. Amazing. At least one thing was normal in my world. I fumbled it out and gave the caller ID a quick glance. Not familiar. "Hello."

"Ms. Bowman? This is Dr. Rasmussen. I'm driving home, so thought it would be a good time to check in on my favorite patient. You are the one I gave a pedicure, aren't you?"

The mood behind his words came through loud and clear. His jocular tone was wonderful medicine. "Yes, and I'm unhappy with the color. Black and blue does not become me. Do you guarantee your work?"

"Hmmmmm. I'll have to check with your insurance. I view pedicures, like lobotomies, as irreversible. No do-overs allowed."

I chuckled, couldn't help myself. "Thanks, Doc. You may be just what the doctor ordered."

"Oh, bad. Leave the funnies to me. How

do you feel? I could swing by and check that lump if it's bothering you."

"I have a better idea," I said, feeling emboldened. "If you're off work, you could buy me a sundae. I checked my horoscope this morning. It said eating hot fudge with a person in the medical profession would give me long life and utter brilliance. I'm on Military Trail in Boca Raton, and there's an ice cream parlor calling to me."

"That bump on your head must have made you clairvoyant. That's what I've been craving — ice cream, a banana split. Give me the address."

I did, and he came back with, "I know where the place is. Used to know a delectable Jamoca that chilled out there. It'll take about thirty minutes in this traffic. How about you?"

"I'll be waiting. Heck, I'll even buy. Since I have to pay your tab on the installment plan, this can be the first payment."

Soft laughter answered me. "Thirty minutes. I'm crazy about hot fudge and women who eat sundaes." He disappeared from my ear.

I felt myself smiling, my body relaxing, the tension of the day draining away. My problems hadn't changed, but I felt better. Since I'd never met a doctor who made house calls, much less ice cream parlor calls, I wondered if Dr. David Rasmussen had another reason for phoning. Hell, I hoped he had another reason for phoning. It was worth the price of a banana split to find out.

We settled at an outside table covered by an awning to protect our ice cream from the sun, he with his banana split and I with my hot fudge sundae. Before I could take my first bite, he offered to examine my head. Now, you might think folks would find it strange to see a man fingering his way through the back of a woman's hair at a sidewalk ice cream parlor. Nope. They just traipsed on by as if it was the most common of all occurrences. They didn't even give me the eye like I might have cooties or something. Proves one more time the saying, *It's South Florida,* covers all situations.

Dr. Rasmussen, or David as he insisted I call him, said, "The lump is looking better, not near as red and angry as it was. But the best news is, your roots won't need touching up for a couple of weeks. They're in great shape."

My hand jumped to my hair. "My — ! Watch your mouth. I'm a natural redhead."

"Could be. But not that shade of red. More like strawberry-blond, I'd say."

I grinned. "You're impossible. How'd you ever become a doctor? You'd make a much better hospital clown. You know, going from room to room to make patients laugh."

"Yes, but the pay wouldn't be as good. My way, I get to help them heal with a taste of laughter thrown in on the side. Of course, I save my best for special patients. How'm I doing?"

"Great." I took a spoonful of my sundae. "I feel much better. Now, eat your banana split before it melts and all the flavors run together."

"Ah, a great prescription. Have you ever considered medicine?"

"Only from the being-jabbed side."

We ate in silence for a few minutes while my curiosity about and interest in Dr. David Rasmussen grew. I eyed him while trying not to get caught doing it. My guesses were thirty-five to forty, six feet tall, hundred and ninety pounds. The rest was fact. Good-looking in an outdoorsy way, wavy brown hair worn moderately long over the ears, and no visible puncturings or tattoos.

I figured he had a little black book the size of the tri-county yellow pages. Miami-Dade, Broward, and Palm Beach Counties housed thousands of beautiful young women with enhanced body parts looking for an available doctor — and not just for plastic surgery. He probably dated overtime just to please the most demanding. My entry was most likely the newest in his phone listing and would soon be the most ignored.

I must have sighed because David said, "What produced such a forlorn sound?"

Rats. Caught in the act. Thinking fast, I said, "Frozen brain syndrome."

"Uh-uh. Too lame. The ice cream's not that cold, and you're not eating that fast."

He had me. May as well give it up. "I was wondering about you. Are you a native Floridian?"

"No. North Carolina."

With that began the usual *I'll tell you mine if you tell me yours* routine. By the time we reached the bottom of our dessert dishes, I'd told him enough to chase off any man. He didn't run, but he did ask why I referred to my ex-husband as Sonny-the-Bunny. I must have been high on artificial sweetener because I told him that was my special behind-his-back nickname. He was on and off in a flash — and it didn't matter whom he was on. Of course, the whom-he-was-on was any female he could lure into bed, and there had been many of them. Several came forward after I filed for divorce. They were all apologetic, saying they didn't know he was married. Yeah, right. Anyway, the judge sided with me, and I moved away from the embarrassment of Dallas.

In exchange, I learned the most important thing a woman needs to know about a good-looking man. Dr. David Rasmussen was single. Better yet, he'd never been married. He picked up a bachelor's from the University of North Carolina along with an ROTC commission in the Army. Following his four-year hitch, he returned to UNC and entered medical school. Then he set up shop in South Florida, waiting for me to come along. Well, I might have added the last part.

I studied him, remembering my dear mother's advice. Marry a lawyer or a doctor. Since Sonny-the-Bunny was a lawyer, perhaps I could look forward to a change of luck with a doctor. Okay, so I was jumping ahead a bit. But, you can't be a good PI without imagination. And he had mine working overtime.

Then he wrinkled my bridal gown by asking, "So, why were the cops after you when we met?"

"Uh . . ." I reflected a moment, fiddling with my spoon, wondering how much I should tell him about my being duped. May as well find out if he scared easily. I gave him the whole story, including footnotes, finishing with, "I feel so stupid. She played me like a cheap keyboard, and I sang to her tune. Karaoke is not my normal style."

"So," he said, studying my face, "what are you going to do about it?"

"Do? I'm going to find her and pull her hair out by its mousey brown roots. After I've jerked her bald, I may hurt her. Then, if my cravings for revenge are satisfied, I'll turn her remains over to the cops as an accessory to murder. That's what I'm going to do — dead or alive."

He chuckled, returning to the personality I found more enjoyable each moment. "Sounds like a plan. Should I infer that you're upset with her?" His eyes shifted from jolly to serious. "And I bet you're tough enough to do it."

"You bet I'm tough enough. She can run, but there's no hole deep enough to hide her. I'll find her and when I do . . ."

We lapsed into an uneasy silence.

I wondered if I'd come across as too bent on revenge, too forceful. I should have known better. I had chased men off before by intimidating them. But he didn't make an excuse to leave, just raked his spoon across the bottom of his dish. That changed my thinking to whether he'd jump and run if I asked him to dinner. No, that would be stupid. A good-looking, single doctor in South Florida? He was probably booked solid for the next year. And, while I considered myself moderately attractive, no one had ever accused me of being a beauty queen. I resigned myself to finishing my sundae, then he'd ride off into the night for his next rendezvous.

"Beth," he said, staring at his dish. "I don't usually mix my medical practice with my social life, but you pique my curiosity — and you definitely stir my interest. Since I referred you to a colleague for follow-up, I feel unencumbered by medical ethics." He stopped and scraped his spoon along the bottom of the banana split boat. "I've never met anyone quite like you. Are you free for dinner tonight? I know it's late, and I'll understand if you already have a date, but —"

"Oh, hush," I said, relief flooding over me. "I was afraid you'd never ask."

"So, do you have a favorite place?"

Remembering my earlier conversation, I said, "I understand there's a steak house nearby. Can't vouch for it, but it received a solid recommendation from a homeless guy I recruited to help me find Garcia."

"A what?" He laughed. "Yeah, I suspect

hanging with you will teach me a whole new world. I love it. It's about time I took off my stethoscope and enjoyed life as a normal South Floridian. Let's find that restaurant."

We did. It wasn't a Morton's, but not as bad as it could have been. Several steps up from Joe's, you know the one with the big neon sign flashing, *FOOD . . . FOOD . . . FOOD.* We laughed, ate, chuckled, drank, chortled, and, at least for me, had a wonderful evening. When he dropped me at my car, his lips felt wonderful on mine — warm and caressing, as if they belonged there. He promised to check the lump on my head again in the next couple of days if I wanted. I most certainly wanted and told him so. I missed him even before he drove out of the parking lot.

FIFTEEN

Unlike the previous night, I had no problem
sleeping drug free. Not even an aspirin
crossed my lips. There was one minor situation, but I managed to work my way through
it. Brushing my teeth was difficult because
of the smile dominating my face. Yeah, I
know it was stupid, but I kept thinking,
maybe Mom was right after all — Ms. Dr.
David Rasmussen. I felt like a freshman in
high school, and the starting quarterback
had asked me to the prom.

Now, don't get me wrong. I wasn't some
young thing with no experience. I told you
about Sonny-the-Bunny. That was marriage,
the whole *till death do us part* bit. And there
were times when death, *his,* would have
pleased me. But I lived through it and put
him behind me. In addition, there had been
a few other men in my life, pre and post
marriage — none while married. I was
mature enough to know it was only one

brief evening with David, but it was sufficient to send my heart in hot pursuit of Tchaikovsky's *Romeo and Juliet.*

After dressing, I settled with a cup of coffee at the kitchen table and checked my calendar. It was nails day, a standing appointment every two weeks. There are some luxuries a girl should never give up, and I didn't plan to. Not that my manicures were a luxury. More like a necessity. Other than that, my day was empty until late afternoon. That's when I planned to tour the mall again, hoping someone had news for me.

Just as I poured a second coffee, the phone rang. I jumped to answer, hoping it was David.

"Ms. Bowman? This is Detective Bannon. Is it okay if Detective Sargent and I stop by to chat?"

Talk about dumping ice in your bathwater. The cops were about the last people I wanted to hear from. "Why? Sargent think up some new insults?"

"No, ma'am, nothing like that. We have news for you."

"So tell me." If he could do it over the phone, I was pretty sure it wasn't an arrest warrant.

He chuckled. "I told Major, uh, Detective Sargent that might be easier, but he said he owed it to you to go face to face."

Crap. It was an arrest warrant. "Sadistic bastard, isn't he?"

"Believe it or not, he's a good cop. Best I ever worked with. Now, what time would be convenient for us to stop by? Or, if you'd prefer, you can come to the station."

Sure. I was going to rush downtown so they could clang a cell door on me. They must believe the red on my neck came from my heritage rather than a normal reaction to Sargent. Maybe I should explain to them I was not a redneck. I checked my watch. "It's eight thirty now. I have an appointment at ten. Your window is one hour until the door will hit you in the ass."

"We're on our way."

Fifteen minutes later, the doorbell rang. Through the peephole, I saw Bannon and Sargent standing there, each wearing a grin. As I peered, Sargent waved. I didn't see any papers, but they could be in a pocket.

"Get in here," I said, swinging the door open. "You've got ten minutes."

"My watch says thirty," Bannon said. He led the way with Sargent on his heels. Sargent stopped, looked around the room, then sat on the sofa. Bannon took the most comfortable chair. That left me the third seat in the room — an ugly thing I hated. I picked it up at a yard sale because I thought the room needed something. Only when I moved it in did I realize why it was so cheap. Green and brown plaid velour clashed with everything. However, at that moment, I was glad I bought it. Without it, I'd have had to sit beside Sargent.

Bannon said, "My friend has news for you." He nodded at Sargent. "Don't you, Major?"

"Ms. Bowman, I'm here to apologize. I came on a bit strong, and I'm sorry."

I looked from one to the other. "I know good cop–bad cop. I took a class in how to play on a guilty conscience. I've heard of rubber hoses. I read about water boarding. I've even been on both sides of a two-way mirror. But what the hell is this routine?"

That brought laughter from both of them while I sat and seethed.

"Maybe this will help," Sargent said. "Your gun fired the bullets that killed Jacobs."

"Oh? That's supposed to make me feel better?" I said, wondering where they drank breakfast.

"Yes, because someone wiped it clean. There wasn't the slightest hint of a print. Since you had a significant lump on the head and a concussion, we're pretty much convinced you didn't do the Windex routine. Ergo, you didn't kill him. Your story might sound strange, but it's wacky enough to be true." He paused, then added, "Lady, someone did a job on you." The smirk on his face said he was enjoying himself.

I stared at him, debating whether to shout hurray or be insulted. I compromised on sarcasm. "It's nice to know you can arrive at the obvious . . . given enough time. Seems like that's what I told you yesterday. Now, have you located Ms. Garcia?"

"Uh . . . no," Sargent said, ducking his head. "Without something more than a name, it will be very difficult. We'd like you to come down to the station with us. We'll hook you up with one of our sketch artists. If you can give a good description, we'll have something to put out."

"Idiots," I mumbled, shaking my head. "Maybe I should look at your badges."

Bannon quit grinning. "Why? You saw them before."

"Yeah. But then I assumed you were on the level. Now I think there's a good chance you're imposters." I couldn't help it. A chuckle escaped me when his face went red.

"Here." He handed me his credentials case.

I examined the picture, looking back and

forth several times between him and his image. "It looks enough like you to qualify for a government ID. How about your partner's?"

"Give her your creds, Major," Bannon said in a resigned voice. "After she gets her jollies, maybe we can head downtown and get some work done."

"Ah, shit," Sargent said, handing over his case.

Sixteen

I used the same routine on Sargent's credentials as I had on Bannon's while trying hard not to smile. Judging from Sargent's expression, I may not have been successful. But it was so much fun jerking him around, I kept it up. Revenge is ever so sweet.

"You finished yet?" Sargent said, a bit of a snarl in his voice. "I don't have all day for you to play games."

"Maybe if you stood on your head, so I could get a better look. Your hair's mighty slicked down in this picture — not the wild, just-got-out-of-bed style you're wearing now."

"Enough —"

"Easy, Major," Bannon cut in. "She's got a right to have some fun at our expense. We messed with her pretty good." He shifted his attention to me. "Will you come with us? We'd like for you to work with one of our sketch artists. The sooner we get a picture on the street, the sooner we'll have something to look for."

"Oh, hell," I said. "Stay where you are." I rose and walked into my bedroom where I'd dropped my briefcase the previous night. When I returned to the living room, I held a sketch for each of them. "Here she is. Now, get out of here and find her."

"How'd you —" Bannon stopped and grinned. "Damn, Major, she might be better than we thought. I'm not going to ask the hows and wherefores. I'll just be thankful we have a lead." He stood. "Thank you, Ms. Bowman. We'll be on our way. If we get a hit, we'll let you know."

"Wait," I said. "What about my pistol? When do I get it back?"

"No time soon," Sargent said, smirking. "It's a murder weapon. You might consider replacing it. Once things go into the evidence room, they often stay there."

"He's right," Bannon said. "However, I'm betting you already have a replacement — maybe more than one." He gave me a hard look. "Just make sure they're registered and your permit is up to date."

He headed toward the door. "C'mon, Major. Let's get out of here. The city still expects us to find a killer."

Sargent followed Bannon's lead, but when

118

he reached me, halted and stuck out his hand. "Like I said, ma'am, I might have come on too strong. I'd be honored if you'd forgive me with a handshake."

Damn. What's a girl to do when a guy she pegged for an asshole turns out to be a gentleman? Only one thing to do if you're Texas born. I smiled and gave him a firm handshake. "Nice to know I'm off the hook."

Bannon had stopped and now watched us. "Sorry to say this, but we didn't mean to imply you're off the hook. Your gun killed him, and you were present in the room. The lack of prints means you're not the primary suspect anymore, but you remain a person of interest. We're hoping you'll remember something that helps solve the case. Keep thinking. Anything could come to mind. We're not the enemy."

Before I could come up with a fitting remark, the phone rang.

"You can get it," Bannon said. "We'll let ourselves out."

As I headed toward the kitchen and my wall phone, I heard the door close.

"Hello," I said, not recognizing the number on the caller ID.

"Hey, Lumpy. You had me worried when you didn't answer your cell."

"David? Is that you?"

"It's been such a busy morning, I can't be sure. But I know David stared at me from the mirror this morning. Of course, he was hard to recognize because of the happy look on his face. Are you feeling all right?"

"Yeah. Almost back to normal. But it's good of you to ask." I reflected a microsecond. "What did you mean about happy look and my cell?"

"The first shall remain my secret, but a clue to tease your investigative genes is it has to do with last night. On the second, I called a couple of times, and you didn't answer. Good thing you're not unlisted, or I'd be knocking on your door."

"You called . . . Oh, my cell must be in my purse. And I left it in the bedroom while I entertained two of Coral Lake's finest."

"The police? Why are they there?"

"They're not. They just left. Kind of a strange visit."

"How so? What'd they have to say?"

I paused, thinking through the visit. "They don't think I killed Jacobs, but are keeping me on the persons of interest list. I guess it means I'm innocent unless they can find something to hang on me — and they'll keep digging. Makes me feel better — I think." I hesitated a split second and came

120

back in a softer voice. "It was sweet of you to call. How long can I expect this personal medical follow-up?"

He chuckled. "Just standard practice, Ms. Bowman. Remember my Hippocratic oath. However, we could discuss it over dinner tonight. You had me so fascinated last night with your adventures I forgot to eat dessert."

"What? We had dessert before dinner. Or was that another doctor I shared an ice cream appetizer with?"

"Touché," he said. "But let's do it in the correct order tonight."

"You're on. But you'll have to come by and pick me up like a proper escort. No more meeting at a neutral site."

"Sounds perfect to me. See you at seven."

We hung up, leaving me thinking, wow, the day was getting better and better. First, the cops tell me I'm no longer the prime suspect, then the man of my dreams pursues me. I should stop by Publix and pick up a lottery ticket. I felt sure I'd hit big.

Then reality returned, and I remembered I had to rush. Had to have fresh nails for David, and appointments were hard to come by. I grabbed my purse and ran out the door.

SEVENTEEN

At two o'clock, after changing into my canvassing clothes, I headed for the mall with high hopes. I wasn't dressed as fancy as the previous day — I only had so many expensive outfits — but I felt professional. A white knit top showing a modest amount of skin, brown slacks, and a pair of flats to match. The slacks were among my favorites and showed it. Soft and comfortable, I wore them more often than any others in my closet. I knew I'd have to retire them soon — shrinkage, I called it. Truth was I'd put on a few pounds since buying them after hitting Florida. They were tight around the hips. The outfit came from Penney's, my favorite department store. Not only did it seem that everything was always on sale, but its corporate headquarters was in Plano, just north of Dallas. Made me feel at home even though I was thirteen hundred miles away.

As I drove, I admired my nails in their new blood-red color. Wicked, the manicurist called it, and *wicked* I felt. I was no longer the prime suspect in the murder, dinner with David filled me with anticipation, and I had wicked new nails. I was on a roll. With the wonderful day I was having, surely someone would have news about Maria Garcia. No way was I going to let her get away with setting me up for a frame — even if it was a lousy effort. And there was the matter of her check for the thousand-dollar advance that someone — I suspected one of her friends — had lifted from my purse.

I parked in front of the Starbucks, exited the car, and started at the last store in the strip. By the time I worked my way to Madam Bergeron's Dress Salon, my enthusiasm had entered a droopy phase. No one had seen Ms. Garcia. They knew no more than the previous day.

I stopped at the entrance, checked my nails to boost my confidence, fixed a smile on my face, then pushed the door open.

"*Bon jour, ma cherie,* I am so glad you *arrivé,*" Madam Bergeron said, charging at me. "I have *les news merveilleux. Vitement,* come with me."

Ah, my earlier optimism had panned out. My phony-accent friend had what I needed.

She spun and strutted through the dressing room into her office as she had on my previous visit. I followed, not saying a word. It was obvious she was savoring the moment, and I didn't want to do anything that might cause a memory lapse.

She settled behind her small desk, and I took the straight-backed chair. After a deep breath — for dramatic effect, I figured — she said, "Sarah remembers the woman you're looking for."

"Sarah is your floor clerk?" I wanted to be sure whom she meant.

"*Oui.* She tends the customers."

"And?" I lifted my eyebrows to let her know she could continue.

A knowing smile. "After we closed last night, I sat her down and explained that I expected full cooperation." Madam Bergeron's French accent was on vacation again. "She pretended to think, then asked if the information was worth anything. I laughed at her and told her it was worth her job. When I spoke to her before, I had a feeling she might know more than she said. So I was not surprised when she remembered the lady in your picture." She leaned back and crossed her arms, a satisfied look on her face.

I guessed she waited for congratulations,

so I gave them. My adrenaline flow was so intense, my next words came out in a rush. "Who is she? Where can I find her?"

She leaned forward and held out her hands in a helpless gesture. "*Alors.* That was not what she knew. She says the woman came into the shop last Monday afternoon about four o'clock. She checked the dresses near the front, but Sarah believes the woman was more interested in staring through the window than in the merchandise. Sarah offered to assist her, but the woman said she was browsing. Because of her strange behavior, and we had no other customers, Sarah kept an eye on her. After several minutes, the lady left." Madam Bergeron stopped talking.

"Does she know where she went? What kind of car she drove? Anything that can help me find her?"

"*Non.* The phone rang, and Sarah went to answer it. By the time she looked through the window again, your *poulet* had vanished."

I leaned back and took my own deep breath, realizing I'd hardly breathed at all during the telling. "So, all we really know is she was here last Monday afternoon?" Yeah, disappointment probably showed in my voice.

"Oui. She was here. She went away. But, since she was here once, she may come again, *n'est-ce pas?"*

I agreed, but without much conviction. My guess was she ducked into the dress shop until I left the area. After I departed, she did her disappearing act. Nothing to go on there. But I wanted to walk away with something. "Is Sarah convinced the woman she saw is the woman in the picture?"

"Oui."

"And you think she's on the level with you?"

"Ms. Bowman, I *know* she needs this job. She has a six-month-old baby, no man, and no family in the area. Lying to me would be stupid, and she is not stupid. Slow, maybe, but not stupid. She wouldn't dare lie to me."

I went quiet for a moment, seeking another question to ask. None came to mind, only continued disappointment. After thanking Madam Bergeron, I walked to the front of the shop and thanked Sarah. When we shook hands, I palmed her a ten-spot. I'm a sucker for babies and mothers who struggle to raise them. Or maybe I just had a guilty conscience. I doubted Madam Bergeron paid her much more than minimum wage.

The rest of my trek through the mall was

less enlightening. No one had seen my woman. Of course, Starbucks had a third set of teenagers working. I went through my quest from the top, only to learn they knew nothing.

Maybe my homeless news vender would have something for me. One last stop, then I'd go home to get ready for David. That thought brought a smile to my face. I might be striking out as an investigator, but I rode high as a woman.

I walked out to Military Trail and stopped at the corner, waiting for the little sign to flash WALK . . . WALK . . . WALK. The homeless guy was either ignoring me or hadn't seen me yet. I assumed the latter since there was money on the line. No one hawking newspapers at fifty cents a throw would ignore the possibility of a hundred bucks — especially with no work involved. The light changed. I lifted my left foot to step off the curb when a flash of white filled my peripheral vision.

Instinct took over, and I launched myself backward as a white car screamed by in a hard right turn. It passed through the space I'd occupied a microsecond earlier. This took place in that slow motion we hear about and see in movies and on TV. As my head turned to track the white sedan, my backside found the sidewalk in a skid followed by my head slapping the concrete hard. Familiar stars and fireworks replaced the vehicle before blackness took over.

EIGHTEEN

Light seeped through my eyelids as I opened to a squint. The day seemed incredibly bright, but I could make out several people hovering over me. Everyone wore a concerned expression — you know, the look you see at a funeral. Since the lump on my head — yeah, same head, same lump — hurt like someone was using it to crack Brazil nuts, I assumed I wasn't dead. I read somewhere there is no pain after death. I decided to conduct a test. "What happened?" Okay, not very original, but the question was uppermost in my mind.

"A car almost ran over you," a bald man with a paunch said. "You came close to stepping in front of him when he was turning. It doesn't look like he hit you though. You made some backwards leap. I never seen anything quite like it. Bet you would have gotten a ten in the Olympics."

Memory flooded through the mist of pain.

"No. That's not right. Uh, I don't think it's right. Didn't the car run up on the side-walk?"

"That's what I saw," a lady in her thirties wearing shorts and a T-shirt said.

"I didn't see it that way," the bald man said. "Why would he do that? Plain silly, I say. You can bust a tire doing that. Not to mention denting a wheel. And those things are expensive."

The woman shot him a glare that said he didn't have a clue, then returned her concerned look to me. "Maybe we should call 9-1-1. You might need an ambulance." She fumbled in her purse.

I assumed she was going for a phone so I sat up — too fast, my head said. "No ambulance. I'm okay . I just need a moment to get my bearings. Here." I held my hand out to the man. "Help me up. I'm fine."

He took me by the elbow and forearm and, with his support, I gained my feet. I wobbled a bit, but gradually, the world around me slowed its rotations, then stabilized as faces came into better focus.

"You sure you're okay?" the lady said. "You ought to have someone check your head."

"I'm fine . . . honest. Happens to me all the time. I keep a lump on the back of my head to use as a cushion. See?" I rubbed the bump then held out my hand. "No blood. I always say no blood, no foul."

She gave me a funny look, shook her head, and walked away. With her movement, the small crowd dispersed. Their faces said they'd come to the same conclusion — I was nuts and didn't deserve sympathy. Or maybe they were disappointed by the lack of serious injury.

I glanced down the street and was not surprised to see a dozen or more white sedans racing away, but none I could identify as my assailant. What did I expect — he would park and wait to see if I was okay? No way. He'd be long gone by now. I shook my head, trying to clear it. The world was still a bit dizzy. Did I step out like the man thought? Did the car jump the curb like the woman saw? Whichever, it didn't matter now. The car and driver were well out of the area. Time to get back to normal.

I remembered why I'd been ready to step onto Military Trail and looked toward the median. The stack of newspapers was there, but no sign of the homeless guy. I could hope he saw what happened and rushed to get help. Or, as I suspected to be closer to the truth, he saw it and ran in the opposite direction, not wanting to be involved. In any case, my head hurt too much to care. I needed aspirin, the more the better.

I started into the strip mall toward my car, walking gingerly. As far as I could tell, nothing was broken, but things just didn't seem right. I chalked it up to the bump on the lump.

There was a low wolf whistle behind me followed by, "Red's always been my favorite color. Too bad they're ripped like that."

I took three more steps, listening as someone closed on me. When I thought he was within range, I spun, my hands up, ready to defend myself.

He jumped back. "Whoa, missy. I'm on your side. Remember?"

"Why are you following me?" I asked, recognizing my homeless recruit. "Where've you been?"

"Right here. I seen that car knock you down and rushed over. You was so busy playing Wonder Woman to the crowd you didn't see me behind you. But that's not the important thing right now. Do you know you're mooning the public? Now mind you, I enjoy looking at a well-shaped tush, but —"

"What are you talking about?"

"Feel your rear end . . . or maybe I could do it for you."

"Don't you —" I reached behind me where I should have had pants, but felt skin, two bare cheeks. Minimum exploration told me my pants had split and my panties were shredded. Both my hands rushed to my butt as I backed away from him. "You, you get away from me. You . . . you." I went speechless. What could I say? I was at the intersection of two of the most heavily traveled streets in Boca Raton, with my ass hanging out, my car a block away, and a bum ogling parts I considered most private.

"Here, missy. You don't have to thank me."

While my predicament blinded me with embarrassment, he had peeled off his top shirt — he wore several — and was now holding it out in my direction.

My first reaction was revulsion. There were stains I didn't wish to identify, but that passed in a hurry. I grabbed the shirt and wrapped it around my waist, tying the sleeves in front. "Thanks. Uh, sorry I jumped on you."

"Oh, that's all right. Man in my position don't get to see a sight like that very often — not near as often as I'd like. I mean, you look good from the front, but from the back —"

"Enough. I said thank you. I'll bring your shirt back tomorrow." I turned to walk away.

"Don't bother. I got others. Ain't you going to ask about your mystery lady?"

"Huh? Do you know something new?" He had my full attention, no matter how much breeze caressed me where it shouldn't.

"Same as you — soon as you get your wits back. You're just not putting it together yet. Maybe because of the way you're . . . uh . . . *un*dressed."

"Please. No games. I have a splitting headache." Then a vision of the near miss jumped up. "You mean that white car?"

"Yep. Think about it."

I squinted in concentration, rolling my memory tape. In the video, I saw my foot lift to step off the curb, then a white sedan bore down on me. A Toyota, definitely a Toyota, expensive model. My eyes lifted from the front-end emblem to the windshield. A woman, brunette, familiar features. "You think it was Garcia driving that car?"

He had a *gotcha* look on his face. "You don't stay alive on the street by guessing. You can't afford to be wrong. But I did see a white Toyota Avalon with dark side windows. I could make out that the driver was a woman. And I saw that same car make a beeline toward you. Now, you got any other enemies that want you taken out?"

He paused while I gnawed on what he

said. "You're thinking about it," he said. "That's good. Keep it up, and I figure you'll come to the same conclusion. So I'll just get back to work unless you want to buy me dinner." He stepped into the street, mumbling loud enough for me to hear, "Love them red panties. My favorite color on a woman. Mighty nice ass, too. Been a long time . . ."

NINETEEN

I managed to get to my car and drive away
without another catastrophe — or another
free skin show. While I replayed the incident,
the *Anvil Chorus* clanged away in my head.
Was it Maria Garcia, or whatever her name
was, driving the Toyota? Did she try to kill
me? It was possible. The bash I received in
Jacobs' room was no accident. Maybe my
head was so hard, the assailant didn't realize a simple sledgehammer wouldn't do
me in. My stomach roiled with the realization I might be a target, while common
sense said there was only one solution. Find
her and her accomplices before she found
me again. Simple to say. Accomplishing it
promised to be far more difficult.

Once I accepted the premise that Garcia
came after me, the question became how
she knew I'd be there. The only possibility
was she saw one of my flyers. That solution
led in two directions. The first was that

someone I'd questioned didn't level with me. Possible. Especially when I considered no one in the strip mall owed me any loyalty. The other was she returned to one of the shops and was not recognized. Mr. Homeless told me the picture wasn't right, her hair was different from the way she normally wore it. I knew from personal experience how a woman can change her appearance by changing her hairstyle. It was one of my favorite tricks when conducting surveillance.

There are times a person needs someone else to discuss a situation with — a partner, a husband, or a best girlfriend. This was such a time, but I had none of them. Since escaping Sonny-the-Bunny, I had shied away from close relationships, concentrating instead on establishing independence and enhancing my reputation as a PI. My case-load said I'd been successful. At that moment, though, I'd have exchanged some of my success for a friendly ear. David came to mind, but I nixed him. Far too spooky to share with a new love interest. Probably scare him back to North Carolina.

I shuddered. If Garcia tried once, how soon before she tried again? I'd have to stay on my toes. Be alert or be dead would have to become my mantra. Maybe I'd invent a fancy logo to represent it. A round yellow face with big searching eyes. Stupid? Yeah, but in spite of my predicament, I could still make myself smile.

The smile disappeared when I noticed a broken fingernail and scratches in the polish on several others. Talk about adding insult to humiliation to injury. Was this the same day that started on such a high?

I grabbed my cell phone, called my manicurist, and explained my dilemma. She understood and said I needed to get to her shop as fast as I could. She had a small window she could fit me in if I hurried.

I briefly considered that the homeless guy's shirt was all that stood between my bare butt and the world, but priorities were priorities. And perfect nails for the evening were my priority. I made a beeline for her emporium where she put me through triage and restored my dignity.

Once at home with beautiful new wicked nails, I took Mr. Homeless' shirt from around my waist and dropped it in the washing machine. I stared at it a moment, then set the machine for large load, hot wash, hot rinse, heavy-duty action, and super ultra-clean minutes. I put in a full complement of soap and bleach, then added more. I wasn't taking a chance that anything living in that shirt would survive. If the whole thing disintegrated, the residue would at least be clean and sanitized.

After feasting on three extra-strength Tylenol — and not once considering my liver — I wandered into the bedroom to examine the damage to my wardrobe. Turning my backside to the mirror, I saw the view I gave my homeless contact. As advertised, the slacks showed everything, the panties hid nothing, and both cheeks glowed with scratches and abrasions from the slide along the sidewalk. Although I wanted to scream at the destruction of my clothing and bruising of my body, I had to smile at the compliment he gave me. Maybe I did have a nice tush. After a last look, I dropped my clothes in a heap and headed for the shower. Time to get ready for my big evening. Judging from the way the day had gone, perhaps picking blood-red polish was an omen — a bad one. Made me wonder if I should warn David and postpone our date. That took a microsecond to consider. Not a chance.

Dinner with David wasn't all I hoped it would be. Oh, he was handsome, gracious, and funny, but the pounding in my head returned with a vengeance, and my irritated backside kept me squirming. I caught myself fingering the lump and tried to hide my actions by stroking my hair. I wondered if I'd done serious harm to myself this time, but sloughed it off behind a big smile — or so I thought. Apparently, my eyes refused to smile with me.

During dessert, mixed fruit for me and double chocolate cake for David, he said, "You've been squinting and fidgeting all evening. And I can see a vein jumping in your forehead. In most people, that means a headache — major pain. What's wrong?"

"Huh?" There I went again with one of my-*I'm-an-idiot* responses. I bit my lower lip while trying to find something intelligent to say.

"I was right, wasn't I?" he said, a note of compassion in his voice. "Is this a condition you get often — migraine, sinus . . . guilty conscience?"

I jumped. "What makes you say guilty conscience? I have nothing to hide. It's just a headache. Nothing special. Well, maybe a touch of sinus, but nothing more." Oh, darn. Could I have spouted words that sounded more stupid?

"Uh-huh." He stared at me. "Did you forget I'm a doctor? I spend every day looking at people's faces expressing their pain."

"You act like I'm trying to hide something

from you. Is that what you think? Well, I'm not. Well . . . not really." I felt my voice getting weaker. I was always a lousy liar. All my mother had to do was give me *the look,* and I crumbled.

David pulled on his earlobe, then gave me the eyebrows waggle. "Okay, I believe you."

That did it. I couldn't keep up the façade. I caved and gave him a sanitized version, playing down how close the Toyota came and leaving out my exercise in mooning Boca Raton. When I finished, he sighed. "I wondered why your hair looked . . . uh . . . less under control tonight, especially in the back."

My hand shot to the offending spot. It felt like a bird's nest. Bedroom hair I'd have called it except I hadn't had my head on a pillow since that morning. I grinned what I knew was a weak attempt and shrugged. What could I say?

"Okay, let me check your head." He rose and came around the table. Once again, we did the *he rummages through my hair* routine. And once again, no one seemed to find it unusual. Kinky world out there.

TWENTY

David returned to his seat. "The lump doesn't look too much worse. I can tell it got an extra bang, but I think you'll live. If you were a normal human being, I'd suggest you check into the hospital for tests, but I assume that would be wasting my breath." He stopped and gave me a quizzical look, then added, "And the medical facilities can be used by someone who appreciates them."

"Hey, I am normal — just like my parents. They didn't believe in hospitals either." I hesitated. "Uh . . . do you have any aspirin?"

David ran his hand over his face while peeking at me through his fingers. "Can I afford to get involved with you? If my interest continues to grow as fast as it has so far, must I pack a medical bag every time we meet?"

I shrugged.

"I don't suppose you called the police."

"What would I tell them? They already have me on their persons of interest list. If I came in with a story about an attempted hit-and-run, they'd assume I was trying to mislead them. No, I didn't call them."

It was David's turn to shrug. "Come on. I'll take you home. Then I want you to take your painkiller of choice — not too many of them though — and go to bed. I'll check in with you tomorrow."

I protested, but he insisted.

He was quiet as he drove toward my place. When we pulled into the driveway, he turned to me. "I don't suppose you'd give up your hunt if I asked you to let the police handle things. Seems to me someone might be playing a game with you, and they're pitching a shutout. This latest is just another example. I don't want you hurt anymore."

I took his hand and held it between mine. "David, please try to understand. I can't stop. This is what I do. I'm a private investigator. The only difference this time is I'm also the client. Garcia and whoever she's working with set me up to take a fall for murder. I take that personally."

David rubbed his thumb along the back of my hand in a soft caress. "That's what I expected you to say. I suppose the question I must answer to myself is whether I can handle your lifestyle and the danger you put yourself in."

We walked to my front door, and he turned me toward him. His kiss was a soft, gentle buss with little romance, leaving me wondering if it would be our last. However, his hug was long and possessive.

I pressed myself into his chest. "I'm not always getting banged up in my job. I go days, even weeks sometimes without anything happening."

"Uh-huh. Goodnight." He kissed the tip of my nose. "Sleep well and sleep late. I'll call you mid-morning." He walked away shaking his head.

TWENTY-ONE

The next week was uneventful. Each day, I drove to the shopping center, hoping someone had information. Each day, I received the same headshakes. My Ms. Garcia had not shown herself. If she had, no one was admitting it. Fortunately, no one tried to run me down again.

My taskings from Bergstrom and Bergowitz were minimal, taking little time. I suspected that Sly was taking it easy on me, knowing my head was engrossed in tracking Maria Garcia.

David and I went out three of the intervening evenings. His pretense was he wanted to keep an eye on my lump. Mine was more direct. I wanted to be with him. I hoped he was trying to be funny and being with me went beyond a medical reason. I didn't want to be his lab mouse. I wanted to be his woman, but he kissed me goodnight on the wrong side of the door each night. My invitations for him to come in for a nightcap went unaccepted.

My dreams persisted. In one, he stood at the altar waiting for me to walk down the aisle. In another, I held a baby in my arms while he stood by, grinning from ear to ear. Each of the others was more of the *live happily ever after* variety.

At two on Monday, a full week since my meeting with Ms. Garcia, I headed toward the strip mall, hoping my posters would produce results this time. I came to a stop near my homeless recruit, realizing for the umpteenth time I didn't know his name. His back was to me as he talked to a motorist. Somehow it didn't seem appropriate to roll down my window and say, "Hey, you," to get his attention.

After a moment of indecision, I rolled down my window. "Hey, you."

In days past, he simply looked at me and shook his head. This time his face lit with recognition, and he rushed to my car. "Ah, lovely lady. Hoped you'd come by today. My palm's been itching. That's a sure sign there's money coming in, ain't it?"

I studied him. He looked different, not as beaten down as before. He wore a clean shirt and jeans and the beard stubble was gone. He even smelled better, but that might have been because my air conditioner was blowing cold air past my nose. "Do you have anything for me?"

He smiled. "Great question. But if you want a great answer, you gonna have to meet me at Bobby's Bar, two blocks up. Beer's on you."

"I'm not going into some bar with you."

"Your loss. Guess you're not interested in that woman in the picture you gave me. Must not want to know who and where she is right now." He moved toward the next car in line. "Paper, sir? Can't know what's happening without a paper."

Damn him. He had me, and the light was going to change any second. "All right, the bar — Bobby's, you said. Your info better be good."

His grin said he liked winning, even a small matter like this. "I figger it's so good you gonna wanna pay me double." He forgot to smile.

The light changed and a horn sounded behind me. I gave Homeless a last look, more like a glare, and drove away, my good feelings toward him in the landfill.

Since I didn't know which side the bar was on, I'd have to be ready to turn either way so I swerved into the center lane. A driver who was now behind me didn't seem pleased with my move. The one-finger wave he gave me probably was not a *hello.* Ah, one of the glories of living in paradise. My spirits lifted a bit when I saw the sign on the right. It read *Bobby's Bar,* words spelled correctly and no foreign translations. The parking lot held a couple of cars, neither of them junkers. Maybe it wasn't a dive catering to the homeless like I'd envisioned. I pulled into an empty space and got out to wait for my contact. There he came, huffing up the sidewalk.

"Hey, missy, you found it. Of course, I knew you would — being a smart PI and all." He stopped talking and gave me the once over. "You don't look happy. Not to worry, I'm well-known here."

I bet you are, I thought. "Let's get this over with. But you'd better have some news I can run with."

He grinned. "Follow me."

We walked into the bar, and I was surprised again. Nice place, well lighted, everything spic and span. My homeless guy was way ahead of me, and I don't mean just in entry position. I looked at the back of his head and realized he had a fresh haircut to go with his fresh clothes. Apparently, he'd had an appointment with his grooming consultant.

He signaled the bartender. "Judy. I'd like a Killian's." He turned to me. "What would you like?"

"Water with lime," I said to Judy. "I'm working." I didn't want her to think I was with Homeless for social activities.

"We'll be in my office," he said and led me to a booth in the back corner, farthest from the entrance. He paused and motioned for me to sit first.

I sat, not sliding across the seat. My intent was to *not* leave space beside me. Either he got my message or had no such intentions in the first place because he took the bench across from me.

Judy showed up with my water and his beer, a frozen mug dangling from a finger. After setting the water down, she laid a bar napkin on the table, then picked up the salt shaker. Without hesitating, she sprinkled salt around the napkin, then set the mug on it. She gave him a big smile while pouring the beer, tilting it so the head was negligible. "How'd I do?" she asked.

While I examined him, wondering if there was more than my eyes had initially seen, he checked the beer and nodded. "You're improving. Not like that first one you poured when the foam overflowed onto the table."

They enjoyed a laugh while I sat and wondered just what was going on. Judy walked away, and he returned his attention to me. "Now, Ms. Bowman, before we start, why don't you level with me? I spent my business life listening to people, having to separate their truth from their fiction. What you've been telling me smacks of a lot of fiction, or my talent is slipping." He leaned back and gave me the proverbial *I'm ready to listen* look.

Now he really had me going. His demeanor and his language had reversed itself. He was no longer the helpless beaten-down man I faced previously. He was confident, in control of himself, and thought he was running the meeting.

"Mr. . . . What is your name? I can't sit here with you unless I know what to call you."

"Names aren't important for homeless people. We're just blank faces in a sea of urban living. You didn't need a name that first day when you demanded I drink a latte. And you haven't needed a name when you've driven by me each day. But, if you think it's important, you may call me Bob."

His smirk said he thought he was scoring points in whatever game we were playing. And the hell of it was, he was right. Somehow, the meeting had swung against me. I felt like a teenager applying for a job. My palms had slickened with sweat as I stared into his confident eyes. I couldn't let the situation stand. It was time to regain control.

Twenty-Two

"Okay, I'll call you Bob, Albert, or Harold. I'll even call you Rumpelstiltskin if you like. Frankly, at this point, I don't give a damn what your name is. Forget I asked. But I demand to know what you are. When we met, you sounded like a . . ." I swallowed the rest of my words.

He let me flounder for a moment while sipping his beer, then said, "Like a bum. Is that what you were going to say? And, of course, in your saying it, you really mean an *un*-person. Right?"

Again, he had me. This had to stop. "Bob, or whatever your name is, let's get to the point. Do you have information for me?"

"If you mean the identity of the woman in the picture, yes." He leaned forward and placed both hands, palms down, on the table. "However, I'm thinking you need help. You have a personal, not professional, interest in finding her. For example, the car that almost ran you down. It was no accident it came so close. You only survived because when she jumped the curb, it redirected her away from you a bit. That was more of a personal attack than a professional one. Also, I see pain behind your inquiry. What is it? Knowing the truth might affect the price of the information."

I was flabbergasted. What had happened to the faceless, invisible, homeless man I met? This man was a force, a man who read me like a well-written newspaper. I was almost afraid to question him anymore. He might tell me about my nights dreaming of David. A shift in strategy was demanded.

"Bob, you're perpetuating a scam on society. You're not homeless, are you? If you are, it's by choice, not necessity. Why are you selling papers in the street?"

He smiled and did a palms-up gesture. "Why do you ask? Have I suddenly developed a face?"

I hated his smirk. "Yes, dammit, and it's one that's pissing me off."

"Good. But since that's not my intent, we'll move on." He swiveled toward the bar. "Judy. Bring me that paper I asked you to keep, please."

"Yes, sir."

I stared at him again, questions and

doubts swirling through my mind.

Meanwhile, Judy approached us, carrying a newspaper. "Here it is." She laid it on the table and walked away.

Bob flipped it open and spun it toward me. "There she is."

I looked. There was a picture of a woman. It wasn't quite like I remembered her, but close enough. It was either my Ms. Garcia or an identical twin. The caption read, *Hit-and-run victim identified as Deborah Ann Goldstein.*

I stared, not wanting to believe. I zeroed in on a section circled in red.

The hit-and-run victim killed Friday evening has been identified as Deborah Ann Goldstein of Deerfield Beach. Ms. Goldstein, age 43, was struck while crossing Hillsboro Boulevard. Her body was thrown 25 feet before hitting a royal palm tree. Paramedics said she was dead on contact. She has no known relatives in the area.

There was more to the article, but my eyes had quit focusing. I had already learned more than I wanted to know. My Ms. Garcia was dead. It was a strange time for it to happen, but the problem with my police sketch, the one that had nagged at me since my friend finished it, became clear. Ms. Garcia did not look Latino — not in the slightest.

My face must have reflected my disappointment because Bob reached across the
table and laid his hand over mine. "Tell me
what's happening. Maybe I can help."

I blew up. "Help? Help? How the hell are
you going to help? This bitch," I pointed at
the picture, "set me up for murder. And she
was my only lead to prove I didn't do it.
Are you some damn high-powered lawyer
masquerading as a bum? Where'd you hang
your shingle, under a bridge?"

He leaned back and grinned as I continued to rant. I don't remember everything I
said, but it didn't wipe the patient look off
his face. That just made me madder. Within
minutes, I didn't know who I was madder
at — him, Ms. Garcia-Goldstein, or my
predicament. If I'd been at home alone, I
might have broken out in tears of frustration. But with Bob across from me, I wasn't
about to let it happen. Not sure how long I
went on, but finally, I blew myself out and
wilted.

"Is she okay?" Judy said. "Can I get you
something, ma'am?"

I hadn't heard her approach, but I'd been
so loud the fire department could have
driven old number one through the place,
and I probably wouldn't have known it.
However, the *ma'am* following her question

did little to improve my disposition. "I'm not your ma'am. I'm —" I couldn't continue. From her age, mid-twenties at the oldest, I probably did look like a ma'am, a shriveled up, blue-haired ma'am in need of a walker. "I'm sorry, Judy. I'm just a bit upset. I'll be fine." Someone inside me added, "Bring me a beer. One of those will do." I pointed toward Bob's Killian's.

"Yes, ma'am." She disappeared toward the bar, a smile plastering her face.

"Have you finished blowing off steam?" Bob said. "If you have, maybe we can figure out what to do. All I know is a woman you wanted to find is dead. If you read the rest of the article, it says the police have no leads, no description of the vehicle that hit her." He sighed. "Not like my day when folks stepped up to help solve crimes. But we must deal with what we have. Want to tell me the parts of the story that happened before I entered the scene?"

Judy appeared beside the table with my beer and a frozen mug. She repeated the salt on napkin routine, then poured the beer. Before she set it down, she showed it to Bob, pride on her face. "No head. Just like you taught me." Turning to me, she said, "It's more difficult than it looks. Bob says it's the mark of a good bartender —

knowing how to pour a beer without letting all the fizz out." She set it in front of me and said to Bob, "I'll get you another. Then I'll make myself scarce. Looks like you're having a business conference."

Bob patted her arm. "Thank you, Judy. You're very perceptive"

"Hold it with the bullshit," I said. "What's with the salt? Why'd you salt our napkins?"

She looked at Bob and grinned. "He taught me that, too. You see, if you sprinkle some salt on the napkin before you set a frozen mug on it, it won't stick to the mug. And the mug doesn't drip on you either. That's what Bob said, and it works."

I must have looked pretty dumb because they enjoyed a communal laugh as she walked away.

TWENTY-THREE

While I sat, feeling like the sidekick in an old western, a revelation hit me. I looked first at Bob, then toward Judy's retreating back as she swished away from us. "Bobby's Bar. Bob. The way she treats you," I said, confidence building with each word. "This is your place, isn't it?"

Bob glanced toward Judy, then back at the table, and sighed. After what appeared to be a moment of reflection, he said, "I suppose you'll dig at it until you come up with the truth, so I may as well lay it out. Yes, I'm the Bob of Bobby's Bar. Guilty as charged. But I hope you'll keep my secret. In return, I'll look into your case and, with my contacts and vantage point, we just might discover what's going on around you. At least, it won't hurt to try."

I let the clock tick a couple of minutes while I wrestled with what I was hearing. Somewhere along the way, I'd lost control and was now a pawn on Bob's chessboard. He was ambushing me with ease, while the best I could do was castle to move my king out of his queen's attack. But that was about to come to a screeching halt.

"Ms. Garcia is dead, Bob. That means I don't need you or anything from you. And about all your report is worth is the beer you're drinking." I fumbled in my purse and came out with a twenty that I dropped on the table. "I've had enough of your games. You've had about all the fun with me you're going to have." I stood, ready to walk away.

"Hold on, missy. You're right. But you're also wrong. I can help you. And for some strange reason I don't understand, I want to help. First time I've felt this way in a long time." He paused and sipped his beer. "I have to admit, it feels pretty good. Allow me to start with an explanation. If you'll sit back down and finish your brew, I'll give you an abbreviated version of Bob Sandiford's life."

I glared at him, then settled into the booth. "It better be good."

He raked his hands over his face, then leaned forward, his elbows on the table. "It starts a long time ago, a time when I had the best that life has to offer — a wonderful family and a job I enjoyed. My wife, June, was gorgeous, loving, loyal, and a marvelous mother. I worshipped her. Every day I wondered why she picked me from all the men she could have had. We had one child, an eleven-year-old daughter. I know every father thinks he has the perfect daughter, but in my case, it was true. Samantha was smart, pretty, talented, popular . . . a bright future ahead of her. Everything a man could hope for. My job? I was in my early thirties at the time, but was already a vice-president in my bank. The world was flush for me, the sky the only limit."

His face went somber as he paused, visibly swallowing. I sat frozen, feeling as if he were reaching deep inside himself to tell his story.

He focused tear-filled eyes on me. "Then the bottom fell out. In one brief instant, everything collapsed. I was working late, and my wife and daughter were coming home from ballet practice. Samantha had the lead in an abbreviated version of *The Nutcracker.*" He smiled a sad smile. "She was so graceful." He turned his head and rubbed his eyes, then took a deep breath. "A drunk driver crossed the centerline and hit them head-on. June and Samantha were killed instantly — or that's what the doctors said. I can only pray they didn't suffer. The

160

funerals were closed casket.

"Can you imagine what that did to me? I lost my reasons for success. I lost the reasons for staying alive. The glitter, the shine was gone from everything I saw. Oh, I stayed on the job for another year, but I knew I was just going through the motions. I had no heart for it. And going home to that empty house every evening was agony."

Bob stared at me, a plaintive look on his face. "I hope you never go through the kind of loss I felt. I hope no one does." He paused again, then continued, "After about a year, I knew it was over, life was not worth continuing as I'd known it. I liquidated everything and moved to Florida. I wanted to get away, to escape anything that reminded me of what I had been, what I lost. I quit running when I reached Boca, bought the bar, and converted a storage room to my master suite." He chuckled a sad chuckle. "Some suite. A twelve by twelve block room with no window. However, it did connect to the original restroom. I added a shower, and with that done, became a drunken bartender. I opened the bar at three, then drank all night and slept all day. Eating became an accident that occurred when severe hunger drove me to it. My solace was in a bottle.

"Now, don't think I drank alone. That's the sign of an alcoholic, isn't it?" He gave what appeared to be a forced smile. "Well, that's what I told myself during the few moments when I was lucid enough to think about it. I drank with my customers. Didn't matter who they were, I'd match them drink for drink. My place became a watering hole for husbands on the way home from work. They'd stop in to let the rush hour traffic die down, and I'd have whatever they ordered." He stared toward the bar. "Husbands and fathers sat on those stools, sharing their familial happiness with me. Every one of them broke my heart into smaller pieces. It got to the point I'd hang out the closed sign if I saw one of them pulling into the parking lot. I couldn't take it.

"But I had one customer I liked, one who was as sad as I, a homeless *bum.* He called himself Jupiter. Said he liked being the biggest something, even if it was only a planet no one knew much about. He sold papers on the corner down the street, the same one I use now. I don't know much about him, and he didn't know much about me. We respected one another's privacy. We didn't need to pry, we had a common friend — booze. Didn't matter what kind. Beer, wine, whiskey. We shared it all. Whatever my hand settled on was what we had. We bonded through our misery and our love of the empty-mindedness of being drunk." Bob stopped talking, lowered his head, and held his face in his left hand.

I could see pain etched across his forehead. This was not the man I met. This wasn't even the man I spoke to moments ago. This was a man baring his soul to me. My intuition said he needed to finish the story, needed to use it as a cleansing. I couldn't tell if I was the first person he'd told it to, but I felt he shouldn't stop. "Bob," I said in a soft voice. "What happened next? How did you get yourself sober?"

He looked at me, then took a deep breath. "One night, it was July thirteenth, actually more like early the fourteenth. As usual, Jupiter and I drank ourselves into a stupor. At some point — I was too far gone to know — he left the bar. The police investigation said he staggered into the path of an SUV. Since it was after two a.m., and traffic was light, the vehicle was moving fast. Jupiter was dead before his body quit bouncing — much like your Ms. Garcia."

He stopped and wiped a hand across his eyes. "I didn't find out until the next day. I woke with my head resting on the bar, a whiskey bottle turned on its side, my sleeve soaked with the liquor, and my head pounding. After a little of the hair of the dog, I noticed a note. It was from the police and said I should contact them when I sobered up. Later, I discovered they had canvassed the neighborhood, found my front door unlocked, and me passed out. They said they were unable to wake me so they left the note. That's how I found out my only friend was dead — dead because of me, because of my drinking. Again, I'd lost the person closest to me."

He paused, straightened his shoulders, and seemed to grow an inch or two. "I took that as a wake-up call. I knew I had to get my life back on track, or people who cared about me would continue to die. So, I buried Jupiter, shook off the booze, and pledged my life to his memory."

He raised his hands, his palms open to me. "That's it. That's the sorry life story of Bob Sandiford. Not very pretty, is it?"

I took his right hand between mine. "I'm so sorry. I can feel your pain. No man should ever have to go through what happened to you."

"Many people go through worse and don't fall apart," he said. "There are so many horrific stories out there."

"Yes. I suppose there are. But you still

haven't explained why you're fooling society, why you're making the world think you're homeless."

"You'll never understand, but I'll try." He sat for a moment, appearing deep in thought. "No, I can't find the words. Just accept that it's something I promised Jupiter."

His failure to explain made me wonder if this was another charade, another attempt at jerking me around. "Then why did you tell me your story? What's your gimmick?"

He shifted on the cushion and scratched his scalp. "Nothing I can explain. Again, I find myself at a loss for words. All I can say is your problem has affected me like Jupiter did. For one of the few times since my family died, something interests me. That something is your situation."

I lifted my mug, realizing I had emptied it while Bob told his story. I didn't remember a single sip. That was an indicator of how engrossed I was in his words. Despite my earlier reservations, respect for him flowed into me. This man with so much pain in his background was sharing with me. I was convinced. For something to do, I signaled Judy to bring another round, but Bob waved his off. "I'm buying," I said.

"Two is my limit." His eyes focused on a

place far beyond me. "Those were my last words to Jupiter as they lowered his casket. I promised I'd clean up and sober up. No more than two a day, no matter what the occasion." He took a deep breath. "There are days when it's hard to live up to that oath, but I do it. I do it for him and for me. Now, do you want my help?"

With no hesitation whatsoever, I said, "I'd be honored," and reached across the table, hand extended.

He grinned and shook it. "Okay, partner. How about you start by telling me why you were chasing this dame? The whole story this time."

"She set me up . . ." I gave him a condensed version of what transpired from the time I received the phone call from the alleged Maria Garcia until I met him that afternoon.

When I finished, he nodded. "Sounds like something you'd see in a movie — if I went to movies. Of course, her being dead doesn't help us any." He toyed with his beer bottle for a moment, peeling the label with his thumb nail. "Hillsboro Boulevard, Deerfield Beach. I'll put out the word. There are homeless all over the area. Maybe one of them saw something — something they'd never tell a cop. You'd be amazed what we see and keep to ourselves. Saves a lot of hassle."

"Good. While you do that, I'll make contact with the detectives who put me on their short list. The communities here in Florida are so close together, they must know someone in Deerfield Beach. If we're lucky, her hit-and-run is solved, and the driver is confessing to multiple crimes, including the death of Jacobs." I took my cell phone from my purse.

"Make your calls. I'll use street commo." He pushed out of the booth and took a couple of steps.

"Wait," I said. "I owe you — the reward, remember?"

He chuckled. "Maybe I'm getting a bigger reward than either of us figured on. But you can pay for the beer. Oh, and leave Judy a nice tip. She's really a sweetheart." He paused. "There is one other thing though. Keep my secret. I like the life I lead. If the word gets out, I'll have to change it."

"I will."

He crossed the room and exited through the front door.

TWENTY-FOUR

I called Detective Bannon and filled him in on the death of Deborah Ann Goldstein, aka Maria Garcia. He uh-huh'd me several times, then asked if I was sure. I assured him I was. After that, he promised to coordinate with the Deerfield Beach police and see what they knew. Like me, he hoped they had an ID on the driver.

After a moment of inner debate, I told him about my near miss with the white Toyota Avalon. I gave him time to chew on what I'd said, then let him know I considered it strange the woman that I sought had died on the bumper of a hit-and-run vehicle. I sealed my deal by saying, "Maybe her accomplices had the idea I was getting close, so they took her out."

The line stayed silent for a moment, then I got a noncommittal "Uh-huh. We'll look into it when we have time. Busy week here."

"Thanks, Detective," I said. "It's been a

pleasure talking to you." There may have been a drip of sarcasm in my voice. After clicking off, I stared at the wall a moment, wondering about the whole strangeness of my life. Such a short time ago, I'd been a normal, messed-up PI trying to make my mark in the world. Now, I was befriended by a presumably homeless man I'd probably driven by numerous times without noticing, hounded — or so I felt — by the police who had me on their short list, and totally befuddled by what swirled around me. My life was under control — yeah, right.

The clinking of glasses in Judy's hands took me out of my melancholy. She was keeping busy behind an empty bar. The other patrons had left while Bob kept me engrossed with his story. I rose and walked to where she worked, then slid onto a stool. "I have nowhere to go and an urge to chat. Got a moment?"

Her head was down and stayed there. I thought I saw a drop of water fall.

"Any friend of Bob's is a friend of mine," she said. "Besides, he says a good bartender is there to listen, like a good therapist. Helps sell drinks and makes the drinkers feel like somebody cares."

I grinned at the homespun philosophy, even as she sniffled. She was right on both counts. But something had gotten to her. I know of nothing else that drips like tears. "Judy. Look at me. Is something wrong?"

She turned red-rimmed eyes toward me. "I'm sorry, ma'am, but I was listening when you and Bob was talking. It was hard to hear, but I heard most of what he told you. I had no idea." A tear carved its way down her cheek.

"You mean what he told me about his past?"

"Yes, ma'am."

Damn. Another question mark. Did he make it up just for me, or was it the truth that he didn't share easily? Judy's red-blotched face told me she wasn't faking. Her crying was not contrived.

Time to move on. "How long have you worked here?"

"Two years." She sniffled again, then blew her nose in a bar napkin. "I came here right after Bob rescued me off the street."

"Tell me about it."

"Sure." A big smile broke through, not just lighting her face, but putting a glow in her eyes. "I want everyone to know what a wonderful person he is." She paused, as if gathering her thoughts. "But first, he must think an awful lot of you. I don't think he ever told anybody about his past."

She wiped her cheeks. "Not very professional, am I? Bob would give me a lecture. But . . ." She sighed. "Did he tell you he took over Jupiter's corner as a tribute to him? Did he tell you he splits the profits from the bar and his paper-selling among homeless charities — all as a tribute to Jupiter?"

"No," I answered. "I guess he was too modest. But where do you fit in? Are you just a bartender, or is there more to your story?"

She twirled a glass in her hands and got a thoughtful look on her face. I could tell she was looking backward, and the furrows in her forehead said the memories were not all good.

"I ran away from home when I was sixteen. You don't need to know why or what I did to stay alive. It wasn't the glamorous life I thought it would be. Anyway, Bob found me huddling in an alley on a cold night and brought me here. I lived in his female dorm for a year until he got me straightened out. Now I have my own apartment. It's not much, but it's mine, and I pay all the bills. If it hadn't been for him, I'd probably be dead by now — or in some condition worse than death. He dried me out, got me medical care, and, well . . ."

171

She seemed to search her mind. "It sounds so melodramatic, but he saved my life. Now he wants me to go to college, says he'll help me with the tuition."

My cynicism jumped up. "What do you do for him in return?"

"Do?" Her face changed, pain, then anger taking over. "Don't you ever say stuff like that. I do nothing for him except be the best bartender I can be. Understand when I say I'd do anything he wants. All he has to do is drop a hint. Why not? I did it for other men. You name it, I've done it. I know how to please a man. But Bob won't consider it. I know because I offered — more than once. He's the only true gentleman I ever met." She took a couple of deep breaths. "Now, ma'am, if you don't mind, I need to get back to work."

There may have been extra emphasis on *ma'am* this time. I had obviously jumped the fence with her. "Thank you, Judy. I guess I've seen too much of the dark side of the world. You're a lucky young lady to have a friend like him — and so am I."

I slid off the stool and headed for the front door, not sure what my next move was. It had been a strange afternoon. Some of her words came back to me in the form of a question mark.

"Judy, you said you lived in his female dorm. What did you mean?"

Her face took on an unsure look. "Didn't he tell you? He has rooms in the back, each with bunks. One for men and one for women." She shrugged. "Anybody who needs a bed gets one."

"Why? Why would he do that?"

She shook her head. "I asked him once. He said he helped kill a friend who had nowhere to live. If he had had a room nearby, Jupiter might still be alive, maybe wouldn't have tried to cross that street." She shrugged. "Guess it's just part of paying off his obligation to Jupiter."

"Thank you," I said, then turned toward the door, my mind swirling around this man who had befriended me. Could he be for real, or just another South Florida scammer?

TWENTY-FIVE

Immersed in what I'd heard from Bob, then Judy, I pushed through the front door of the bar into the bright sunshine. Squinting, I headed toward my car while digging to find my sunglasses in the clutter of my purse.

An engine raced, then I heard the squeal of tires. Turning, I saw the blur of a vehicle coming at me from the back of the parking lot. A rush of wind pushed me as I dived between two vehicles, landing on hands and knees. More skin off my palms, and I felt my slacks give. Thank God for my quick reflexes, which were almost too slow.

Scrambling to my feet, I screamed, "Come back here, you bastards. I'm tired of this crap." Simultaneously, the thought jammed its way into my head that a new line of work might be a good idea. Followed by, did I really want them to come back?

I looked for the car, but saw only a flash

of white as it tore out of the parking lot and hid itself in the far lane behind a huge SUV. It caught the left turn signal and raced away. My closest guess was a Florida plate. Beyond that, nothing except it was white. It might have been the Toyota again, but I couldn't be sure. I hoped it was. The thought of another car trying to run me down was discouraging. I didn't have that many enemies — or did I?

I checked my hands, seeing new scratches, but nothing severe enough to justify calling David. Darn. What was the point in getting hurt if you couldn't consult your favorite physician? I wiped my palms against my hips, thankful I hadn't landed on my butt again. First, it didn't need any more punishment and second, I was still embarrassed about mooning Boca Raton the last time I encountered a white car.

"You all right, ma'am?"

I started, then spun and saw what under any other circumstances I'd have called a reprobate. Today I wasn't sure. "Yeah, I'm fine. Who're you?"

"Bob told me to watch for you. Said take care of you. Folks call me Street."

I studied him. Dirty beard, disgusting dreadlocks, a penetrating smell, and clothes from a low-class dumpster. Teeth that hadn't visited a toothbrush in a long time. Had to be one of Bob's friends. "Nice to know you, Street. I'm okay. Just getting tired of jumping for my life. Did you see that vehicle?"

"Yes'um. One of them Toyota Avalons. White with gold trim. Lot of 'm 'round here. Two men in the front seat. Couldn't tell about the back. Windows too dark."

I figured he was of the *short-choppy sentences school of education* — or lack thereof. What the heck? Who needed subjects and verbs? "Don't suppose you got the license number."

"Yes'um. QQ3984. Florida, with one of them oranges in the middle. Bob said I should watch for it and 'member the number."

If Bob had been there, I would have kissed him. I suppose I should have offered one to his friend, but I couldn't find that much gratitude. I dug into my purse and came out with pen and paper. "Give me the plate number again."

He did, and I wrote it down, a grin splitting my face. With this, I could burst the case wide open. My grin faded. Unless the license was stolen. But I wouldn't know until it was run. And even if it didn't match the car, it would prove once and for all that someone was out to get me. And if they were trying to get me, it meant I was innocent. Even Bannon and Sargent could follow that logic — if they believed me. I shook my head. Too many ifs. I was making myself dizzy.

I flipped open my cell phone and punched in Detective Bannon's number. Just my luck. He didn't answer. I left a message and hung up feeling better than I had in several days. Then I checked my knees. Another pair of ripped slacks. I needed to solve the case soon. My wardrobe was taking a beating, and it had its limits.

After assuring Street at least five more times that I was okay, I offered him a five-dollar bill and thanked him.

"Oh, no, ma'am. You Bob's friend. I do anythin' for him. You won't see me, but when you in this area, I be nearby. Don't you worry none."

I climbed into my car and headed out of the parking lot, my mind working to find a crease in the zone of confusion that clouded it. Twice, three times if you count my meeting with Deborah Ann Goldstein, aka Maria Garcia, I'd had opportunities to land solid clues to the mess. Each time I failed. Either I was slipping or the bad guys were lucky. I refused to consider they might be faster and smarter. Not a chance.

I replayed the two attempted rundowns. Nothing I could hook my blouse on. White Toyota Avalons were a dime a dozen in South Florida, and every car had tinted windows. The bright spot, if I could call it that, was they might try again and my luck might improve. I frowned, realizing that if they tried again, their luck could improve. Since the choice of time, place, and method was theirs, they held the advantage. All I had was . . . was . . . not much. Then I remembered Bob and Street, and my spirits lifted. Were there others? Maybe I wasn't as alone or as helpless as I felt.

As I drove south on Military Trail, my cell phone played its ditty. A quick look at the caller ID window brought a smile. "Hi, David. I was hoping you'd call."

"Are we still on for dinner, or are you on your way to the emergency room?"

I heard humor in his words, or hoped I did.

"I'm headed home to get ready to spend the evening with my favorite doctor. When are you making my house call?"

"Suppose I meet you there. I'm only a couple of blocks away. I can kick back and rest while you change. It's been one hell of a day. Do you have a beer?"

My heart jumped, hoping this meant he'd decided I wasn't too big a risk. "Extra key under the flowerpot. Beer's in the fridge. Go ahead in and get comfortable. I'll be close behind you."

"Don't be long. I'm counting the minutes."

He clicked off, leaving me hovering above the seat, my foot barely touching the accelerator — or so I felt. I had a wonderful night with a gorgeous doctor in front of me. Life was good.

Thirty minutes later, I reached my house, parked, and rushed toward the front door. The grin I wore was so big I could feel it. An evening with David seemed far more important than a trivial thing like white cars trying to run me down. As I walked, I unbuttoned the top two buttons of my blouse. Yeah, it was a cheap move, but tonight I felt lucky and wanted every advantage. And I was sure David would appreciate a nice cleavage. Don't all men?

I popped open the door. "David, here —" The words froze in my throat.

David sat in a straight-backed chair facing the door. The chair belonged in the kitchen, not situated as a key part of my living room décor. Gray tape covered the lower part of his face. In the next moment, I realized it was duct tape, and it also bound his hands and legs to the chair.

"Good evening, Ms. Bowman."

Those words came from a man leaning against my bookcase. His manner appeared as relaxed as his clothing — tan slacks and a dark blue pullover. He was clean-shaven, no visible scars or tattoos, nothing about him to scare me, yet he did. Perhaps it was the pistol he held in his right hand, its barrel angling downward. Common sense told me he could rectify that situation long before I could reach into my purse.

I grappled for calmness while forcing my eyes away from the revolver. "Who are you? What are you doing here?"

"You may call me Bruce, but I am unimportant. Only the man I work for is important, and he wants to talk to you."

I studied him, wondering if he was as laid-back as he acted. "Your boss has an interesting way of extending an invitation. Was it his idea to truss my friend like something from a bad movie? Or was that yours?" As I said it, I looked at David. He did not look happy.

Bruce smiled, showing a lot of white teeth, a nice smile. "Your friend is an accident. We didn't expect him to come prancing in on us. Then he chose not to cooperate when we invited him to have a seat and keep quiet. Seems to be a real loyal type. He thought he should warn you. I hated to do it, but he needed convincing. Pistol barrel beside his head seemed to calm him a bit. But I believe in going the extra mile, so . . . I couldn't take the chance he'd get you excited before we had an opportunity to extend the invitation."

I noticed a bruise forming on David's temple. My first impulse was to rush to him, but I swallowed the urge. Probably best not to let Mr. Charm know I had strong feelings for David. That could make him a bargaining chip. I went for tough, not caring. "This is a bunch of crap. Turn him loose. He's a friend who drops in sometimes to filch an after-work beer from my fridge. I have nothing to say until he's free and out of here." To David, I said, "Sorry. Today's not a good day. Maybe some other time. But call first."

More smile, more casual leaning on the bookcase. "Nice. I bet you had the lead in your high school play. Suppose we compromise. I'll remove the tape from his face — that does look uncomfortable — and undo his arms and legs from the chair. Of course, I'll have to re-tape the hands for our trip. But if he promises to keep a civil tongue about him and not interfere, I'll leave his mouth untaped."

Was it possible his relaxation had increased since I entered? Perhaps my tough-gal persona wasn't working. He didn't seem to perceive me as much of a threat. Time to step it up a bit, and let him know I was not impressed. I took a deep breath and forced my voice down an octave. "Let me guess. You drive a white Toyota Avalon and specialize in running down pedestrians. But since your aim is not very good, you miss a lot. I bet your boss was so unhappy he sent you to ambush me here at my house. How'm I doing?"

He frowned, then laughed. "Great theory, but doesn't work for me. Do you write pulp fiction when your PI cases dry up? If so, I suggest you plant a dead body somewhere. Folks like that."

His body language had not changed. He was as cool as if leaning on a bar in his favorite pub. Now I was the one frowning, while trying not to. Had I run into a different someone who didn't like me? I mean, I knew I was a nice person. How many people could want me dead? Nah, had to be the Toyota gig. "I'm on to you. You made two runs at me and missed, right?" I said, not really wanting the truth.

"No. But if you're on the level, I'm glad you survived. My boss does not like disappointment. He's not prone to quick forgiveness."

This guy was just too cool. There must be some way to rattle him. I had to recover lost ground, make a dent in his façade. I walked to my couch and sat down. "I hate to make your boss unhappy or get you in trouble, but we're not going anywhere with you. Furthermore, I suggest you take yourself out of here on the double. It just so happens that Detective Bannon of the local police is on his way over."

"Ah, Ms. Bowman, you disappoint me. Your reputation says you're more imaginative than that. If it were true, would you really tell me? Tsk, tsk. You must have a case of the shilly-shallies, as you girls say around the bridge table. Now, do I turn your friend loose so we can leave, or will you continue to argue?"

It only took a moment to figure he had insulted me, inferred I was a coffee klatscher who spent her time gabbing with the girls. The truth was I had few close female friends. Everyone I knew had a husband or children. The lucky ones had both. "Dream on, Brucey. I'm not leaving this house with you."

If my words had any impact, he didn't show it. "Oh, my. I was certain we'd be able to skip the false bravado part. I know you're going, your friend knows you're going, and, of course, you know you're going."

"How 'bout me? Don't I know they're going?" a new voice said.

I looked and saw another man had entered the picture. He stood just inside the doorway, carrying a pistol like the first thug. However, the barrel of his weapon stared straight at me, reminding me of the one-eyed bogeyman I feared under my bed when I was young. For reasons that made no sense at all, I noticed he was dressed different — blue jeans with sneakers and a button-up shirt. Somehow, his attire made him seem more sinister. Maybe it was the grubby week-old beard.

Bruce said, "Have the car brought up, Gerald. We'll be ready to leave in a moment."

Gerald flipped open a cell phone and punched at the numbers. "Lodo, bring the car into the driveway. We're almost ready."

Their use of names bothered me — along with their nonchalance about my seeing their faces. I hoped it didn't mean they figured I wouldn't have a chance to pick them out of a lineup.

"Untie the doctor, then redo his arms," Bruce said. "Leave his mouth untaped. I'll gamble he learned his lesson."

A muffled sound came from my purse, my cell phone ringing.

"Must be Detective Bannon," I said. "Told you he was on his way. Want I should answer it? If I don't, he'll know something is wrong."

For the first time, I saw a slight crease in Bruce's affectation, a hint of hesitation. His eyes flicked toward Gerald, at David, then back to me. "Ah . . . yeah. Answer it." His voice picked up strength. "But make sure all that comes out of that bag is your phone. Gerald, be ready to shoot her boyfriend if a pistol appears."

As the phone rang again, I glanced at Gerald. He had stepped forward, only a couple of feet from David, his gun pointed at David's head. Bruce's barrel now stared at me. "Relax," I said, forcing strength into my voice — more strength than I felt. "Only the phone."

The fourth ring sounded as I fumbled it out. "Hello."

"It's me, Detective Sargent, returning your call to Bannon. What's this about somebody trying to run you down again?"

"Hi, Detective." I covered the phone and

whispered at Bruce, "It's the cop I told you about. He's on his way."

"Get rid of him," he replied, "or your boyfriend dies before he gets here."

Into the phone, I said, "Sorry, but I can't talk now. I have company and the steak is about to burn."

"Steak? Ms. Bowman, what are you talking about? I don't have time for games. Call me when you're sober."

The phone clicked in my ear. You handled that well, I thought. Some investigator you are.

"So?" Bruce said.

"He thinks I'm drunk."

Bruce laughed and lowered the gun. "Me, too. Steak? That may be the lamest excuse I ever heard. Now, back to our preparations to get out of here."

TWENTY-SIX

"Do we have a deal on your boyfriend?" Bruce, the chief kidnapper, said. "Does he keep his mouth shut if I take the tape off?"

I stared at David, hoping my eyes warned him to keep quiet. He was busy firing daggers at Bruce, who had resumed leaning against the bookcase in my living room.

"He'll behave," I said. "Won't you, David?"

He glanced at me, then returned his glare to Bruce. Any moment I expected to see blue smoke pour out of his ears.

"Let's find out. Gerald, prepare him for travel."

Gerald picked up a roll of duct tape from the table and walked to David. He ripped the tape from David's arms, leaving bare areas where I knew there had been hair. Then he demonstrated his professionalism as a thug by re-taping David's hands behind him. David didn't even have time to rub his wrists. I had to marvel at Gerald's skill since not only was David still sitting in the straight-backed chair, but his ankles were attached to its legs. If I ever chose to stage a kidnapping, I wanted Gerald on my team.

Interrupting my admiration, Gerald grabbed David's head with his left hand, and without ceremony, ripped the tape off David's mouth. The sound of the stickum turning loose was so loud, I flinched.

"You bastard," David said. "Undo my hands, and I'll —"

"Shut him up again," Bruce said, shaking his head. "Some folks you just can't be nice to."

In the flash of an eye, Gerald had replaced the tape, leaving David making mmmph, mmmph sounds. I hated the result, but admired the execution.

Gerald stepped away from David. "Whenever you're ready. All I have to do is snip the tape around his legs, and he'll be mobile."

David quit with the mmmphing sounds and went quiet except for a soft groan.

Bruce smiled at Gerald. "In a moment." He turned toward me. "Ms. Bowman, what will it be? Travel or argue?"

"Must be tough going through life hearing-challenged. I distinctly remember

188

telling you I'm not going any place with you."

Bruce sighed. "Okay. It's on your conscience, not mine. Break his pinky, Gerald. He's wearing his watch on his left arm. Must be a righty. Do the left hand first."

Before I could process what Bruce said, there was a cracking sound and David let out a super mmmph, this one containing pain.

"No. Stop. What the hell are you doing?" My mouth ran ahead of my mind.

"It's called the art of persuasion and team work," Bruce said. "I talk, Gerald breaks, and your friend suffers. Saves a lot of arguing. He has nine other fingers before we switch to other parts of his body. Probably affect his medical practice if he loses his hands. All the trial lawyers lined up to sue him will be heartbroken."

I looked at David, whose eyes reflected anguish, but what I could see of the rest of his face showed a determined set. He shook his head.

What could I do? What would any woman do if the man she wanted to father her babies was in that position? "We'll go with you."

Gerald's cell phone rang. He looked at it. "Lodo."

Bruce nodded. "Suddenly he can't live without us. Answer it."

Gerald flipped the phone open. "Yeah." He listened, his forehead furrowing. "What? Say that again."

More listening. Deeper furrows.

"Hold on." He spoke to Bruce, a mystified tone in his voice. "Lodo says there's a bunch of people headed up the sidewalk. He thinks one of them might be a guy he saw snooping around when we got here. They're carrying sticks and other clubs."

Bruce stared at him. "Bullshit. Give me that thing."

Seemed like David and I had bottomed on their interest list as Gerald handed over the phone.

"What the hell's going on, Lodo? Don't give me any shit, or you'll pay for it later." He quieted, a carbon copy of Gerald's expressions flitting over his face.

Frowning, Bruce said into the phone, "Are you drinking?"

Silence.

"You damn well better be sober. How many?"

More silence.

"Keep the line open. If they turn into the yard, we'll go out the rear. Boss said keep it simple, don't make a fuss. He'll kick our

190

asses if we end up on the eleven o'clock news. Back the car out and be ready to pick us up one block over. Then you're going to show me your army — and they'd better be there."

TWENTY-SEVEN

Bruce returned the phone to Gerald. "Keep it by your ear." To me, he said, "You know anything about a bunch of bums working this neighborhood?"

"Could be undercover cops. You know, they can be pretty sneaky. Maybe the detective sent them for one of my grilled steaks."

"No way, bitch." He wiped his hand over his mouth, a puzzled look on his face.

I struggled not to smile. Could Mr. Cool be losing his composure? I sure hoped so. From his antics, I assumed he had not anticipated anything going wrong, especially something like an invasion by the homeless.

"They're in the yard," Gerald said.

"Headed for the house?"

"Yes."

"We're out of here. Let's go." He ran toward the rear door, then stopped and turned toward me, his gun waving. "This is not over. We'll meet again." He grinned. "It may be your loss. The boss will not be happy at this development."

The slam of the back door found me untaping David's wrists, then ankles. I grabbed the edge of the tape over his mouth and, closing my eyes, followed Gerald's example. Worked like a charm.

But David would not be shaving for a few days. He'd look Hollywood scruffy. I wasn't sure of his opinion of an unkempt appearance, but the real loss, I feared, was his sore lips would keep him from kissing any time soon.

"Owwww," David said, rubbing his mouth. "Whoever invented duct tape should be sentenced to this chair forever."

"How's your finger?"

"Hurts. We need to splint it. Got a nail file or something?"

"In my purse." I rummaged through and found an emery board. Following his instructions, I used it to stabilize his finger. I had just finished taping both to the third finger when a soft tapping sounded from the front door.

I grabbed my purse and fished out my revolver. No more surprises, *no more damn surprises.* I was up to the top of my head with surprises. If another son-of-a-bitch bothered me, I intended to blow his ass into

Palm Beach County — the north end.

I sidled to the edge of the doorway, then glanced at David who sat holding his hand, his eyes wide, staring toward my pistol. After only a slight hesitation, he stood and moved to the other side of the door and nodded.

"Who's there? Identify yourself or I start shooting," I said. Okay, so it sounded like a B-movie. I was in no mood for originality. But I did add, "I'm not kidding. I'll blow your ass to hell if you don't speak up."

A nervous voice responded, "Bob sent me. Is everything all right in there?"

Glancing at David, who still appeared fascinated with my gun, I shrugged and flipped on the front floods as I opened the door. A man fitting the description of one of Bob's friends stood in the spotlight. Suffice it to say, he wouldn't be welcome in any of Broward County's finer restaurants. On second thought, fast food joints might bar the doors. He had his hands clasped on his head.

With a slight stutter, he said, "The bad guys are gone. They cut through the yards over to the next block and jumped in a car. We watched them drive away. Are you okay?"

I lowered the gun. "For the most part, yes.

Come on in."

"No'm. We'll watch out here. They might come back."

We? I looked around and saw no one else. "Who's we?"

"The others are there. You just can't see 'em. And that means the bad guys can't see 'em either. Trust us."

"Well . . ." I hesitated and looked over my shoulder at David. He held his bad hand in the good one, pain creasing his forehead. "I have to get my friend to the hospital," I said to my benefactor. "I'll call the police from the car."

"We'll hang out in case those crooks come back, keep an eye on your place until the police get here. When they git here, me and the others will disappear, if that's all right by you. My friends can watch for my signal but not be seen. The police and us don't move in the same circles, if you know what I mean."

He lowered his hands, turned, and walked away, soon lost from sight around the edge of the house.

"Damn," David said. "That was spooky. Glad he's on our team. Now, if you have no other drama in mind, I'd really like to go to the hospital. There's a slight debilitating throb coming from my finger. I fear my sense of humor could be seriously impaired if I don't get medical attention."

"I'll call nine-one-one."

"I don't think so. How would that look — a doctor being carried into the emergency room on a stretcher — diagnosis, broken pinkie? I'd never live it down. I prefer to risk my life with your erratic driving."

"Let's roll then. Doctor, you need a doctor."

He gave me one of his lopsided grins and waggled his eyebrows. "Better leave the jokes to me. I have a medical degree."

Twenty-Eight

A couple of hours later, David and I sat in the doctors' lounge off the hospital emergency room. Bandaging secured David's pinky to the ring finger. The break was not compound, but, as David said, every broken bone is serious. He figured it needed a month in the splint and another couple of weeks without stress to mend. In the meantime, the hand would limit his activities.

I was thrilled to see that his lips had regained their normal color. However, the redness and irritation around his mouth signaled that shaving soon was out of the question. Oh well, what's wrong with beard burn from the man you crave?

Otherwise, my luck held — all bad. Detectives Bannon and Sargent had shown up about halfway through David's x-rays, setting, and splinting. While they hadn't exuded patience, they agreed to wait until the doctor released David.

Now they were in full interrogation mode. Note, I said interrogation rather than interview. They were not happy. Bannon didn't say a word when Sargent took the lead.

He stared at his notes, then shifted his gaze to me. "I want to make sure I have this exactly right. Okay?"

"Of course," I said.

"And, in chronological order?"

"Go ahead. I have no place to go."

"Thank you, Ms. Bowman."

His tone was officious and overly formal, as cold as a tax collector's heart.

Bannon stood and strolled to a picture on the wall. He appeared fascinated with the cheap print of an Italian harbor scene as he examined it from different angles. I had to smile. I'd seen the same painting in numerous inexpensive motel rooms during stakeouts.

Sargent studied his notes, flipping between pages. He must have done well in the *let the suspect cool his heels* phase of his training. Finally, he cleared his throat. "A white Toyota Avalon attempted to run you down a week ago in Boca Raton alongside Military Trail, barely missing you. You believe the driver was the woman who tried to *frame* you. You have a witness, a newspaper vendor on the corner. Do I have that right?"

"Yes. That's the meat of it."

He looked at David. "Is that what she told you?"

"Yes. Well, close enough."

Sargent returned his attention to me. "Since then, the lady who tried to *frame* you," he glanced at the page, "Ms. Maria Garcia, has been killed in a hit-and-run, and is now identified as Deborah Ann Goldstein."

He acted like I should agree with him, so I did. David stared at me with wide eyes. I remembered he didn't know this part of the story.

Sargent must not have noticed. "Today, another attempt was made on your life. Again, by hit-and-run. This time, there was another witness, someone you call Street. He told you it was a white Toyota Avalon, license number QQ3984, with two men in the front seat. I take it I can assume Ms. Garcia, aka Goldstein, was not the driver. Is that accurate?"

"Yeah," I said, sensing there might be a tinge of skepticism in the air. "Tough to drive when you're dead."

"Why didn't you tell me?" David said. "That's the second time someone tried to run over you?"

"Sorry," I said. "I was going to tell you

tonight, but we had a minor interruption."

"Oh." He held up his hand. "How could I forget?"

Sargent rolled his eyes and turned to Bannon. "Looks like the new way to eliminate someone is to run them down. The anti-gun nuts will be thrilled. We won't have to worry about shootings anymore."

Bannon's back stayed to us, but he ducked his head while rubbing his face. Seemed like he and Sargent found my situation amusing.

Sargent came back to me. "After the latest attempt on your life by blunt force trauma, i.e., a car grinding you into the pavement, you went home where you walked into an ambush. Dr. Rasmussen was bound to a kitchen chair with tape over his mouth."

He glanced at his notes. "The chair had been placed in the living room facing the front door. One armed kidnapper was in the room. He told you his name was Bruce. A second kidnapper, equally armed, but more scary, joined him. Gerald, you said his name was. There was a third member of the gang in their car — someone called Lodo. The two inside guys communicated with Lodo by cell phone. Their stated intent was to take you and the doctor to some unknown location to meet *the boss*. When you refused to cooperate, Gerald broke the doctor's finger." He cut his eyes toward David, then back to me. "Am I on target?"

I nodded. I didn't know where he was heading, but his skepticism had morphed into sarcasm.

"But, in keeping with your record of last-second escapes from tragedy, a mob of homeless types armed with various home-made weapons stormed the house. The three thugs panicked and ran away. One of your rescuers told you he'd keep watch until the police arrived." He yawned. "You loaded the doc in your car and hightailed it for the hospital, calling us en route."

"That's right," I said. "Just the way the evening went down."

"And you never had the opportunity to thank your benefactors, other than the one you spoke to at the front door. By the time you and the good doctor came out of the house, there was no one in sight."

"Yes, they had —"

"Well, one part of her story checks out," Sargent said, looking at Bannon, who had finally turned toward us. "When the uniforms arrived, they reported no evidence of anyone in the area — and no evidence of a break-in."

"Is there a problem?" I squeaked, realizing

my story was not quite *Law and Order* material.

"No. No problem a boilermaker won't solve," Sargent said, closing his notebook. "Ms. Bowman, have you ever considered moving to another town, maybe one in Wyoming or Montana? Alaska is a possibility, too."

"Now, Major," Bannon said, walking toward us. They were his first words since Sargent began the interview. "I'm sure Ms. Bowman has a good reason for spinning her yarn. We mustn't be too tough on her. That concussion she received could have affected her lucidity. And she did give us a license number. Perhaps we should run that before we recommend her for the loony bin."

"That's right," I said, ignoring Bannon's patronizing tone. "Find the owner of that plate, and your case is solved. If you don't believe me, ask David who broke his finger."

"It was like she told you," David said. "Beth does not lie."

Sargent gave him a look of resignation. "You may be right. But do you have any idea how many cases are charged to us now? There have been two murders and a rape since Mr. Jacobs' death. Not to mention a dozen burglaries, car thefts, and miscellaneous felonies. Then there are the ones we had before Ms. Bowman entered our lives. Those are serious cases with real leads affecting," he glared at me, "*real people.* My question to you, Dr. Rasmussen, is if she's so sincere, why do I feel like a bit player in *Alice in Wonderland*?"

TWENTY-NINE

Detectives Bannon and Sargent left David and me sitting in the doctors' lounge after saying they'd check the license plate number. Their attitudes said it would not be a high priority.

I stood in the doorway watching their backs as they walked through the exit. "I don't think they believed me, David. Does my story sound as strange as Sargent made it out to be?"

"First, come over here and sit down. There's nothing to be gained by trying to read their minds — especially from behind. But, since you ask, I was with you, and I'm not sure I believe it. You really think there was an army of homeless rushing the house to rescue us?"

"Yes," I said. "You saw the man at my front door. And the thugs must have seen them because they took off."

"But why? Why on earth would they save

us? Do you know any of them?" His look said he found the whole situation doubtful.

I considered my promise to Bob not to give him away. Sometimes we have to compromise with ourselves. At that moment, my integrity took a hard hit. "If you promise to keep the secret, I'll tell you about Bob Sandiford." After he nodded and squeezed my hand, I told him. When I finished, his face bore the same skeptical look as Sargent's.

He stared at his damaged hand, then said in a resigned voice, "Well, my finger *is* broken. That part of your story is verified."

The clock ticked away several hours — or so it seemed. I suppose it was only a couple of minutes. Finally, I couldn't stand the silence. "What now? I still owe you a beer."

David looked up, a smile breaking through the gloom on his face. "Yes. You do, don't you? Not one from your fridge though. I have reservations about hanging out at your place."

"Me, too. Which begs the question of where I stay until this mess is over." I paused, waiting for David to speed to my rescue. My knight didn't rise to the occasion, so I said, "Look out, Motel 6. I'm on the way."

We sat without saying anything for a moment while I wondered how much slack there was in my credit card. Then I felt David squeeze my hand again. When I looked at him, there was a mischievous twinkle in his eye.

"There's always my condo. I have an extra bedroom."

Hallelujah.

He continued, talking fast. "We can swing by your place while the cops are still there. You can grab a few things, then we'll have dinner. After we eat . . ." He shrugged.

I stared at him, wondering about that extra bedroom. My druthers were to stay out of it. The master suite was more to my liking. "Sounds like a plan to me. What say we get started?" I hesitated, then plunged on. "I don't have any clean pajamas."

"So?"

"I might get cold."

"Only if you choose to sleep alone."

"Not a chance."

I awoke to sunlight filtered by the sheers over the window. Stretching, I felt luxurious and sated from a wonderful night with David. Without going into details, I'll simply say he was everything I expected — and more. And we only bumped his bad finger once.

When I rolled toward his side of the bed, I found it empty. Instead of the man I wanted to cuddle, there was a note on his pillow. *Early rounds this morning. Cereal on the table in the kitchen. Coffee in the carafe on the counter. Thank you for a wonderful evening. See you tonight. Don't get hurt today.*

It wasn't exactly a love note, but close enough for now. I'd have liked it better if he hadn't reminded me there were people out there who thought injuring me was a priority.

I stretched again and considered switching to his side of the bed and going back to sleep in the fragrant aroma of his manly scent. But reality checked in, and I knew it was time to roll, time to find out why I had become such a target. I plumped the pillows and sat up, thinking, evaluating. It had to start with the death of Jacobs and the attack on me in his hotel room.

I had a white Toyota trying to turn me into Spam and three thugs wanting me to meet *the boss.* The leader, Bruce, denied knowledge of the Toyota. Did this mean I had two groups on my tail? That thought didn't give me an elevated sense of security. What was the story? I needed answers.

One thing was for sure. I wouldn't find any satisfaction sitting in David's bed —

well, unless he came home early. I threw back the covers and climbed out, shivering in my nakedness. First a shower, then a bowl of cereal. After that . . . Hey, I'd think of something. I was Elizabeth Angeline Bowman, Private Investigator. Said so right on the badge I carried. The key word was *investigator.* With that reassuring thought in mind, I headed for the bathroom.

While standing under the hot spray, I considered where to start. After yesterday and the protection I received, Bob Sandiford seemed the best direction. I owed him my thanks, perhaps my life. Plus, I wanted to get his permission to bring David by to meet him. I thought they would hit it off, and David would know I hadn't exaggerated about my newspaper vendor/bar owner/philanthropist.

I wondered if Bob had a cell phone. Did he think he could get through life without one? If that's how he thought, I would strongly suggest he change. We couldn't work together if I had no way to contact him other than driving past his corner. How was he to keep rushing to my rescue if I couldn't call him?

When I opened the bag I'd thrown together at my place the previous evening under the protection of a uniform, I realized

I'd either have to make another trip or go shopping. Under the best of circumstances, I'm a lousy packer. However, with the evening's expectations driving me, I'd done worse than usual. Of course, that depended on where I stayed. I had enough for the day, but hoped I'd have to acquire a change for the next day.

I dressed, then went to the kitchen, smiling when I saw the cereal on the table — Fruit Loops. My macho doctor-lover ate *Fruit Loops*? Bet he never prescribed those for his patients.

THIRTY

After giving myself a sugar overdose on David's cereal, I filled a travel mug with coffee and headed out to find Bob. I hoped it wasn't too early for him to be on his corner. If he wasn't there, I could try the bar, but felt pretty certain it would be closed. Judy told me there were sleeping accommodations in the back, but didn't say Bob used them. My impression from her was he maintained those for his homeless friends. In short, I had no idea how to find him if he wasn't selling papers.

I considered killing time by cruising past my house first. If the way was clear, I could slip in and pick up another change or three of clothing. Then, if David suggested I stay over, I'd be ready. That sounded like a plan more to my liking, so I blessed it and made a left turn.

When I reached my neighborhood, I started five blocks out and circled, closing the radius with each trip around the area. I didn't see any cars that held ominous-looking thugs on surveillance or any white Toyota Avalons with gold trim. A couple of Camrys and three Corollas, even two Priuses, but no Avalons. Kind of disrupted my illusion that I lived in an upper middle-class neighborhood.

Satisfying myself there were no thuggeries about to take place, I pulled into my driveway. Big mistake. As I slid out the door, a large sedan coming fast slammed on its brakes, blocking me in. Caught with one foot on the ground and the other inside the car, I was at a disadvantage fumbling behind me at my purse. Someday, I'd learn to carry that blasted gun where I could get to it. However, it was probably to my advantage that I didn't pull it. A man stepped away from the edge of my house holding either a howitzer or a semi-automatic pistol. From my vantage point, it looked more like the former. Once I tore my eyes away from his hand and up to his face, I recognized Gerald.

Two others jumped from the white Mercury that blocked my driveway. I groaned as I recognized Bruce. My best guess was the third man would be Lodo. Shit. Déjà vu all over again. My opinion of the key word on my badge — *investigator* — sailed downhill as I realized I'd fallen into a trap like the ditziest heroine in the lowest budget movie. If I escaped this one, I vowed to change my hair color to platinum blond. Might as well appear the way I behaved.

"Good morning, Ms. Bowman," Bruce said.

Apparently, he'd recovered from his flight the previous night and again displayed his gentlemanly persona.

"Good morning, Bruce," I said, proving I could also be gracious. "I see you didn't injure yourself when you dashed out my back door." Never hurts to rub it in a bit.

"No, but it's kind of you to notice. Now, can we pick up where we left off? You were about to join us on a trip to chat with the boss." He waved his jacket pocket like in the movies, then scanned the neighborhood. "You're not expecting any guardian angels this morning, are you?"

Instead of answering, I stared at him. I assumed the pocket waving was to convince me his hand held a pistol. Probably the same one he had the previous night. I could well remember the business end of that one. Ominous.

When I inspected the man beside Bruce, I saw the same hand position. Non-surprises filled the day. And Gerald, who I knew had a cannon suitable for taking out tanks and fortified positions, now had his hand in his pocket. Guess they were bashful about neighbors observing my abduction. I have days when I'm not the brightest bulb in the marquee, but that day was not one of them. That day I was brilliant. Only used a few seconds to make the right decision. "Your car or mine?"

Bruce smiled. "Mine. Lodo enjoys the feel of the Mercury, and you know the rule. Driver gets his choice." The pocket wave again. "Shall we go?"

"By all means." I marched toward his vehicle, acting like we were off to a business brunch. Maybe they'd relax around a woman acting like a compliant wimp.

A moment later, I was in the middle position of the backseat squeezed in tight between Bruce and Gerald, the muzzles of their guns pressed into my sides. Guess they thought pinning me with their bodies meant I couldn't escape.

"Hey guys," I said, "you get any closer, and I'll have to name my firstborn after you. Which do you prefer, Bruce Gerald or Gerald Bruce?"

That produced strange looks from both of them, but they did scoot over a bit — not much, but enough to allow a deep breath. I took one.

Bruce leaned away from me far enough to say, "Gerald, check her purse. We wouldn't want her to get hurt by trying anything silly."

Gerald followed instructions and displayed my pistol, pepper spray, and handcuffs. "Looks like we tied into one tough lady."

"Facsimiles," I said. "I got them at Toys R Us."

"Uh-huh." That came from Bruce, who didn't seem to believe me. He switched topics. "I'm sure you understand you have to wear a blindfold. A professional like you probably has a photographic memory. The boss doesn't want you to know where we're meeting. He's a nut on his privacy."

"Of course," I said like it was a situation I encountered every day. "Not too tight though. I'd hate to miss anything he says because you gave me a headache. That's happened in previous kidnappings, you know."

He gave me a look that said I was a kook, but played the game. "I understand. Your comfort is my most important consideration."

The world went black as he slipped a sleep mask over my eyes. Then I felt him fumbling behind my head. I assumed he was adding a blindfold. Probably afraid I had X-ray vision or something. When he finished, I knew I'd have no clue where we were going. Total darkness.

To add insult to injury, I felt cold steel slip around my wrists. Handcuffs. I wondered whether they were mine, and if the key was in my purse.

The car careened along as I tried to keep count of rights and lefts versus time spent without turning. That proved to be as impossible as it sounds. Soon, I'd lost track of time and location. For all I knew, we could have been in Palm Beach or in the middle of Homestead. About the only thing I was sure of was we hadn't traveled too far east — there's an ocean out there — or west — the Everglades gets in the way. Had to be north or south. An advantage or disadvantage of living in South Florida, depending on your needs at the time, there's very little land east or west. However, in the north-south axis of the tri-county area, there were still lots of places where *the boss* could live.

One problem I had with keeping track of our trip was my mind kept leaping to what would happen when we stopped. I feared it was no mistake my abductors made no attempt to hide their faces. It might be an indication I'd soon be swimming with the fishes — or feeding the alligators. On the plus side though, was the fact they chose to blindfold me. Doubts swirled.

THIRTY-ONE

After an indeterminate amount of time, the car slowed, pulled onto what I took to be a driveway, then moved at a few miles per hour. I began timing the off-road strip by counting Mississippis. I reached twenty before we came to a stop after bouncing over what felt like two speed bumps. A grinding sound followed — garage door, I thought — then the Mercury lurched forward again before stopping and the engine dying.

"Home," Bruce said. "Now, Ms. Bowman, watch your step as we go into the house."

From the other side of me came a chuckle. "Not possible. The blindfold stays on. She can't watch anything."

I held out my wrists. "I walk better with both hands for balance. You can take these off."

"Wish I could. But certain protocols must be followed. If you prefer, I could cuff your arms behind you."

"That's okay," I said, chuckling. "I'll live with what we have."

Gerald laughed. "You gotta like this chick. She's got balls." He hesitated, then broke out in louder laughter.

Bruce joined Gerald in the mirth. If Lodo had a reaction, it was lost to me.

"Yes, she is gutsy," Bruce said. "Now, Ms. Bowman, you'll have to trust me. Lean on me, and I'll keep you from falling. When I tell you to step up or step down, do it. There are stairs to negotiate. We're in the garage, and you'll have to step up to enter the house — one step. Next, we encounter three down. We'll go up again, four of them. Don't worry about remembering. I'll prompt you as we come to them. And," he hesitated, "if you tell the boss what he wants to know, we'll have the same situation coming out. If not, you won't have to concern yourself with stumbling."

"I don't suppose you'd like to give me a forecast of what happens if *the boss* is not happy with my answers."

"Remember when you were in school and the motto was *Cooperate and Graduate*. Graduation for you will be my dropping you at your house. No cooperation, no graduation." His words carried a note of finality.

I forced a smile. "Well, graduation sounds like the best alternative. Lead on, McDuff."

"Yeah, we'd better get in there. Undoubtedly, the boss heard the garage door open and is waiting for us. He wasn't in the best of moods when we left this morning. He's still upset that I didn't deliver you last night."

Several stumbles later, Bruce settled me onto a soft leather chair in what felt like a spacious, multi-windowed room. Either *the boss* was using a sunlamp or the sun streamed in. Thinking of the time — mid to late morning — I assumed the windows faced east. But what did I know? Since the blindfold remained in place, it could have been a sunroom with windows on three sides, a tanning salon, or a gazebo. We hadn't walked across grass, but could have negotiated a breezeway without my knowing it. I had considered counting my steps, but threw the idea away. What purpose would it serve?

"Ms. Bowman. So nice to have you as my guest," a new voice said. "Would you like something to drink — water, maybe a soda? I assume the hour is too early for anything alcoholic. You need only name your choice, and Lodo will do your bidding."

The speech was well-modulated, a bit

gravelly. It reminded me of the bass-voiced types who do voiceovers or read scripts to the ostensible movement of an animal's lips. If there was an accent, I didn't find it.

"A diet soda would be nice," I said, playing the game. "And removing this blindfold and the cuffs will make my day much brighter."

My host chuckled. "A wonderful play on words. I enjoy a person who understands the art of repartee. I should have brought up the visual impairment. Lodo, get Ms. Bowman a diet cola while I apologize for my bad manners." There was a distinct change in his tone — from one speaking to a guest to one commanding a servant. He continued. "Bruce, take off her blindfold and the handcuffs. I'm sure Ms. Bowman will be more comfortable without them."

"Yes, sir."

I felt someone fumbling with the knot behind my head, then the sleep mask lifted. Light flooded in, blinding me. The first thing that came into focus was Bruce standing in front of me with a handcuff key in his fingers. A moment later, my hands were free. Next, I saw Gerald leaning against a doorjamb, a revolver cradled in his large right hand. So much for my initial thought of making a break for it. My internal alarm cranked up a couple of notches. The situation did not bode well for my spending the night with David as I preferred.

"Thank you," I said, rubbing my eyes, then my wrists. I've always believed you are as you act. If I didn't let them see my fear, I wouldn't be afraid — or something like that.

"You're welcome. You realize they must be replaced when you leave."

I looked for the voice, but saw only a speaker above the door. Mr. *Boss* was not in my presence.

Lodo entered from outside and handed me an iced soft drink in a plastic cup, then assumed Gerald's position at the door. I took the opportunity to study Lodo, memorizing his features. African American with a shaved head. Brown skin tone, not dark. He towered above me. I figured about six-two with a body that bulged his clothes — and not from fat. Attractive guy except for a nasty scar on his cheek. Looked like he came in second in a knife fight. Or maybe he won, but only after receiving a mark for life. If he decided to give up his career in crime, he fit the profile of a professional wrestler.

I scanned from Lodo to Gerald to Bruce. Not a trio to make a girl's heart go pitter-pat — except in abject fear.

A quick look around told me my luck continued its downslide. We were in a room with cement walls, fluorescent lighting, and one door, against which Lodo leaned. The lighting reminded me of a tanning salon — brilliant. That explained the sunlight I thought I felt when we entered.

My three roommates wore sunglasses. I assumed it was not to hide their identities since we were well past that stage.

I squinted at Bruce. "How about a pair of shades for me?"

"Sorry, Ms. Bowman," the speaker above the door said. "Your eyes will adjust in a few minutes. I've often found that studying a person's eyes tells me more than their words." He hesitated. "If you've finished examining the place, you know there is no way out except through Lodo. And I assure you, Lodo is an impenetrable obstacle. Also, inspect the area carefully and you'll see there are enough cameras to ensure I have a clear shot of your face at all times. The eyes, remember?"

"So, you're sitting someplace comfortable while I swelter here with your friends?" I said as I followed his suggestion. I did a quick count and spotted eight lenses before I quit. I had heard that the camera puts five pounds on a person. That meant I was in danger of gaining a quick forty.

"Don't overact, Ms. Bowman," he said in a colder tone. "It doesn't become you. The room is seventy-two degrees. My employees are there to make you comfortable. If you need something, you need only ask. Of course," he interrupted himself by chuckling, "I reserve the right to say no."

"First thing you can do is show yourself. Second is tell me who you are."

"It's bad manners not to please a guest, but I have to refuse you on count number one. I have no intention of letting you see me. Enjoy your view of Bruce, Gerald, and Lodo. I'm sure you've memorized their features by now. As for who I am, I'll meet you halfway. You may call me Mr. T."

THIRTY-TWO

My first thought was how insipid the whole situation was. Locked in a room with three thugs and a boss who hid from me. Then the utter stupidity of everything rushed in, and I laughed. "You must watch too many reruns. Mr. T? Is that a take-off from *The A-Team*?"

"The what? Oh, I get it. No, my people often call me Boss. Since that might seem farfetched for you, I thought you'd like something simpler. So, Mr. T it is."

"Fantastic," I said. "Okay, why are you hiding? I suppose it's so I can't pick you out of a police lineup."

"Astute. Very astute. You're living up to your reputation."

I sipped my drink, thinking how polite everyone was. Not the types who'd try to turn you into a greasy smudge in a parking lot. More likely, they were of the long-swim-in-cement-boots persuasion. Everything civil until they pushed you out of the boat.

I set my glass on a small table to my right. "I don't mean to sound like an ill-mannered guest, but I have plans for this afternoon. Could we move on to the reason I'm here? If it's to waste *me,* you're wasting valuable time."

A gravelly chuckle came through the speaker. "Yes. I'm sure you're curious, therefore I'll get right to it."

I let my eyes wander the room, taking in Bruce and Gerald who sat in chairs similar to mine. They looked relaxed, almost bored, but not so much they couldn't raise the pistols they held. Lodo continued to lean against the door, scowling. A straight-backed chair was vacant. Best to take it slow and easy.

The boss continued, "You interfered in my business, and I take that personally. My assumption is that it was not on purpose, or you'd be fish bait now. Don't do anything to make me think I'm not a good judge of people."

"Mr. . . . uh, T, you lost me. I assure you anything I did was quite unintentional. That is, if I knew what you're talking about."

He laughed, and his minions joined him.

"You were witness to the murder of one Benjamin Jacobs. He was an associate of mine. I wish to know who killed him."

"Well, I sure don't know. I've been trying to find out, and when I do . . ." Whoops. Intuition jumped in and said maybe that wasn't the best line to pursue.

"I'm well aware of your efforts. That's why I had you brought here."

I heard the clink of ice cubes as he went silent. My guess was he had taken a sip of his drink. I did the same, figuring I may as well play the good guest.

He continued. "Bruce reported on your investigation of the woman who hired you, and the sketches and your conversations with the shopkeepers in the strip mall. The idea was good. Did you have any luck?"

"Nothing worthwhile," I said, wondering at the tone of his questions. Did that mean he didn't know about the death of Ms. Goldstein, whom I met as Maria Garcia? If so, I had an edge. All I had to do was find the best way to use it.

"Here's what I suggest, Ms. Bowman. You're only one person, albeit a talented one. However, what you lack, I have in abundance — manpower. We're both look-ing for the same thing, Jacobs' murderers. If we combine our efforts, we'll have better luck and resolve it in a shorter period of time." The clink of ice cubes again. "Does that sound logical?"

I assumed he was examining my eyes, waiting for an answer. Stalling seemed like a good move. "You mean, your . . . uh . . . associates will work for me? They'll follow my instructions? Take orders from me?"

Laughter filled the room and poured from the speaker. Rats. Guess I wouldn't have a core of employees requiring me to subsidize their health care.

I squirmed as I waited for the laughter to die away. Bruce, Gerald, and the Boss seemed to be enjoying themselves. Even Lodo showed the threat of a smile. I won't say I have a thin skin, but I don't enjoy being the butt of a joke. Yeah, I should have expected it, but enough was enough. "If you guys are about finished, I'm ready to go home."

"All in due time," Mr. T said, a last chortle tingeing the words. "But first, we have to establish the rules of the game. They are really quite simple. I make them. You abide by them." He paused amid a breathy sound indicating he had moved closer to the microphone. "Gerald, help her to the straight-backed chair."

Before I could comment, hands slid under my armpits from the rear, and someone lifted me out of my comfortable seat and carried me across the room. Turning my head, I saw Gerald with a smile on his face. While I wasn't thrilled with the trip, it was nice to know I was light enough to lift with little effort. Guess my diet had paid off.

Gerald bounced me onto the hard-bottomed chair, but remained behind me. All I heard was a minor grunt as if someone had set a case of beer into the trunk of a car.

"Don't get too comfortable," Mr. T said. "Gerald, demonstrate rule number one."

I began a turn toward Gerald, but not fast enough. An excruciating pain shot from my right kidney area as I flew out of the chair. My shoulder hit the floor hard, followed by my head. I lay there, hurting all over — or so it seemed — wondering what had happened. Realization came when I saw Gerald who stood beside me, his hand making a fist. He had sucker-punched me.

"That's fine, Gerald. You can relax," Mr. T said. "Catch your breath, Ms. Bowman. Rules two and three coming up." Before I could scrabble away, he added, "Bruce, the pictures."

I cringed when Bruce stepped toward me before registering he'd said pictures. How much could that hurt? As I was to find out, more than a kidney punch.

Bruce held out a photo. "Someone you might know."

I sat up, eliciting a scream of pain from my side, and accepted the picture. It showed David getting into his car, the hospital in the background. He was dressed in a suit I'd seen him wear earlier in the week. "So?" I said. "What's your point? I know where David works."

"You may want to re-look," Mr. T said. "A hint. Look in front of the car."

I did and my stomach rolled. Although the likeness was out of focus, I recognized Gerald staring at the camera. His hand was in his pocket, reminding me of their behavior at my abduction — Bruce, Gerald, and Lodo with their hands inside their jackets. Then, I'd had every reason to think they clutched weapons. Same here.

"I see from your face," Mr. T said, "you recognize Gerald's proximity to your boyfriend. Since you're a smart lady, I suspect you figured out that Gerald could have hurt him had he chosen to. Anything between a simple ass-kicking to killing him. Is that how you see it?"

Still staring at the picture, I opened my mouth, but he cut me off. "Lest there be any doubt in your mind, rest assured that Gerald is a good soldier."

I raised my head toward the speaker. "If you —"

"Don't bore me with idle threats. Next picture, Bruce."

He shoved another in my direction.

THIRTY-THREE

I accepted the picture with trepidation. More shots of David? No. It was a house in an older neighborhood — white clapboard construction, green grass in the front yard, nice landscaping. A man stood in the yard. In the same breath, I recognized the house and the man — my mother's house and Lodo. Nausea assaulted me. I swallowed hard, forcing the bile down.

"Next," Mr. T said.

Another picture floated toward me. I picked it up and an overwhelming weakness gripped me. It showed Gerald putting groceries into my mother's car as she beamed at him.

"Want to see more?" the boss said. "We have others. Your mother is a nice lady. She was grateful when Gerald offered to help her. It would be a shame if she got hurt because her daughter is hardheaded and selfish." He stopped talking, and quiet

231

settled over the room.

I wanted to run and hide, cringe as I had when I saw evil as a young girl. Images of the night my father died rushed at me. Images of his struggle with a burglar. The sound of a gunshot, my father crumpling to the floor, the invader racing out the front door, never to pay for what he did. I was there, I saw it unfold, and all I wanted was to cover my eyes. I cried until my stomach hurt, over and over vowing *never again.* That was the night I decided to become a cop. That dream went down in flames when political correctness became the rule of the day. Police authorities might as well be the ones wearing handcuffs. I became a private investigator, figuring that was the next best thing. I couldn't let the criminals win.

I pulled myself to my feet, knowing Mom would expect me to be tough, just as she was while raising my brother and me after Dad died. I crossed the room at my own pace and sat in the comfortable leather chair, the one I previously occupied. I had to assert myself again. Plus, even though it was only a few steps, it gave me a moment to calm my emotions, set my face, and harden my heart. Mr. T had never met anyone like me. It was time he found out I wasn't some squishy thing that watched afternoon soaps and worried about how much cleavage to flash at the supermarket. "What's your point?"

"My point, my dear Ms. Bowman, is that I can injure your mother. I can leave your doctor friend a cripple. Those would be for starters. It could get worse. I know people who'll do anything for a price."

"And your point is?" I repeated, hoping to conceal how threatened I felt.

"Don't play hard-to-get with me. You know you're going to cooperate. It's only a matter of time — and how much pain I inflict. Let's save ourselves trouble and agree now."

I struggled for ideas, but couldn't find one that showed promise. "What do you have in mind?" Joining him seemed the best of limited poor alternatives. I had no reason to doubt his threats.

"Excellent. I see you're coming around. Here's the deal. What I say from this moment forward is our little secret. I won't tell anyone, and if you do, your mother and boyfriend pay. Understand?"

I gulped, swallowing what I wanted to say. "Yes."

"As I said before, Mr. Jacobs worked for me. I am an importer. I employed Mr. Jacobs to make deliveries. On the day he

233

died, he was to meet with a customer and turn over the briefcase he carried in exchange for a substantial sum of money. Needless to say, it did not go as planned. Someone intervened and took my merchandise."

Jacobs was a delivery boy? A courier? Of what? "And left me unconscious beside the body," I said, my mind swirling.

"Yes. At the time, I wondered where you popped in from. Bruce reported that you came out of nowhere, cut him off, and followed Jacobs around the city."

"Bruce was there? Must have been an important delivery. What was Jacobs carrying?"

Another chuckle. "I learned a long time ago the best way to keep people honest is to watch them closely. Bruce's job was to ensure Jacobs made the meet as scheduled. But you threw him off, and he had to hang back. You see, Ms. Bowman, in a perverse sort of way, you were responsible for Jacobs' death and the loss of my merchandise. If you hadn't gotten in the way, Bruce might have prevented both."

"You forget I was a victim, too. And you didn't tell me his cargo."

"Again, most astute. What he was carrying is none of your business. A smart operator like you should find a clue in that and keep her nose out. As for your victimhood, I didn't forget. I simply don't care. If you hadn't survived, you wouldn't be here. The bottom line is because of you, my merchandise is missing."

I looked at the camera over the door. "You don't seem particularly aggrieved at the fate of your employee."

"One of the costs of doing business, my dear. He was well-paid and knew the risks. But that's past. Let's live in the present. You weren't killed and will help me recover my property. Agreed?"

"We'll see."

"Yes. We will. Gerald, prepare her for the trip home."

In a twinkle, I was handcuffed and blindfolded. "Before you go, Ms. Bowman, be aware that one of my people will watch you every moment. You may find a hint of privacy when you are in the bathroom — but don't be too sure of that." His small laugh was sinister.

Nice to know he was enjoying himself. I wasn't.

"Bruce will give you a phone number. You will report in once a day, more if you uncover anything. Rest assured that if you miss a day, or I have reason to believe you're not cooperating, either your mother or your boyfriend will suffer — a little at first, but enough so you know I'm serious. I hope you won't make me get too drastic with them. While pain is a necessary adjunct to my business, it's not my favorite thrill — money is. Since I feel certain you only believe what you can see or touch, Bruce and Gerald will keep you apprised of what is happening to your mother and boyfriend. They take excellent videos."

He stopped talking. Quiet reigned. It was as if his words had sucked the air out of the room. Even Bruce, Gerald, and Lodo appeared in suspended animation. I felt like if I breathed, the world would come crashing down and something terrible would happen to Mom and David. Evil swarmed around me, causing me to shudder. Chill bumps popped onto my arms. My mind rejected what he said, yet my heart said he would follow through on his words.

"Do you understand me, Ms. Bowman?"

Although I couldn't see, I turned toward the speaker I knew hung on the wall, my mouth refusing to work.

"I had hoped it would not be necessary to prove I do not make idle threats, but if you insist . . ."

"No," I said. "I . . . I understand. I'll do

236

whatever you want."

"Excellent. But before you go, Lodo, another sample."

This time he picked me up and flung me across the room. Blindfolded, I was only able to stick my handcuffed hands out in the hopes of cushioning whatever I hit. Either fortuitously or on purpose, I landed in one of the soft chairs.

"Next time, Ms. Bowman," Mr. T said, "you could hit a concrete wall. All you need is to be ambulatory to do my bidding. A few broken bones won't slow you."

THIRTY-FOUR

The trip home was a nightmare in Technicolor and Cinemascope. The blindfold kept me from focusing on anything that might divert the image of my mother in the parking lot with Gerald. Gerald, who threw people around like beach balls. Gerald, who could tape, handcuff, and break fingers in a flash. Gerald, who was soft-spoken and polite. Gerald, who could act the gentleman and assist my mother with her groceries. Gerald, who worked with evil, who surrounded himself with evil, who was evil. And what did I have to perform combat? My wits. That was it. Nothing more. And my subconscious reminded me their performance in the last few weeks had been less than exemplary.

The car slowed, then stopped, and I felt hands working at the handcuffs. A moment later, Bruce restored my vision.

"You can walk from here, Ms. Bowman,"

238

Bruce said. "This is the telephone number you are to call at least once a day — no later than seven p.m." He shoved a card into my hand. "Don't try to identify the owner. Layers of false fronts block it. Before you penetrate the first, the boss will know you're tampering and go after your mother or your doctor . . . or both." He opened the rear door and started to slide out, then turned back to me. In a softer tone, he said, "Don't toy with him. Don't even think about it. I've learned to respect you. I'd hate to be the one who reduces you to putty by eliminating those you love."

He finished exiting the car and waved me out. As soon as I stood upright, he jumped in, and they roared away. The license plate had a dark plastic cover over it rendering it unreadable.

Looking around, I realized I was a block from my house, so I set off hoofing it, hoping a smart next move would show itself. Best I could come up with was to finish the packing that had brought me home, only to be interrupted by the kidnappers. I studied my watch. Less than three hours had passed. Seemed impossible my world could turn upside down in such little time. But multiple revolutions seemed my M.O.

Turning the corner, I saw my car in the

driveway where I left it. The house looked no different. It needed a coat of paint, and the shrubs deserved a pruning. My neighbors' homes had not changed. The Jendells' son's bicycle lay in the front yard, the spot it occupied when not in use. Helen Jendell yelled at him often about it, Gus Jendell moved it when he mowed, but Gus Jr. never put it away.

On the other side, Ms. Isaacson sat on her small covered porch sipping from a glass. I suspected it was lemonade with a touch of vodka. Not that she was a drunk, but neighborhood gossip had her approaching lush-stage. She waved, and I returned it. Just like any other day.

How could everything be so normal when my life was so abnormal? I took a deep breath, shook my head and shoulders, and plowed on. Although it was probably safe to stay at my house since I had detailed instructions from Mr. T, I still chose to pack a few changes of clothes and complete my toiletries. The comfort of David's arms appealed to me more.

But before I did anything else, I had to do something about Mom. What though? What could I tell her that wouldn't bring out her mothering instincts? I could picture her showing up at my front door, ready to take on those who threatened me.

Once inside, I dialed her number, hoping some brainstorm swamped me and provided words that would move her out of danger. She answered, and we sparred with one another as mothers and daughters do the world over. Then I got serious. "Mom, I have something to tell you and something to ask you. Please don't argue with me. Please just do what I ask. Will you do that?"

She chuckled, actually laughed at me. "Elizabeth, you're running on like you did when you were thirteen and wanted a later curfew. Spit it out. Haven't I always taken care of you? Is it a man? Did you meet someone? Please don't elope. I want to be there this time. You've been single entirely too long. You know I love grandchildren. You —"

"Mom, please," I said. "You're babbling worse than I was. Give me a chance to tell you. First, it's not a man. Well, actually I have met someone —"

"Wonderful. I knew you had. As soon as the phone rang, I knew it was good news. I knew —"

"Mom, you're doing it again. I'm not calling because of him. I'm calling . . ." I swallowed and summoned my courage. "I want you to take a vacation. Grab one of your friends and take a long trip to some place you've always dreamed about. Didn't you say you want to tour Alaska? There are great cruises, and you can get off and cross Alaska by train and dog sled."

"Now who's dissembling? What are you trying to say?"

"Sorry. I want you out of Dallas for a while. Take a tour. Visit Paris. Just get out of town." Ouch, that was not the right way to handle it.

"Okay. What kind of mess have you gotten yourself in this time? Elizabeth, sometimes I just don't think you're going to make it. You're so . . . so . . . I don't even know how to say it."

"Yes, Mom. We both know I'm a mess, but this is serious." It took me another thirty minutes to convince her to get out of town. She finally agreed to visit my brother in Wisconsin, leaving the next day. That meant I would be indebted to him for the rest of my life — and he'd never let me forget it.

When I hung up, I felt better about her, but worse about me. Her repeated suggestions that I find another line of work had hung a guilt trip around my neck the size of the Antarctic glaciers. But at least I could assume she'd be safe. All I had left to worry about was David. Unless, of course, Mr. T had anticipated my move and had someone watching Mom — in which case, I'd accomplished nothing.

THIRTY-FIVE

Later that day, as I drove Military Trail toward Boca, I realized I hadn't spoken to my lawyer, Sylvester Bergstrom, in several days. He needed to know what had occurred in case the worst happened. I dialed my cell phone and after talking my way past Donna — no easy task — briefed him.

He proved my faith in him by asking, "Is there anyone we can sue?"

"No. I have no idea how to find these people and prefer not to ever see them again."

"I see," he said in his legal voice. "Is there anyone who might sue you?"

"Sly," I screamed into the phone. "I don't think legal action has anything to do with their intentions. These are not the kind of people who want to appear in court."

"Yes. You may be right, but a suit is always a possibility. You've had quite an adventure. Did they hurt you?"

New proof of how his mind worked —
money first, then my health.

"No. They didn't hurt me. They just put
me in a world of hurt, but I'll handle it. I
only called to keep you updated."

He said he was glad I called, then asked if
the police had levied charges against me. I
told him they appeared to have lost interest
in my case. Other priorities had replaced
Jacobs' death and my part in it. He let me
know he'd spoken to an excellent defense
attorney who was willing to represent me. I
thanked him and hung up, feeling like I had
assuaged some societal requirement to
involve an attorney.

Approaching Bob's corner, I slowed and
squinted, bothered when I didn't see him
on the median. I felt an overwhelming urge
to talk to him. He was the only rock in this
turgid mess, and I needed him. Hell, why
not? He'd already seen my bare ass. What
else was there?

He stepped from between two cars, newspaper in hand. I smiled, feeling more relief
than was logical. He must have seen me
because he waved and moved in my direction.

"Buy you a beer?" I said when he came
alongside. "Lots to tell you."

He glanced over his shoulder. "I ain't no

touris' bureau. You gonna have to buy me lunch if you want to know. There's a place up the street what makes a good gumbo. Real spicy." He winked.

"I love spicy," I said. "Meet you there."

I took a space in the parking lot of Bobby's Bar and looked around, remembering the last time I was there. No white Toyota Avalons in sight. That made me feel more secure as I hurried toward the entrance. I continued my sweep but didn't see my bodyguard, Street, either. I hoped he'd be there so I could buy his lunch. Little enough payment for his assistance. Before this was over, it looked like I would owe most of the homeless in South Florida — if I lived through it and could find them.

Judy greeted me like a long-lost friend. "Good to see you. Bob said you were on your way. Sit where you sat yesterday, and I'll ladle up the gumbo. Hope you like it spicy. I'll bring a bottle of Tabasco Habanero in case it's not hot enough. That'll heat it up."

I didn't let her see it, but I felt a grimace cross my face. Spicy and on-fire had different meanings for me. However, she had answered one question. Bob must have a cell phone. I'd have to remember to get the number. I dropped into the booth in time to see him walk through the entrance.

He headed in my direction and settled across from me. "Reports say you've been a busy girl since I saw you yesterday."

"Oh, you mean that car thing in the parking lot? Guess Street told you about it. No big deal — well, not now anyway."

"Aren't you leaving a few things out? Like the guys in your house last night, your boyfriend's trip to the hospital, and your disappearance this morning? Not to mention where you slept."

I felt myself blush. "You're thorough. I'll give you that."

"I told you I'd help. That includes keeping you alive if I can. You have attracted some nasty people. When you didn't come home last night, Luther got worried and called."

"Luther?"

Bob chuckled. "Yeah, he's the one who chased off the thugs at your place. Don't let on I told you, though. He prefers his homeless-name of Blister. And before you ask, it's because he burned his feet on the beach his first day in Florida."

"Well, whatever his name is, I owe him. He arrived in the proverbial nick of time."

Bob stared at me a moment. "Tell me about them. Who were they?"

"First, I'd like a bowl of that gumbo. It's been a long time since breakfast — and that was Fruit Loops."

He grinned, then turned toward the bar. "Judy. When you have time, we'll take our lunch."

The gumbo lived up to its billing. Rich with shrimp, scallops, and miscellaneous pieces of fish. There may have been other meats but I didn't bother to identify them. The broth was thick with wonderful flavor. And spice? Enough that I didn't touch the Tabasco sauce Judy set on the table, but I did drink three glasses of ice water along the way.

I took my time eating, my mind swirling around a plan that had begun to shape itself on my drive to Boca. On one hand I loved it, but on the other, it required people placing their lives in danger. What other choices did I have though? My least preferred option was to cooperate with Mr. T. I didn't know what he imported, but suspected it wasn't something that came with a customs tag. Plus, his heavy-handed techniques did not appeal to my softer side.

Mr. T and Bruce had both told me I'd be under surveillance at all times. That, in itself, irritated me. I planned to have a wonderful evening with David, and I couldn't do that if someone watched my every move. Evading the surveillance was a priority. But when I evaluated everything, I had to accept that Mr. T knew where David worked — and maybe lived — so he could get to him at any time. And there was my mother's well-being to consider. No matter how I juggled the facts, they tilted to Mr. T's side. The one thing I refused to consider was that he might know about my brother. He couldn't be that thorough — could he?

However, there was a way to level the board. Perhaps two could play the kidnapping game, two could play the badass game, and the worst badass would win. I planned to be the winner.

I took another sip of water, hoping to quench the last of the gumbo burn. "Bob, how much do you want to help me?"

He rolled his eyes. "Now, you know that's the kind of question from a woman a man should never answer. It fits right up there with, *Does this dress make me look fat?*"

I smiled, then came back serious. "If you decide to help, it could get dangerous. The mess last night and the follow-up this morning upped the ante quite a bit. I may need some heavy work done, not just babysitting."

He leaned back against the booth and gave

me a hard stare. "I'm not sure I like where this conversation is headed. Why don't you quit dancing and say what you're thinking? I'll either be in or out. Either way, you won't have lost anything."

Bob was direct, no doubt about it. And for the life of me, I couldn't imagine why I was being coy. Like he said, in or out, no loss to me. I spent a moment fiddling with my spoon, sorting through ways to approach it. Direct won out. "Fair enough. But first, you get to hear the full story about last night — well, the kidnapping part — and my whereabouts this morning."

I went into as much detail as I could remember while Bob sat and listened. There was no doubt I had his undivided attention. On one occasion, Judy headed toward our table, but he waved her off before she'd taken three steps. When I finished, he said, "Is he outside now?"

"Probably. I don't think they were bluffing."

"Let's find out." He pulled a cell phone from his pants pocket and dialed. "Street, look around. Beth thinks there might be someone waiting for her to come out. Don't be seen." He closed the phone, laid it on the table, then sipped from his glass of water. "We'll have an answer in a couple of minutes. There are advantages to being invisible."

THIRTY-SIX

Without any urging, my eyes ran to the clock above the bar. Big face with beer company advertising across it. Black hands on a white background with a sweep second needle that made an obvious jump between seconds. It jumped . . . and jumped . . . and jumped. On its third revolution, Bob's phone rang.

"Yeah," he answered, his gaze locked on me.

He listened, a frown growing while I squirmed. I was sure I knew what he was hearing, but still didn't want it to be true. In retrospect, I suppose I hoped Mr. T did bluff.

"Stand by, but stay out of sight." Bob closed the phone. "One man in a white Mercury sedan, engine running, parked where he can watch the front of the bar. Street says he's making no attempt to hide."

"That fits," I said. "They want me to know

they're there."

"That fits. What's your idea?"

"You sure?"

"Spit it out, Beth. I've already seen and lost more in life than you can imagine. My wife and daughter were everything to me. Nothing you come up with can get close to that."

I spent the next thirty minutes fleshing out the vague idea that had formed on the drive over. Bob's contributions were tactful, appreciated, and sound. At the end of my dissertation, we shook hands.

"You understand," he said, "these folks owe me nothing. They know that. So, if they walk away, don't let it bother you. Most of them have had rotten lives and feel like the world spit in their faces. They'll have a choice, and we'll accept whatever they say."

"I wouldn't have it any other way."

Bob went onto his cell phone and worked it for the next twenty minutes. I lost count of how many calls he made, but he must have finally reached the end of his list because he flipped it shut and said, "That's it. We'll see how many make the scene. In the meantime, let me show you the back rooms."

He slid out of the booth, and I followed him toward an exit in the rear wall. As we walked, he called to Judy, "If any of our folks come in, send 'em around back to the outside entrance."

We passed through the door into a hallway. Soft yellow paint coated the walls and recessed lighting lined the ceiling, giving everything a warm, cozy glow.

"There are sleeping arrangements on both sides," Bob said.

I followed him, and he stopped at a doorway on the right. "Woman coming in," he called, then opened the door.

Bunks, lockers, and small tables with lamps filled the area. I counted beds for ten tenants, each of whom would have a place to sleep, a place to sit, and a place to stare into space, if that was his choice. The walls were a pale blue, and a sturdy looking carpet covered the floor.

"Is this the dormitory?" I asked. "Judy said you have a place where people can flop with no questions asked."

Bob smiled, a look of pride on his face. "One of them. This one's for the men. Here, I'll show you the other." We exited, then he knocked on a door on the other side of the hall. "Anyone in there?" he said, then waited. When there was no response, he said, "Man coming in," and opened the door.

It was the same as the other room except the bunks were covered in pastel covers and the walls were painted a pale pink. Silk flowers in vases adorned the tables.

"Very feminine — and very cozy," I said.

"Yes. They might live on the street, but that doesn't mean they've lost their femininity. Some really appreciate a break from the coldness of the outside world."

I looked around. "No rules posted. Does someone meet them at the door with a lecture?"

"No. They come and go as they please. No one asks any questions. There are shower and laundry facilities through there." He pointed toward the back wall on the far end.

"Who keeps it clean? Must be quite a chore cleaning up after they've been here."

Bob frowned at me. "Your prejudices are showing. It's quite the opposite. The folks who use it clean it, better than any crew I could bring in. All most of them want is a chance to show they're not worthless."

"Sorry. I suppose I stereotyped them, and that's not fair to anyone." I looked around. "I don't mean to be nosy, but the upkeep has to be expensive."

"The bar supplies some of the funds, and some of it comes from a trust fund I set up several years ago. Also, the homeless who

255

stay here pitch in what they can. We have a contributions can by the door. It's amazing how much accumulates over the course of a month. The secret is trust. I trust them, and they respond."

His words made so much sense, I was surprised it wasn't common practice. "You may have discovered the secret to homelessness in the country. Do you think this template will work in other areas?"

"I think most people respond to the way they're treated. Some are incorrigible, but I believe they're in the minority. Treat everyone like human beings, and the majority will act like human beings. Treat them like animals, and, like animals, they'll cringe in the alleys and hide under the bridges. Tell them often enough they can't make it without welfare, and they'll believe it."

He sighed. "It seems strange. When I see some of these folks, I see how much harm the do-gooders do. There is a segment of our society so bent on helping the homeless they take away their ability to help themselves. They don't mean to, but that's the end result. I mean, I meet men and women who take the path of least resistance — let someone do it for you. They sit back and become dependent on others. But when they come here, they get a bed and a chance to act human. The rest of life is theirs to live. And if the occasional ingrate decides to take undue advantage of my charity, some-one — usually, several — explains the rules to him."

Bob's words fascinated me. Here was a man who had walked the walk and talked the talk. He knew of what he spoke. So different from the politicians who only considered indigents when there was a reporter with a camera nearby — those who wrote off the homeless as a campaign promise to be used over and over again. I promised myself I'd get involved once I dug myself out of my current predicament.

"Where do you sleep?" I asked.

"Across the hall in the men's quarters — when I stay here. Most of the time, I prefer the street with the others. Nothing like being kicked by a passerby to remind me what I need to do. Before you ask, it's part of the promise I made to Jupiter."

That did it. I went speechless. Who was this man who befriended me? Or better question, why had this man with such a huge heart chosen to shelter me? With all he was doing, he didn't need my problems.

"Okay, let me show you another room. I think it'll be perfect for our needs."

THIRTY-SEVEN

We cut back into the hall and headed toward the bar, but took a left. We were in a storage area with no windows — solid block construction, about twelve by twelve. Bar stock, paper products, and other assorted boxes lined the walls.

"We can move this stuff out," Bob said, "and we'll have a perfect place for the conversion of Mr. T's henchman."

"Agreed," I said. "When do you think we can pick him up? The sooner we get this thing on track, the safer I'll feel. And the safer David and my mother will be."

"The ones I called should be arriving within the next ten minutes or so. Then we can lay out the plan. How do you want to handle it?"

A door opened at the end of the hallway, signaling someone's entry. We walked out of the storage room, and I saw two men I didn't recognize standing inside the entrance.

"Street said you put out a call," one of the men said.

"Yeah. Glad you and Manzo heard it. Any of the others with you?"

"Saw a couple headed this way."

As the man spoke, the door opened and three others came in. There were head nods all around, but not much conversation. We moved into the men's dorm, and the newcomers scattered around the room.

I marveled at the discipline these street people showed. They weren't bums, they were human beings. A bit disheveled perhaps, but as human as anyone I knew, and more than many I'd known during my careers as a cop and PI.

Over the next half hour, men continued to drift in — plus three women. Bob played doorman, welcoming each by name. Eventually, thirteen had gathered. They stared at Bob like he was a commander ready to address his troops. He walked me around the room, introducing me to the group. Each of them greeted me with a warm handshake, like they were glad to meet me. Such was the power of Bob's personality.

After we made the round, Bob said to me, "We have a quorum. Are you ready?"

"It's your show," I said. "I'm only along for the ride."

"Friends," Bob said to the assemblage, "you've all met Beth. Rest assured I would not expose you if I didn't have complete faith in her. She is a private investigator, but has no love for our local cops. She's in trouble and needs help. And, like each of us, she must turn inward to find that assistance. None of you have to help her. But I'll consider it a personal favor if you'll hear her out before you make your decision." He turned to me. "Beth, these are my friends. Tell them what you want."

I took a deep breath and stepped forward, knowing my next words were some of the most important I might ever utter. Without these derelicts of society, I would have no choice but to obey Mr. T's orders. "I am honored that you're listening to me. Since I'm sure you have other things to do with your time, I'll keep it short." I paused and filled my lungs with air. "I'm in trouble. I need your help . . ."

After briefing Bob's people on my plan, I left through the front door of the bar, stopping when I reached the sunlight, pretending to be blinded by the glare. I wanted to make sure Mr. T's surveillant didn't miss me. After fumbling in my handbag for about thirty seconds and coming up with a pair of sunglasses, I headed toward my car, taking my time in a casual stroll.

Once in the car, I dialed David's cell phone. As I expected, I got his answering machine. I left a message telling him I had a lead on my case and was off to track it down. With what I hoped was the right amount of promise in my voice, I said I'd see him later at his place, then added, "I'm not sure what time that will be, but I'll call before showing up. Looking forward to it."

I clicked off, then after a moment's reflection, called again. "If you have other plans for tonight, you can leave a message on my cell. Of course, I'm hoping your plans are the same as mine."

As I pulled into my driveway, my phone rang. After saying hello, I heard, "What kind of lead? I want to play. Where are you?"

The voice caused my heart to leap. It was David. "At my house, but you need to stay away. This isn't like your mother's romantic suspense novels. Things could get rough."

"I'll be out of here soon. See you there. Any beer in your fridge?"

"Yeah. And by sheer coincidence, it happens to be your brand."

■ ■ ■ ■

At seven p.m., I leaned back in my favorite chair and punched in the phone number Bruce gave me. The line answered on the second ring.

Mr. T said, "You're very prompt. I like that. But, my dear Miss Bowman, where did you disappear to this afternoon? Lodo said you went into a bar and stayed there too long for a couple of belts. I want an explanation."

During my afternoon with Bob and his friends, we had decided to try to shake Mr. T's confidence in his henchmen. "Perhaps you need to hire a better quality of criminals. There are aspects of my life I do not intend to share with you — or the thugs you employ. If they're so incompetent they can't keep up with one lone female . . ." I allowed my voice to trail away with an upward lilt, hoping to plant a question mark in his head.

There was a moment of silence before he answered my challenge. "I assure you it won't happen again." His voice had taken on an edge. "And I suggest you not play fast and loose with my employees. It could be dangerous. I think you know what I mean."

"Mr. T," I said, "plant your threats where the sun don't shine. I'm not impressed. If you want my help, you'll damn well knock off the bullshit. Now, I've checked in as you instructed. Good night. I've had enough of you for one day." I hung up.

I counted seconds and before I reached ten, my phone rang. I checked the caller ID and saw that the number was blocked. Could my Mr. T be calling? I let it go, and it rang nine times before ceasing. A moment later, it rang again — for another nine rings. I smiled and counted — counted and smiled. Would the next move unfurl as I hoped?

My purse was beside my chair. I slid my hand into it, took out my revolver, and placed it under my leg. I had promised myself I wouldn't be surprised again. I intended to do the surprising.

Three minutes later, there was a demanding knock on the door. Without moving, I said, "It's unlocked. Come in."

The door swung inward with force and Bruce barged into the room. "What the hell are you doing? The boss —" He stopped mid-hiss on the esses in boss, his eyes mutating to huge. My guess was he had noticed my .32 aimed at his forehead.

THIRTY-EIGHT

Bruce recovered faster than I would have. "Ms. Bowman. Put that away. You don't scare me." He took a step forward.

"I hit what I aim at," I said. "Would you like to lose the ear?"

He laughed and took another step.

I fired, clipping his right ear. Fortunately, the .32 has so little power it didn't penetrate the front wall — I hoped.

He snapped his hand to his ear, then brought it down, his fingertips red. "Damn. You did it."

I shrugged. "Can't say I didn't warn you."

He took out his handkerchief and pressed it against his wound. "You're cool. I'll give you that. But do you have the guts to put one of those slugs through my heart? You should know that's the kind of hit it will take from a peashooter like that to stop me. And, be aware, I'm very muscular and the slug might not make it through the pec."

"Want to find out?"

He rubbed his chin and chuckled. "I have to. That's why the boss pays me the big bucks." He took another step.

"If she doesn't kill you, I will."

Bruce spun toward the new voice while I smiled. A man with a scarf wrapped around the lower half of his face stood in my hallway, cradling a shotgun. I hoped Bruce was as intimidated as I was by the opening at the end of the barrel. Even from my angle, it looked the size of a beach ball. And Bruce had a direct view down its length.

Puzzlement swept Bruce's face as he looked from the shotgun to me, back to the shotgun. "What's going on here? Who . . . who is this guy? The boss —"

Two others stepped into the light, their identities hidden from view. One towered over six feet while the other came in at about five-five. Both had determination in their stride.

Bruce's face fell. I could see realization settling in. The worm had turned, the turtle had outraced the rabbit, the ant had outwitted the grasshopper, the prairie dog had scared off the eagle . . . and all kinds of other underdog-wins scenarios.

"May I sit down?" Bruce said. "I have a feeling I'm about to get a lecture and a proposition."

"Of course," I said. "To all three. But not here." I nodded toward Bob, the first who had entered the room. "Prepare him for transport."

While Bob pointed the shotgun, the other two duct-taped Bruce's hands behind him and covered his mouth. The shorter of the two produced a black scarf and blindfolded him, then slipped his hand under Bruce's jacket. He lifted Bruce's pistol. Good move. I should have thought of it.

Bob stepped forward and inspected the taping. "He looks secure enough to move."

I grinned. "You can't know how much I'm loving this. How's it feel, Brucey-baby? Sorry, I didn't have time to find a sleep mask."

I received a mmmf in reply.

David entered the room. His eyes made a one-eighty of the area. "So this is how those who have all the fun live. Makes me wish I'd gone to thug school. I've missed so much."

I laughed as he leaned over and kissed me. If I'd had a choice, I'd have grabbed him around the neck and just hung on. As much as I wanted to be his everything, I had a couple of other problems to sort out first. Releasing him from the lip lock, I said,

"You'd never have made it. You're too cuddly. Why don't you go home now, and I'll come there when we finish with Bruce."

"Not a chance. This is more fun than liposuction. I'm sticking close. Maybe I'll learn how to handle difficult patients."

I looked at Bob. He nodded.

"Okay," I said. "Let's move our guest to his new accommodations."

THIRTY-NINE

Emulating Bruce's kidnapping techniques, we took a circuitous route to Bobby's Bar, driving at a leisurely pace to make sure he had time to sweat. I couldn't tell if he counted Mississippis to keep track of the time. Maybe he accepted that I had outmaneuvered him and was now my pliant captive — or not. I asked a few questions along the way just to disrupt his count — if he was counting, but he wasn't very communicative. All I got in response were a few mmmfs. Perhaps the duct tape over his mouth and the blindfold put him in a bad mood.

We parked at the back of the bar and, after checking to make sure we had no unwanted witnesses, offloaded our passenger. When we helped him into the storage room, one on each side to keep him from stumbling, I did an abrupt halt and looked around. It had undergone major changes during our absence, emptied of everything except a few straight-backed chairs. One of those sat at an angle in a corner with U-bolts anchoring it to the wall. It was the only one with a wooden seat, the others having cushioned bottoms.

Bob led Bruce to the hard chair and pushed him down onto it. The way he landed made my coccyx groan. My two helpers, whom I could identify only as tall and short, were quick to duct tape him to the chair — arms and legs. Bob stopped them when they began to wrap tape around his neck and the back of the chair.

"Leave it for now," Bob said. "If he gets hostile, we'll make sure he doesn't head butt anyone later." He turned to me. "Should we take off his blindfold?"

"Yes, but I want you guys back in your masks first. He can see the room, but not you. I don't want him finding you and evening the score at some later date." I retrieved my pistol from my purse. "I suspect he'll have a better appreciation of the situation once he sees where he is and the hopelessness of his situation."

Bob and the others put their masks into place, then Bob slipped the blindfold over Bruce's head.

Bruce spent the next few seconds blinking

rapidly as he looked around the room. The look in his eyes said he got the message.

I glanced at David, who was leaning against the doorframe, a bemused look on his face. When he saw me looking at him, he held up his bandaged pinkie, then gave me a thumbs up.

I wanted to kiss it to make it well, but Bruce had to be my number-one priority. He had to know it was my show, that I was the ringmaster — in his vernacular, The Boss. "I'm going to ask you a few simple questions. If you're smart, you'll answer. If you're not, well . . ." I gave him time to think it over before adding, "We'll take the tape off your mouth so you can talk." I nodded to Bob.

He stepped forward and the tape made a terrible sound tearing from Bruce's face. I tried not to flinch, but wasn't sure I made it. I could almost feel the pain.

Bruce ticked away a few seconds wiggling his lips and working his mouth. I suppose he was satisfied everything still functioned because he said, "Ask your questions."

"Glad to see you're feeling cooperative," I said. "Nothing too difficult to start. What is Mr. T's full name, and how do I get to his house?"

A slight grin appeared. "That's it? You're

271

right. Those aren't difficult. In a different world at a different time, I could answer in a few seconds. But, this isn't a different world. This isn't a different time. Your third question should have to do with my burial. That's assuming, of course, that there is enough of me recovered to bury. The Boss has ways of dealing with those who cross him." He looked around the room. "I don't get the feeling any of these nice folks are hardened killers, and I know for sure you're not — I've seen you in action. My choices are simple. If I can tell you what you want to know and live to walk out of here, I'll for sure end up in a meat grinder somewhere — or something worse. I've never been curious what it feels like to be snapped in half by a gator. Or I can choose to wait you out. I select the latter."

His response threw me off-track for a moment, but I rallied. "You're right. Two more questions. What kind of import-export business does your boss run, and what was in the briefcase that has him so excited?"

Bruce chuckled and shook his head. "You may as well tape my mouth again. I've said about all I'm going to say. Or," he took a slow head turn around the room, "tell your designated executioner to get on with it. Because, Ms. Bowman, I'm just plain not talking."

Darn. He had me. Killing him had no part in my plan. In fact, marking him in any way was off limits. I intended to turn him over to the police after he told me what I wanted to know. I couldn't have him looking like we'd tortured him or beaten information out of him. Perplexity had become my middle name.

My feelings must have shown because Bruce laughed. "Did you really think I'd just open up and spill my guts? Beth, Beth, you have so much to learn. I'll give you some good advice. Take me back to my car and turn me loose. I'll forget all about the last few hours, and we'll pretend this little episode never happened. Wouldn't do either of us any good if the boss found out you took me like a rank rookie."

That did it. His arrogance stiffened my backbone, and I bristled. "You're not going anywhere — not until I make the decision anyway." I turned toward Bob. "Blindfold him and tape him."

After Bob finished, we gathered in the dormitory. There were David, Bob, Street, Blister, Rose, and Tall and Short, whose names I hadn't learned yet.

I approached Tall and Short, who stood together. "We haven't met yet, but I want to thank you for your help. Without you, Bruce might have been too much for us. I'm Beth."

Tall smiled and didn't say anything. Short said, "It was fun. Been awhile since we been able to do somethin' useful." She pulled her mask down.

I stared at her, and yes, it was a her. I had assumed Short was a height-challenged man, not an average-sized female.

"My name's Dot, deary, and my friend is Bridge. Bridge, take off your mask."

He did as she said.

She continued, "He don't say much, so I talk for him." She cackled. " 'Course some say I try to talk for ev'rybody. He don't want nobody to know his real name. Says it would embarrass his family if they knowed he was homeless. So he picked Bridge cause he's slept under a bunch of 'm. Me? I don't give a shit. Ain't got no family — or if I do, I don't know where they is, and they don't care where I am."

"Nice to meet you," I said sticking out my hand. She looked at it a moment, wiped her hand along her pants leg — men's pants — then took it. Her grip was firm and re-assuring.

"Mighty fine to mee'cha, too, deary. I gotta feelin' you some special lady."

I turned away and felt David's hand on

my back as I lined up beside Bob, who faced the group. "Here's our situation," I said. "The man in the other room is a hardened criminal. I don't want him to see you so keep your mask up whenever you're around him."

Dot said, "What's he gonna do — take away our limousines?" She cackled.

I smiled, admiring her chutzpah. "Our prisoner has information that I need. Information that will remove a threat from over my mother's head." I looked at David. "And from my . . . uh, friend, Dr. David Rasmussen, who promises he'll never turn away a homeless patient."

That drew a chuckle from the crowd and a smile and tip of the head from David. "You have a personal physician any time, day or night." He pulled out his business cards and handed one to each of the homeless. "Just call me." He winked in my direction. "I'll make sure Beth pays."

I waited until the laughter died, then said, "The problem is I want the information that Bruce has, but I can't afford to bruise him. From here, he goes to the police, where I'm sure they have a comfy cell for him. I'm open to ideas about how to encourage him to talk — anything that doesn't leave marks or can be proven as torture."

FORTY

I scanned the room, hoping to encourage someone to speak up. Instead, everyone looked pensive, refusing to meet my gaze. Some scratched their chins while others pulled at their ears. Everyone except Dot, who shoved her way to the front. "Shucks, deary, that ain't no problem. How fast you want it?"

"You have an idea?"

"Ain't no idea. It's a ironclad guarantee. He'll be singing like one of them opera folks before daylight. That's without even hurtin' him none. Now, if you want it faster, maybe in the next half-hour, all I gotta do is appeal to his manhood, if you git what I mean. Ain't met no man yet wouldn't do anything to protect —"

"No," I interjected. "That won't work. Like I said, I don't want him bruised. Add to that, I don't want him missing any body parts."

Dot cackled again. "Hell, deary, you took all the fun out of it. Don't matter, though. I can git him talkin'. Course, I need a few supplies — not much, mind you, just a couple dollars worth."

"Tell me."

She appeared to think for a moment. "Naw, I druther show you. Give me a ten spot, and me and Bridge will get what we need. Then maybe we can play some poker while he cooks. Ain't played in a long time."

Cooks? I hoped she didn't mean that literally. I ran my hands through my hair as my mind raced. Really though, a no-brainer. What did I have to lose? I'd be right there to make sure things didn't get out of hand. I turned to David. "Is it worth ten to watch the show?"

He smiled. "My curiosity is boundless." He took out his wallet and handed me a bill. "Here. This is for a twenty-dollar ticket."

I gave Dot the money.

She shoved it in the front pocket of her pants, saying, "Maybe after you git what you want, I'll have him all to myself for a while." She cackled again, took Bridge by the arm, and they disappeared through the door.

"If y'all don't mind, I got other things I

could be doing," Rose said, walking toward the exit. "Don't seem like you need my help. Everything looks under control here."

"Sure," Bob said. "If you need us, you know where we are. And if we need you, make sure you have the cell with you."

Rose opened the door and called, "Dot. Bridge. Wait up. I'll walk a bit with you."

I watched her leave, then my mind snapped back to Dot. An ironclad guarantee Bruce would talk — without breaking any of his bones or scarring him. Could I trust her? What kind of woman was she? "Bob, do you know what Dot has in mind?"

"Nope. But I have a hunch we can believe what she said. Your Bruce in there will be singing like a lovebird." He rubbed his hand across his mouth. "I don't know a lot about her, but I suspect there is much sadness in her past. I do know she did time for killing a man. From what I heard, she got ten years when she cut his heart out."

"His heart?" I said. "Only ten? There must have been some strong extenuating circumstances."

"Apparently, when the police arrested her, she carried the evidence of his long-term mistreatment all over her body. Anyway, when she got out of prison, she took to the streets. That's where she met Bridge, and they've been together since."

"How sad," I said.

"Yes. And almost every one of these people has a story just as heartrending. They're not homeless because they chose to be. Circumstances put them here. As for Dot, well, I feel like she's never been able to catch a break." He looked toward the door she'd gone through. "But whatever happened in her past, I'd much rather have her for a friend than an enemy."

"Good enough for me," I said. "What about you, David?"

"I'm only here for the education," he said. "This makes my classes on brain surgery seem mundane." He waggled his eyebrows.

"Okay, we wait until Dot and Bridge get back," I said. "She mentioned she wanted to play poker. Can we set up a table in one of the dorms?"

Bob smiled as he surveyed his group. "You might have to bankroll the game."

I turned toward David, whose look said he knew what came next. "Well?" I said. "I'm a bit short."

"It'll speed things up and give me an excuse to sit out. Maybe I can keep an eye on our guest. I owe him one." He held up his bandaged hand. "Besides, my lab partner in med school always said don't play against your own money." He chuckled. "He financed his education at a friendly poker table. Is there an ATM in the area?"

"One in the bar," Bob said.

David grinned at me as he headed toward the front. "This could be fun. I suspect someone is in for a fleecing, and her initials are BB."

"Yeah? Back home, they call me Mississippi Beth, the riverboat gambler."

Bob, Blister, and Street disappeared into the bar and returned to the dorm carrying a round table capable of seating six with space to spare. After moving a couple of beds, things were perfect for poker. Another absence and six cushioned chairs waited for players. Poker chips and two new decks of cards made their appearances. All we needed were Dot and Bridge.

David took a position in the doorway where he could see Bruce held captive in his chair in the storage room. I sat directly across from David so he could tip me if Bruce cracked. If it happened, I wanted to be the second to know.

Dot and Bridge blew into the room carrying a small bag from Office Depot. Its size caught my eye. Don't know what I expected, but the bag couldn't hold a rubber hose or a battery charger. That made me feel better. I still had my scruples about Bruce. Pain was fine, but marks on his body were not.

"Here, deary," Dot said, putting the bag in front of me. "The secret to learning whatever's locked away in that bum's head. I promise we'll know soon."

I dumped the bag. Two boxes of thumbtacks — normal bulletin board standard thumbtacks with flat heads. Not even the fancy ones they call map pins. Only one use of them came to mind. "Now, Dot, I told you we can't mark him. You're not stabbing him in any key parts with these."

She giggled. "Don't mean to, deary. If they's any stickin', he'll be doing it. Is it okay if we git started?"

Even more mystified, I said, "Get on with it."

"Gonna need some help with his legs. Bob, would you take one and, Street, maybe you could grab the other. He looks like the kind that would kick a lady. Bridge, get me a blanket roll from one of them beds."

FORTY-ONE

"Masks up," I said.

While I pondered what she was up to, Dot approached Bruce, sitting in his hard-bottomed chair. "He's a big'un, ain't he? This ain't gonna work. Need something for him to set on, something that'll lift him up. Any old phone books 'round here? 'Bout the only thing they's good for is a booster seat."

"I'll check the bar," Bob said. "There are usually a couple under the counter. Seems like they drop them at the front door at least once a month." He walked out of the room.

I studied the situation. So far, I had no clue what Dot had in mind. Street stood on one side of Bruce, ready to follow orders, I guessed, to keep Bruce from kicking. Bob had been on the other side, but was now rounding up something for Bruce to sit on. I looked at David and shrugged. He returned the motion, letting me know he was as lost as I.

Bob returned to the room. "How about these?" He carried two phone books, each about three inches thick.

"Yeah," Dot said. "They ought to do it. Here comes the tricky part. If you still got that shotgun, better break it out. We gonna have to loose him from the chair. Beth, same for that pea shooter of yours."

I nodded and walked to where I dropped my purse and rummaged inside. My .32 felt good as I assumed a guard position. "Give me an excuse, Bruce. Please, just give me an excuse."

Bruce's head turned toward me. I wondered what was in his mind while wishing I could see his eyes. I had to give him credit, though. He might be defenseless and helpless, but he didn't flinch. He just sat there with excellent posture.

Bob went into the men's sleeping area, then returned with the shotgun, and leveled it at Bruce.

I noticed it was a pump-action. "How many shells does it hold? Is it choked?"

He racked the slide, probably for Bruce's benefit. "Nope. Holds eight and has eight. I used to shoot clay pigeons. It would be a pleasure to drop this pigeon."

"Can we let him see?" Dot asked. "Ain't

nothing he ain't seen before. I want him to know what's comin'."

I figured that between Bob and me, Bruce would get the idea that making a play was not a smart move. "Sure. Do it."

Bridge gave Street a hand in freeing Bruce, including removing the blindfold. As soon as they lifted him to his feet, Dot shoved the phone books under him, then they dropped him back onto the chair. His feet now sat flat on the floor, but not with much to spare.

"Re-tape his arms and chest," Dot said. "I think we're there."

At first, Bruce glared at everyone in turn, but soon, his expression became more puzzled as if he was lost, too. He might have had some worthy questions, but asking was not in the equation because of the tape over his mouth.

"Good," Dot said and turned toward me. "Now, deary, I'm gonna show you a trick that always produces results. I seen some mighty tough characters break on this one. Hold his legs, guys, while I slip this bed roll under his thighs." A moment later, she added, "Oh yeah. That's perfect."

Perfect? What I saw were Bruce's shoes dangling above the floor, his upper thighs resting on the rolled up blanket. He'd have to strain to settle his feet.

"Keep him from kicking," Dot said, "while I spread the tacks." She emptied the boxes in front of the chair, then knelt and began to turn the points up.

I crouched beside her and helped. Seemed the normal thing to do.

When we finished, she said, "Thank you, deary. Soon you'll hear him sing. Hope it's not too fast though. I got some poker to play." She stood, her joints cracking as she did.

Mine didn't feel much better as I rose.

"Okay, now we take off his shoes and socks." She reached over and pinched Bruce's cheek. "Now, listen good 'cause here are the rules. We're going to remove the bedroll and leave your legs free. You'll have the choice to hold them up or rest them on the tacks. While I don't really care what you do, I can tell you those tacks are sharp. Look, I bloodied myself on one." She sucked on a fingertip. "When you get tired of the game, let Miss Beth know, and she'll have some questions for you. Understand?"

Bruce's eyes were so large, I was sure he heard. Whether he understood, I couldn't say. I wasn't sure I did.

"Turn his legs loose," Dot said. "We'll see how long he keeps his feet above those sharp points. He looks like he's in pretty good shape, so I give him a couple of hours. Cover his eyes again and let's play poker."

As Bridge put the blindfold in place, David took a chair near the door. "I'll stay and watch our guest," David said.

"Good." Dot spun and walked into the dorm to the poker table. "Here, Miss Beth. You set beside me where I can keep an eye on you. Oops, forgot something. Y'all just settle on in while I git it."

Bob shrugged and took a seat across from where I'd been directed to sit. "I do believe we've met the real Dot tonight," he said. "When I retire, I might let her manage my bar and the dormitory." His smile radiated admiration.

Dot re-entered the room carrying a round stick, maybe a broom or mop handle, and placed it on the floor beside her chair. Then she sat.

I didn't ask. Neither did anyone else.

"Y'all mind if I loosen them cards a bit? They's always so stiff straight out of the box," she said as if going after the stick were an everyday occurrence.

Bob slid a deck to her. She popped the seal and slipped the cards out of the case. From that point forward, I watched in fascination. She fanned the cards on the table, then rolled them up and back, doing everything but forming them into dancing pairs. If she'd done that, I wouldn't have been surprised. Her shuffles, she named them as she went through them — Hindu shuffle, overhand shuffle, riffle shuffle, and others I'd never seen before — were a blur as the cards hopped in her hands. Before placing them on the table in front of me, she executed a string of one-handed cuts with the cards never stopping. Yeah, I was impressed.

"Cut'm, deary." She nodded toward Bob. "You be the bank. You the only person here we all trust." She looked at me. "Sorry 'bout that, deary, but I ain't knowed you long enough. Now, everybody git their money out. Let's git the chips flippin'."

During the next hour, the pile of chips in front of Dot grew. Luckily, we were playing dealer's choice with a rotating deal. Dot's call each time was five-card stud. She won every hand and picked up enough of the other choices around the table to insure her stack never shrank. I won't say she cheated, but when I hit four tens in five-card stud and lost to her four queens, I became a bit suspicious.

An hour in, David stuck his head in the

door. "You might want to see what Bruce is up to."

Before I could say anything, Dot was out of her chair, the broomstick in her hand.

I heard two sharp cracks, close together, and Dot saying, "We'll have none of that. Don't mess with my tacks. You'll either play by the rules, or the rules will play you. Hold up your feet."

There was a moment of silence before Dot said, "Don't make me come back over here." That was followed by another sharp sound.

She stormed back into the dorm. "Damn fool messin' with my tacks. Don't worry, dearie, he might limp a little, but knees don't bruise. Is it my deal?"

FORTY-TWO

Bridge answered Dot and probably saved at least my ante by uttering his first non-betting words of the game, "Miss Beth's."

I scooped up the cards and shuffled. Dot watched me like she thought I might stack the deck. Not to say I wouldn't if I had known how. Her quantity of chips and mine weren't even in the same hemisphere.

I dealt seven-card stud and found a pair of aces in the hole. Exciting enough to make me take a second peek. Yeah, I know it's a no-no, but I needed a winning hand — I wanted a winning hand. My up card was a king, giving me dealer control.

Checking around the table, I saw nothing that bothered me. But with Dot's run of luck, who could tell? She showed a ten of diamonds. I made a moderate bet, and everyone stayed in.

When the pot was right, I ran another round of cards. Caught a trey to go with my king and pair of aces. Whoopee. Gave Dot a nine of diamonds, Bridge a queen of clubs that didn't help his eight of hearts, doubled Street on Jacks, and didn't do much for anyone else. Things looked fine.

"Your bet, Street," I said. "How much are those jacks worth?"

He scratched his jaw. "Not much, the way my night's gone." He bet the minimum, taking himself out of my wave of concern.

Bob took his time eyeing his hole cards, then folded. "It'd take a miracle to make something out of this mess."

"One more round, but you better be kind," Blister said. "Adding a face might help."

Dot studied everyone's cards, then raised a moderate amount. "Since everybody's bettin' on the come, might as well make it worthwhile. Dang pot's too skinny." Her witch's cackle sounded again.

When everyone had called, I laid out the next cards. Eight of diamonds to Dot. Now, her hand appeared dangerous. Straight flush building, or a straight, or a flush. Whatever, not in my best interest.

Didn't improve anyone else until I got to my hand. Ace of clubs. Three aces with two cards to go. I felt good.

Street's pair of jacks were still high.

"Check to the power," he said, staring at Dot.

She cackled some more. "The timid never win." She tossed in the maximum bid.

Bridge never hesitated. His cards landed on the pot with Blister's right behind.

Street shook his head and said, "I gotta be nuts." He called the bet.

I stared at Dot's hole cards, trying to see through the backs of them. No matter which of her threatened hands she hit, I was in trouble unless I improved. I needed a pair to ride my aces into a full house. I called her bet.

One more up card. Street didn't improve again and groaned, frustration evident.

The six of diamonds landed at Dot's place, and I joined Street in groaning. She was doing it again.

Me? Damn jack of hearts. I'd have happily given it to Street if I could. Didn't help me any.

Street checked, and Dot bet the max.

One card to go and Dot and me left. Without much enthusiasm, I met her bet, then before anyone could say anything, raised the max. I might lose my bra, but she wasn't chasing me out.

Street folded. Dot grinned and met it.

"Last one down and dirty," I said. "And

papa, you better treat mama right."

Dot giggled. "If you want, you can have mine, too. I don't need it."

I slid her last card across, laid mine on my cards, then tossed the remainder of the deck onto the pot.

Dot stared into my face. "Deary, your ace controls the table. Can you bet without looking?"

"No problem," I said, and slid the maximum bet out. "Don't ever doubt me, Dot."

She didn't hesitate. She simply grinned, met me, then raised.

Time to check my last card. I peeked and felt as if my eyes bugged out like the yolks of two jumbo eggs, sunny side up — ace of spades. Four aces. That beat everything except a straight flush, but Dot showed four to hers with the inside open. I repeated my vow not to let her bluff me. "Nuts to bet into a big winner, but I have to do it. Want to raise the cap?"

Dot studied my cards, my small pile of chips, then her stash. "Table stakes?"

"Suits me." I slid everything I had into the middle. Dot gave me a toothy smile and matched it. The room was silent. Even the breathing was quiet if anyone was doing any. I'm sure I wasn't.

David tapped me on the shoulder. "I think the show is ready to start."

FORTY-THREE

Bob and I rose and crossed into the storage room to Bruce's chair, stopping far enough away that he couldn't kick us.

"Ready to tell me what I want to know?" I said.

He nodded, his forehead a mass of wrinkles.

"Bob? Would you do the honors?"

"My pleasure." He ripped the tape from Bruce's mouth.

Bruce groaned. "Please. My legs are on fire, every muscle is cramping. I have to get up. Please help me to my feet. Let me walk'm off. I'm dying here."

I had to give Dot her due. She had been right-on from the beginning. Her nonviolent technique had reduced Bruce to the equivalent of melting Jell-O. He was mine now.

I turned to Bob, then to Street and Bridge who'd followed us. "Cut him loose from the chair and help him stand. If he tries anything, kick him in the legs. That'll slow him down."

With my foot, I swept the tacks out of the way, then realized Dot wasn't there. I turned and saw her coming through the door.

"Damn, deary, you had four aces. I sure didn't see them comin'. Beat the heck out of my little straight. You woulda took me for everything. Too bad we didn't finish the hand. You just go on with what you're doing. I'll divide the pot 'tween us since we didn't git to show the cards. Rules is rules."

All I could do was hope I had better luck with Bruce. Dot was way beyond me.

David and Bob each held one of Bruce's arms and escorted him around the room. He wasn't exactly limping, more of a hop, hop — one foot to the other. Street and Bridge walked behind them, Street with Dot's stick and Bridge with Bob's shotgun. Things appeared under control.

When his hop-hops had transitioned to shuffle-shuffles, I said, "Put him back in his chair. I'm finished with the show part of the evening. It's time for tell."

They followed my instructions with no resistance from Bruce. "Do I need to tape you down?" I asked.

Bruce shook his head. "I've met my

match. Ask your questions. I'll answer any that I can."

I pulled a chair over and sat. "From the top: Who's your boss? Where does he live? What kind of import/export business is he in? What was in the briefcase that disappeared?"

Bruce took a deep breath. "Diamonds. A million dollars worth of diamonds. Enough to turn any man into a thief. His name is Anthony Tomasco, and he's the owner of Tomasco Import/Export Limited. He brings in anything he thinks he can sell — legal or illegal. He has homes all over the country. The one you visited is in Boca, but there's also Dallas, Los Angeles, Seattle, and Long Island." He paused. "Did I answer everything?"

"Yes, I think so. You gave a good summary. Now —"

"Want I should help, Beth? I'd love to mess up his face. I hate pretty boys."

Without my hearing her, Dot had moved beside me. The expression on her face said she meant every word.

"No," I said, letting my annoyance slip in. "There'll be no rough stuff. He's cooperating."

"Deary, if the shoe was on the other foot, you can bet he'd be slappin' the shit outta you. You too soft. One of these days, it'll come back and bite you in the ass."

"Maybe, but we'll do it my way." I looked at Bruce. "At least as long as he answers my questions."

"Well, when you wake up, I'll be standin' by." She stared at Bruce. "Ever had a tack driven into the palm of your hand? Hurts like hell. Wanna see the scars?" Without waiting for his response, she walked toward the door, chuckling under her breath.

I leaned toward Bob and whispered, "Would she?"

He nodded.

Putting Dot out of my mind, I returned my attention to Bruce. "Okay, let's begin to flesh out some of those answers. Take it from the top and don't leave anything out."

"I didn't know you existed until you stuck yourself in front of me when I was following Jacobs. I had no idea what the hell was happening, just that you were interfering with my mission —"

"Which was?"

"Follow Jacobs, make sure he made the meet and traded the briefcase for another one. I didn't know what was in either of them, but I found out when I reported back to Tomasco. He was furious that I broke off the surveillance. I told him you went into the room, then shots were fired. To me, that meant the cops would soon be on the way, so I got the hell out of there."

Not the information I needed. I knew what happened in that room, or thought I did. If Bruce couldn't stick with a surveillance, that was his problem. "Back to Tomasco. He's my target."

"Okay. You've got the junk yard dog. Where'd that crazy woman go? Is she still here?" His head swiveled as if he hoped to see through the blindfold.

Over the next two hours, I asked and re-asked every question I could think of, trying to learn as much about Tomasco as I could. The more I knew, the better plan I could develop to get him out of my life. Bruce's answers carried the ring of truth, satisfying me I didn't need Dot again.

When it was over, I was confident I knew everything about Anthony Tomasco that Bruce knew. A disappointment was that Tomasco used cell phones and had no fixed communications. He had latched onto throwaways as soon as they became available because they did not give his location away. When I spoke with him the previous evening, he could have been in Boca Raton or Rio de Janeiro, and I wouldn't have known the difference. Bruce didn't know

Tomasco's current whereabouts, only that he'd last seen him during our visit to the Boca mansion.

Since my original plan had been to confront Tomasco, not knowing where he was put me in a quandary. I needed a new plan, and that meant I needed time to think. "Sorry, Bruce, but the tape goes back on." I studied him. He was a beaten man. "If you promise to keep your mouth shut, I could skip it — but the blindfold stays on."

FORTY-FOUR

Bruce gave me a look of surrender. "I'll stay quiet. Do what you have to do."

Once he was secure, I walked over to Bridge. "Please keep an eye on Bruce while I speak to the others." I switched my attention to Bob, David, and Dot. "Can we talk?"

We walked into the dormitory, and David and I sat on one bunk while Bob and Dot sat across from us. "My problem is I need to confront Tomasco. He has to know he can't mess with me and those I care about."

Bob stared at me as he pulled the scarf off the lower part of his face, then turned away, a frown crinkling his forehead. "I like you, Beth, and I think you're a pretty capable woman. But facing down an international criminal seems a bit out of your range. Why don't you just go to the police with what you know?"

"Ha," Dot said.

I wasn't quite as derisive as Dot, but my

skepticism won the Day. "To the cops? So far, my track record with the authorities has not been sterling. Even if I threw the missing briefcase filled with diamonds on the counter, they'd laugh." It was my time to go silent as I let the events of the past few weeks filter through my mind.

"I understand how you feel," David said, "but Bob has a good point. This Tomasco character is most likely well-protected. Bodyguards, alarms, and who knows what-all. You're out of your element."

My expression must have carried images passed down by my grandmothers, who were two tough ladies. In a world run by and for men, they had cut wide paths.

David added in a rush, "I don't mean just you. I mean anyone would be over their heads with this situation. It's just not possible."

"Yeah?" I said. "Stand back and watch. Anthony Tomasco has met his match this time. He's going down."

"Easy, kids," Bob said. "Don't go hostile at one another. If Beth's serious, we'd best concentrate on a plan to penetrate his protection."

"I'm serious," I said. "You can bet on it."

"Yeah, we're serious," Dot said.

"Dammit, Beth," David said, exasperation

oozing from his tone. "You are the most frustrating woman I've ever . . . uh, uh . . . treated for a lump on the head."

I gave him my sweetest smile. "Yeah, I feel the same."

"Seems pretty simple to me," Bob said. "Nothing has really changed. Sooner or later, Tomasco will return to Boca. When he does, if she hasn't come to her senses, Beth does her thing. I know a few folks in that area who can keep an eye on the place and let us know when he shows up."

I chuckled. "Is there any place you don't know a few folks?"

"Well, let me see. Most of those in Tallahassee moved over to New Orleans to work in the hurricane cleanup. So, I reckon I'm a bit thin there." He stood. "Let's go ask our new friend about the security arrangements at the Boca estate."

Bruce's briefing consisted of the proverbial good news, bad news. The bad news was Tomasco's house was like a fortress. He employed perimeter guards and had alarms in layers. Four men patrolled the grounds during the hours of darkness, one at each point of the compass. They were members of a local gang who spent most of their spare time knocking off 7-Elevens and bragging on street corners. Most had criminal records and had done hard time.

After hearing that, I was ready for better news and Bruce came through. On a scale of one to ten, Bruce rated the local gang members no more than a three. He figured their bravado and loyalty would last as long as they held the upper hand and had superior numbers. They were armed, but for bragging purposes only. They couldn't hit a 747 at seven paces. They'd do more damage if they threw their fancy weapons.

He continued. "Tomasco won't allow the guards inside his house and is lax about using the alarms when he's in residence. He lives alone with an occasional female visitor." He winked at me. "The bought-and-paid-for kind. He trusts no one — he has no friends. Anthony Tomasco is a modern-day Midas — only gold interests him. His greed knows no bounds."

"So, how do I account for you, Gerald, and Lodo? You were inside the house."

"True, but that was a special situation. And, I'm not one of his local thugs. I have my own security company and a day-to-day contract with Mr. Tomasco to perform, uh, certain activities. I allowed him to make you part of the deal. I made a mistake, one I deeply regret. And, before you ask, Gerald

303

and Lodo work for me, not Tomasco."

I felt like going into the other room and spending an hour or so meditating on what Bruce was telling me — or banging my head against the wall. How much truth was he giving me? How much should I trust him? Since I didn't have the luxury of time, I plowed on. "What are Gerald and Lodo doing now?"

"Probably home with their families. It is past the bewitching hour, and they're off-duty."

My befuddlement factor was rocketing skyward. "If I hit Tomasco's house, where do you stand?"

"Depends. I usually sell to the highest bidder."

"Gerald and Lodo?"

"Like I said, they work for me."

I looked at Bob, who shrugged, then both of us shifted our eyes toward David. He gave us a *beats-me* gesture.

I leaned back in my chair and studied Bruce, the first wisps of an idea forming.

FORTY-FIVE

"Bruce," I said, "let me recap a bit. You have a private security company with Gerald and Lodo on the payroll. Is that right?"

"Yes," he said, then followed with, "Why don't you take off this blindfold? You can see I'm neutralized."

"Maybe after a few more questions. What kind of contract do you have with Tomasco?"

He said nothing for several seconds. "Take off the blindfold, and I'll work with you any way I can. Like I said, Tamasco is no friend of mine."

I nodded at Bob, who freed Bruce's eyes.

After a few moments of blinking and squinting, he gave me his full attention. "Day-to-day. Personal services. Specific duties undefined. He asks, and I either say yes or no. Of course, if I say no, I don't get paid."

"Seems reasonable. Suppose you got a

better offer?"

"It would have to be something I couldn't turn down. Even in my business, there are credibility issues. If word gets around that I switch sides at the drop of a dime, I'll soon be unemployed."

"Pretty words that didn't answer my question. Let's suppose someone offered you your freedom for a one-event contract. What would you say?"

Bruce chuckled. "Somehow I suspected we'd get back to my survival." He glanced at Dot. "Let's just say I didn't make it this long by acting like an idiot."

"So, in such a situation, you'd be free to work with someone else?"

"Basically. But there would be stipulations."

"Such as?"

Bruce grinned. "Look. Can we stop peeking around corners? If you want to hire me, it can be done. However, for my professional standing, I could never go against him one-on-one. The best I can do is help in some unseen capacity."

"Hold that thought," I said. "I need to consult with my associates." Nodding at Dot, I said, "Don't let him leave." I stood and started toward the door, waving David and Bob to come with me. Oops. Had I left

306

the cat watching the canary? "Don't hurt him. Okay?"

"Shit," I heard as I walked into the dormitory. David and Bob joined me.

"I'm not going to like this, am I?" David said. "You're going to do something stupid and dangerous."

"Me?" I said, taking his hand and squeezing. "You know better."

For the next twenty-four hours, the hands on the clock moved like they were blazing trails through molasses on a cold day in Alaska. The first couple of hours went the fastest as Bruce and I arrived at a meeting of the minds. He called it a contract while my choice was an accommodation. We agreed I wouldn't turn him over to Dot, and he would do what I needed.

I had a few calls from blocked numbers, but ignored them, assuming it was Tomasco calling from some place in the world. Likewise with Bruce's phone, which I kept in my possession.

At daylight, Bob dispatched Street and Blister to make contact with their friends who worked the beach in Boca Raton. We had to know if Tomasco was in residence. I hoped he was. The tension was killing me. I needed to get it over with so I could go back to hunting the slobs who left me with a severe headache and set me up for murder — not to mention assorted attempts to turn me into roadkill.

David left soon thereafter to clean up and make his rounds at the hospital. He had a full day of appointments ahead but promised to return as soon as he could. We both hoped it would be by six, no later than seven.

Dot and Bridge kept an eye on Bruce. Since he was now an ally, or I wanted to believe he was, he was loose and free to move around. However, I felt confident he wouldn't pull anything with Dot on his case. She'd like nothing better than to cut him off at the knees, or maybe a bit higher.

Bob and I watched morning TV, catching up on the news. It only took about thirty minutes to learn what the cable news stations knew and commercials filled twenty minutes of that. Then, it was the same thing in a repetitious loop — different faces, same teleprompters.

The day dragged on.

Mid-afternoon, there was a knock on the back door. Bob opened it with me in backup position, my .32 by my leg. Gerald and Lodo stood there. Their expressions told me nothing, except they had followed

Bruce's instructions to show up at the bar.

"Come in," I said. "Bruce has a new contract. Follow me."

I walked toward the storage room, knowing Gerald and Lodo followed, with Bob bringing up the rear.

"Dammit, old woman," I heard Bruce say. "You cheat. You had that same ace two hands ago and the cards haven't been shuffled."

Dot cackled. "I knowed you couldn't take losing to a lady. Told you blackjack was a girly game. Now, if you want to switch to five-card stud, we can play some real poker."

Bruce said, "Okay, but the deal changes with each hand. No way you're going to keep bottom dealing me. At least half the time I'll know my cards are from the top of the deck."

"Hold the game," I said. "Bruce has company."

"Not now," Dot said. "We was jist upping the ante to five dollars. Right, Brucey?"

He handed her twenty dollars. "Take it. I'd rather give it to you than have you cheat me out of it. Hello, Gerald, Lodo. Come on in. We have some planning to do. But don't play poker with this woman."

"Keep your money, deary. Jist cut me in on the action. I ain't had this much fun since . . . Well, better not tell you when that was." Her cackle rang through the room again. "You best git over here, Bridge. Brucey's gonna give us our assignments."

Bruce looked at me with a *do I have to* look. I smiled and shrugged. "Better to have her working with you than working against you."

Bob's cell phone rang and he walked into the sleeping area to answer it. A few minutes later, he was back. "Tomasco is in residence."

FORTY-SIX

Three a.m. Somewhere I read or heard that three in the morning is the best time for burglaries and other skullduggery. Normal people are sound asleep behind their locked and alarmed doors and windows. The hour belongs to those who take it.

Guess that meant my small group was not normal. We crept along the beach working our way toward Tomasco's Boca mansion. The Palm Beach County Sea Turtle Protection Ordinance worked to our advantage. Its no-lights-allowed kept us bathed in the darkness of the moonless night. Of course, the sky was clear and the stars and the luminescence of the ocean made things brighter than I wished them to be.

"This is it," Bruce said. "Gerald, Lodo, come with me as we planned. The rest of you stay put until I call you in. If I'm not back in ten minutes, run like hell and find a new plan for another night."

Bob, Dot, and I hunkered down against the concrete wall along the beach line of the property while the three of them made their way toward a personnel gate. "Cross your fingers," I said, "and wish them luck. I really want to get this over with tonight."

"I shoulda gone," Dot said. "I ain't got no trust for him. They might just walk right in and sell us out."

"We'll know in ten minutes or less," Bob said. "Bruce is opening the gate, and the others are going over the wall now."

Bruce, Gerald, and Lodo disappeared from view and we, at least I, spent the next minutes staring at the spots I'd last seen them. The waves splashed onto the shore, paying no attention to the rapid thumping of my heart.

If I'd taken the time and looked around, I might have spotted a sea turtle making its way onshore to lay eggs. But I had no thoughts of wildlife, other than the kind that walks upright on two legs. The turtles would be back next year and in future years. I had my best shot at Tomasco tonight.

More upsetting to my plans would have been a beach patrol stumbling onto us. Palm Beach County was serious about its illumination ordinance and enforced it with vigor. Possible answers to their inevitable questions never entered my mind. I couldn't tear my concentration away from the gate Bruce walked through. My whole world centered on the swing of those hinges.

After what seemed like an eternity, but was only seven minutes, Bruce came through the gate and waved us forward. "Coast is clear," he said. "We neutralized the guards and shorted the alarms. Are you ready?"

"What did you do with the guards? Are they still there? What should I expect from them when I enter the compound?"

"They decided to take the rest of the night off. Seems Tomasco insulted their gang colors. With a little persuasion from Gerald and Lodo, they decided there are things more important than money. Now, do you need me to unlock the door?"

"No, I can handle the lock. Thanks, it's time —"

"Not so fast," Bruce said. "There is one other issue. Tomasco has company, a female companion."

"Darn." That was the last thing I wanted to hear — well, maybe not the last, but way down the list.

"The guard said she arrived about ten and hasn't left. That makes me assume she's sleeping over."

I hesitated, hating his words. My quarrel was with Tomasco, not some local call girl. I did not want to involve an innocent person, no matter how she made a living.

"I'll go with you," Bob said. "If there's a problem, I can hold her out of the picture while you do your thing."

"No," I said, perhaps too sharply, then mentally cursed myself. He only wanted to help. "Sorry, thanks, but Tomasco has to know this is my show. If you go in with me, he won't see it that way. His male chauvinism will kick in, and he'll write me off as a threat."

"I see your point," Bob said. "What's your alternative?"

"Hey, what am I — seaweed?" Dot said. "Just some hooker in there. I'll take care of her."

Now that put me in a dither. I couldn't use Bob, Bruce, or any of the other men. If one of them showed up, Tomasco wouldn't take me seriously. As soon as the men were out of sight, he'd go back to treating me like a piece of fluff. But taking Dot was a risk I didn't cherish. She'd already proven she could be a loose cannon, and that was the last thing I wanted behind me. I studied her face, trying to discern intent. "Will you do exactly what I say? No questions? No arguments? No rushing off on your own?"

"Of course, deary," she said, as if she always listened to others. "You jist hand 'er over, then worry 'bout Tomasco. Maybe she'd like to play a bit of two-handed stud."

"Uh-huh." I thought a moment longer but didn't find another solution. "Okay, Dot. But I swear you'd better do what I tell you."

"So, tell already. You're windier than an old man after a can of pork 'n beans."

"Let's go. We can walk and talk."

"Hold it," Bruce said. "You still carrying that pea shooter?"

"My .32? Yeah. What about it?"

"Trust me. It won't impress Tomasco. Take this one." He pushed a pistol, grip first, in my direction. "It's an M9 Beretta, standard military weapon. Carries a fifteen-round magazine, which is full. Lightweight enough for a woman and enough stopping power for a cop." He turned the weapon slightly. "Here's the safety. It's on now. Take it off when you decide to shoot him. There's a round in the chamber."

Ignoring his supposition, I accepted the weapon and hefted it. The weight was good, and it had a nice feel. I slid the safety back and forth, feeling a spring pop it into position. "Thanks."

"Can I have the little one?" Dot said. "He

315

took back his .38." She glared at Bruce. "Never know when a lady might have to defend herself."

I shrugged and handed the .32 to her. Worst she could do was shoot me.

"Okay, I'm ready," Dot said. "Let's go." She took off in front of me waving the pistol around like she was Al Capone looking for the St. Valentine's Day Massacre.

FORTY-SEVEN

I stood for an instant, then raced after Dot, catching her before she barged into the back yard. I grabbed her shoulder and scooted past. "Stay behind me. And be quiet."

I inched my way across the rear of the house to the porch. The lock wasn't difficult to pick. Only took a minute or so. I could have done it in seconds if Dot hadn't hung over me, breathing in my ear, and bumping my back and arm. I was already regretting my decision to take her along.

The door swung inward on quiet hinges, and we were in. The sketch of the layout was as Bruce said, and I found the stairs at the end of the foyer. I didn't worry about the floor or the stair treads squeaking — they wouldn't dare. Beach mansions coddled the very rich, those that wealthy politicians love to excoriate for having too much money, those that politicians of both parties visit Florida to cultivate.

There were several doors leading off a hallway at the top of the staircase, each of them closed — a development that did not please me. I hesitated. "Which do you think is his bedroom?" I whispered.

"Move outta the way, deary. I'll find him." Dot shoved by me and before I could grab her, pressed her ear against first one door, then another. She made a round of the doors then returned to the fourth and waved me forward. "All yours," she whispered. "They're in here. Two of them. Sounds like they's asleep. Ain't nobody in the others."

I listened, but heard nothing. Maybe Dot's street living had given her super hearing. I twisted the knob, pleased that it turned, and the door opened with a gentle push. Muted light filtered into the room from the stars outside. There were two lumps in the bed, a man on the near side and a woman on the far. The sheet was down around their waists, and there was no doubt which was which. Also, there was no doubt she had been medically enhanced. Even lying on her back, they pointed straight up. No sliding under the armpits for her — ever.

I turned to instruct Dot, but saw she was making her way to the woman's side of the bed. Shaking my head in frustration, I flipped on the light and went after Tomasco. Slamming the barrel of the Beretta against his temple, I said, "Okay, asshole. Party time."

He came awake with a start, his eyes glassy, so I withdrew, backing off a couple of steps. Didn't want him flailing around in surprise and knocking the gun out of my hand. Beside him, the woman's eyes flew open and grew large as they focused on the barrel of Dot's weapon, hovering a couple of inches from the tip of her nose.

"You'n me going for a walk," Dot said. "Get up."

The woman didn't move. She appeared fascinated by Dot and the .32.

"Now," Dot said, shoving the pistol into the woman's boob. "Want me to blow silicone all over the room? I can give you a blowout that will take a NASCAR pit crew to reinflate that boob."

"I'm getting up," she said, swinging her legs from under the sheet.

Staring at her bare ass, I wondered what guys find so fascinating about naked women. Didn't look hot to me. With a bit of prodding from Dot, she headed toward the door and out of the room. I hoped Dot would find her something to wear before she dealt the cards.

"Who . . . who are you?" Tomasco said. "What do you want?"

I saw a pair of glasses on the nightstand and picked them up. "Here. Put these on and try again." I tossed them at him.

He slipped the specs on and stared at me. His features relaxed. "Oh, Miss Bowman. Not my normal office hours, but I gather you have business with me. Speak. You have the floor."

So much for intimidating him with my grand entrance. I stepped forward and rested the barrel of the Beretta between his eyes. "You bet your ass I have the floor. Now get your butt out of bed. And if I don't like what I see, I might shoot it off."

That produced a flinch and a look of fear. Mention doing harm to a man's pride and joy, and you get his attention every time.

He slid his legs off the side of the bed and rose to his feet, wrapping the sheet around his waist as he did so. Guess he wasn't taking any chances I had higher expectations in men than he could meet.

"Sit over there." I motioned toward a wingback chair with a reading lamp crouching near it.

He shuffled forward and sat. "Okay, you have the gun. What's on your mind? Better make it fast. My men will be here soon. I hit the silent alarm when I rolled out of bed."

I chuckled. "Glad you did. Your silent alarm will only find silence. I own your house and grounds. The guards lost interest and I neutralized the alarms. My people are all around your compound. Even if you had a connection to the police department, they won't be answering."

His confidence seemed to slip a bit, but bravado took its place. "You're bluffing."

"If that's the best you can do, don't ever play poker. You can't tell the difference between truth and a bluff. How long would you like to wait?" I studied my watch. "Been almost five minutes since I popped the lock on the back door. Not a very efficient alarm system. Guess you bought the Blue Light Special." I sat on the edge of his bed, my gun leveled on his chest. "I have lots of time."

FORTY-EIGHT

If Tomasco wanted to believe his guards were rushing to his rescue, I was willing to allow it. The longer he waited, the more he'd sweat. I didn't have all night so, at some point, I'd have to speed things up. "I have twenty-five after three. What say we wait ten minutes? Will that give your rescuers enough time?"

His face said his confidence level had dropped again. It looked like he was beginning to accept his predicament — maybe I wasn't bluffing.

I stood and walked around the room. Someone had spent a lot of money furnishing it. The paintings were originals. Since I'm no connoisseur of the arts, I didn't recognize any of the names, but I could see they were quality. The furniture appeared solid, no veneers for this man. And even someone as uneducated as I could recognize a Persian rug covered the center of the room. The best that money could buy was my guess.

"The import/export business must be doing okay for you," I said. "Of course, when your imports are mostly high-dollar items smuggled in, it does enhance the profit margin, doesn't it? No splits with Uncle Sam. Too bad about that attaché case filled with diamonds."

That got his attention. "What do you mean? I run a legitimate business."

"Sure you do. Just like the female who's entertaining my cohort is in love with you and shares your bed because you're such a wonderful, romantic lover. How much do you pay her? One of those things I've always wondered about. If things get tough in the PI business, I might be tempted to turn a few tricks — if the money's right."

"You'd never make it. Too flat."

I looked at my chest. "Guess you can't tell the difference between what Mother Nature gives a woman and what the medical profession supplies. Mine are natural C's. That honey of yours is probably a natural A. The rest is silicone, a fancy name for sand. I've been told there's a delicious difference in the taste, but I wouldn't know. Seeing you here, you probably wouldn't know either."

"That's ridiculous," he said. "Tiffanie is

here because she wants to be. Money is not the motivation."

I stared, feeling a bit sorry for him. Apparently, he had all the money he could ever need, but had no one to share his life. To even the stupidest male, it must be demeaning to hand over money for sex. In Tomasco's case, was it lack of trust or lack of anything other than cash to attract a woman? I wondered, then decided I didn't give a rat's ass.

I said, "Possible that she just drops in to share the mattress with you because she respects you so much, but somehow I doubt it. I'm thinking the only way you can get your rocks off is by hand or a prostitute. Tonight, you chose the latter."

While sparring with him, I had continued my inspection of his bedroom. I tried not to show it, but I was impressed. Someone had good taste and the money to indulge it.

I checked my watch. "Okay, time's up. Haven't seen any white knights charging through the door. Guess you were wrong about your *boys* riding to the rescue. Any other tricks in your little box — or that you think you have?"

"What do you want? Money? Name your price."

"No. I'm not interested in money. Here's

the deal — simple and straightforward." I leaned against the dresser. "I walked in tonight like I own the place. That's because I do own this place. I have as much run of your house as you do. Your gate didn't stop me. Your alarms didn't stop me. Your piddling guards were no challenge for me. Hell, even your bimbo didn't put up a fight. I could blow you away and stage it any way I want. Ever consider suicide? It could happen, then I walk out of here, and no one would ever know. Do you agree?"

He glared at me, then nodded. "Get on with it."

"You threatened my mother. You threatened a friend of mine. You threatened me. You also had your people invade my house and humiliate me. You dragged me here and put me through your dog and pony show in your little room with the big speakers. Remember all that?"

His complexion had gone a bit green. "What do you want?"

"Simply this. I can enter your house and your bedroom any time I choose. You can't erect enough barricades to stop me. You can't hire enough guards to intimidate me. I can get to you no matter where you are. Understand that. Accept that." I grinned. "But don't let it interrupt your sleep. I'd hate for that to happen."

I hesitated, giving him a chance to smile. He didn't, so I dug the tines in deeper. "Tonight, I only brought a pistol with me. If you bother me again, if you bother my mother again, if you bother my friends again, I will be back. And next time, I'll bring a scalpel. You know I can get one from my doctor friend. Whenever that night is, you'll hope you got laid because it will have been your last. I'll neuter you like a puppy."

I paused to allow my words to sink in while keeping my pistol pointed at his head. I wanted him to absorb the full impact of what I said. Also, staring down the barrel of my Beretta would soften him. I've seen pistols from the business end, and no one can walk away without an appreciation of how big and ominous they look. It appeared to work with Tomasco. I could see his eyes enlarging with each tick of the clock.

After an appropriate number of seconds passed, I said, "Do you understand? Are we clear on what will happen if you *ever* bother me or mine again?"

His eyes stayed locked on my pistol, but his head went up and down.

I accepted that as agreement but took a step in his direction so he could better examine the inside of the barrel. I wanted it to be the first thing he envisioned every morning. After giving him time to memorize the rifling, I walked to the door. "Dot. You and the bimbo can come in now."

Tiffanie led the way in with Dot behind her. Tiffanie had wrapped herself in a sheet, leading me to believe they'd been in an adjoining bedroom.

"You. Get into the bed," I said to the woman. "Pull the covers over your head and don't let them down — ever. Dot, keep Tomasco covered." I handed the Beretta to her. "Try not to shoot him unless he wiggles or breathes too deeply. Give me your pistol."

As the woman crawled into bed and followed instructions, I took the .32 and walked into the hallway. Once out of Tomasco's view, I flipped the cylinder open and extracted the five shells. Then I reentered the room.

"Pull the sheet back," I said to him.

"What? Are you —"

"Pull it back," I said pointing the .32 at him and thumbing the hammer. "Don't take a chance with me. I could be having PMS. You don't want to test me."

With quivering hands, he uncovered his lap, revealing his bare crotch.

"I've seen a lot better," I said, chuckling. I addressed the lump on the bed. "How about you, sweetheart? Or does your business cater to the size-challenged?"

No response, just a shaking of the sheet. Either she was laughing at how funny I was or quaking with fear. Didn't matter which.

Dot cackled. "Size-challenged. That's a good'un. You good, deary, you good."

FORTY-NINE

I returned my attention to Tomasco. "Here's the deal. This weapon holds five rounds." I waved the pistol. "When I went into the hall, I unloaded four of them. Now it's time to play Beth's version of Russian roulette. You can guess the game, can't you? I spin the cylinder, point and pull the trigger. If we have an empty chamber under the hammer, nothing happens. If it's the one with the bullet . . . well, oops, we have a boom."

I pointed the pistol toward his limp manhood as I talked. Its shrinkage increased with each word. "However, instead of holding the gun against my temple as in the normal game, I'll just point it at your Mr. Happy. Ready?"

He covered himself with his hands and closed his eyes.

"Damn, deary, you are tough," Dot said. "Hell, even I ain't never shot a man's dick off." She cackled. "This I gotta see. Hope that bullet's in the right hole."

I cut my eyes at Dot and grinned, then back to Tomasco. Without taking my eyes off him, I spun the cylinder. "Open your eyes, you creep. You made me look at your photographs. You can face this."

He didn't move.

"You either open your eyes and move your hands, or I use the automatic. I know there's a round chambered in that. It'll leave holes in your hands and still take off all they cover."

His eyes crept open and stared at the .32. His face was greener and tears trickled down his cheeks.

"Much better. Now, move your hands so we can get on with the game." I took careful and slow aim.

His hands stayed in place.

"You're still doing it. Do you want me to shoot through them? Then, not only will you have no penis, but your hands will be useless."

Slowly, his hands moved to the side and rested on his thighs. "Please don't do this. I'll do whatever you want. I'll give you anything you want. Please, please." His head bowed, and the trickle on his cheeks became a flow. Mucous ran from his nose as he bawled like a two-year old.

I hesitated, enjoying his suffering. He was the bastard who put me through hell worrying about my mother and David. I waited until his eyes came back to me, then pulled the trigger.

The hammer slammed down on the empty chamber. At the instant of the click, he flinched and cringed, looking like he was trying to shrink inside himself. He stayed that way while the clock moved. I held my position.

Dot whispered, "Damnedest thang I ever seen."

The bimbo never moved under the coverlet. You have to love people who follow orders.

After giving him a moment to thank his lucky star, I said, "You were lucky this time. Understand me though. If you bother me, anyone around me, or anyone I know, I'll be back, and we'll repeat this exercise with a fully loaded pistol, an automatic. You know I can do it, and rest assured, *I will.* Mr. Tomasco, if you give me the slightest reason, I'll blow your nuts off with the first round, your dick with the second. After what I consider the right amount of time for you to consider your gender change, I'll put a bullet through your gut and hang around to watch your life trickle away. Your only solace will be knowing that when I leave, you'll be a dead man, never to suffer again. I can't make it any simpler than that, and I doubt I need to. Do you understand?"

His head stayed down.

I nudged his chin upward with the barrel of the .32. "I hate to repeat myself. Do you understand?"

He nodded.

"Not good enough. Say it, you bastard, or I start now."

He refused to meet my eyes. "Y . . . yes. I understand."

I stared, wishing I could inflict more pain without killing him. Nothing came to mind. I was out of my body, a person I'm not sure I would have recognized had I been able to observe. I turned away and paced the room, getting myself under control. When my turmoil settled a bit, I came back to him. "Since I suspect you need to go, get in the bathroom. Sit there until your butt goes to sleep."

Tomasco stood and, walking with a staggered step, followed orders, his head down. The sheet stayed in the chair, but he showed no thoughts of his nakedness. He was a beaten man. The door clicked shut behind him. I foresaw no more problems with him.

"Let's go," I whispered to Dot. "Our job

is finished for tonight."

"Whatever you say, deary. I ain't never messin' with you agin."

FIFTY

As Dot and I exited the rear door of Tomasco's mansion, I set the lock. It seemed like the right thing to do since he was in no condition to defend himself against an intruder. I suspected the next one out would be the prostitute. I hoped she'd secure the house as she disappeared into the night. Be a shame if a burglar broke in.

Bob waited for us on the beach. There was no sign of Bruce, Gerald, or Lodo. "Everybody split?" I asked.

"Yeah. Bruce said he figured you were even. He left his card though, and said if you need him again, just call. Of course, he'll charge for the next service."

I took the proffered card and studied it. "Langston Security Services, Inc. Pretty nebulous name for what he does. But general enough to get him business from all kinds of customers. Who knows? I may have to hire him down the road. At least I know he can do the job."

"You're kidding," Bob said. "You wouldn't really hire him."

"Don't you bet on it," Dot said. "You didn't see what I did. This is one badass woman. Her and Bruce are two of a kind."

Bob gave me a look. "Do I want to know?"

"No," I said. "But I think Tomasco's out of the picture as a threat, at least for a while. He discovered there are things more important than harassing me."

"Yeah, his dick," Dot said and cackled.

Bob looked at her like he expected an explanation, so I jumped in. "It's time to get moving. We've been lucky so far. A beach patrol could come along any moment. Besides, I'm tired. It's been a long day." I started toward where we parked my car.

Behind me, I heard Dot whisper, "I'll tell you later. Damnedest thang I ever seen."

I dropped Bob and Dot at Bobby's Bar and continued to my place. While I preferred to curl up next to David, I decided that might not be my best destination. He needed his sleep, and I might not be inclined to let him have much. Besides, it was almost five and he'd have to get up soon to prepare for hospital rounds. However, that didn't change the fact I was still hyper, and he knew how to relax me.

At home, I changed and crawled into bed, replaying the scene with Tomasco, wondering what I should have done differently — if anything. I figured he would take one of two courses after he recovered his equilibrium. He would leave me alone, believing I had the capacity to follow through with my threats. Or he could come after me. Either way, he shouldn't bother Mom and David. If he wanted vengeance, it would be against me and me alone. That's how I'd work it if I were in his shoes. I'd have to stay on my toes for the next few weeks — at least until I could turn the whole mess over to the police.

It was reassuring to know I wouldn't have to face Bruce, Gerald, and Lodo again. After watching them operate, I was even more impressed than I'd been when they staged the kidnapping and hauled me off to Tomasco's audio-visual room.

I forced my mind to clear, then allowed an image of David to slip in. That man had definitely gotten under my skin, and I wanted him where he could scratch long and often. Reaching across the bed, I dragged the extra pillow to me, hugging it as I wanted to hug him.

Sleep came. I dreamed I slept with a huge smile on my face.

I woke with a start, sunlight streaming into the room. I lay there, every sense functioning at full capacity. What had awakened me? A noise? Listening as hard as I could, I heard . . . nothing. I glanced at the clock radio — seven thirty — then slipped out of bed. Imitating a church mouse, I rummaged in my purse for Bruce's Beretta.

Door or window? Where should I start? I chose the door, and crept to it, shouldering in close alongside the opening, squinting with the effort to hear. No sound. No breathing except mine. I peeked into the hallway. Only the ticking of my clocks. They were a weakness of mine. Wall clocks, table clocks, watches. Even one grandfather clock. I liked them all and bought far too many. Moving the collection from Texas had doubled my expenses.

After a moment, I decided whatever woke me must have come from the outside, so I inched my way across the room. Again, nothing out of the ordinary. A few cars and kids on their way to school.

Grimacing, I accused myself of being paranoid. How long would I jump at imaginary situations? I took several deep breaths, then crawled into bed after stuffing the pistol under my pillow. Somewhere, I read that being paranoid doesn't mean they're not out to get you. And, with the humiliation I'd heaped on Tomasco, it could well be true. Somehow though, I didn't think he had recovered that quickly.

I lay there, my hearing attuned to any sound out of the ordinary. There were none. Only the ticks of the clocks and the expansion noises of a house heated by the Florida sun. Yet, something had awakened me — what?

Perhaps a dream. I searched my mind, trying to find a thread. Nothing appeared. Two-thirds of me begged to sleep, however the other one-third, the common sense third, said get out of bed. I had work to do.

Shoving the idea of sleep behind me, I puttered into the kitchen and made coffee. After it reached a satisfactory drip stage, I sneaked a cup and headed for the shower. With minimal thought, I chose my clothes for the day. Jeans, sneakers, T-shirt, and a large purse. The clothing because it blended in and the bag to carry the M9 Beretta. I wasn't sure where Bruce obtained it, but I didn't want to give it up just yet. When this was over, I'd look into getting one for myself — one I could register without fear of having a SWAT team descend on me.

By the time I dressed, the hands of my kitchen kitty clock had worked their way around to eight thirty. I figured it was late enough to call David, even though I might interrupt his hospital rounds. To heck with it. I needed him more than his patients did.

FIFTY-ONE

"David," I said when he answered the phone. "I just wanted to hear your voice."

"Are you okay? Why didn't you call me when you got home? I was awake all night worrying. Darn you, Beth. You're the most frustrating, most —"

"Music to my ears," I said. "Is this your way of telling me I'm more than a one-night stand?"

"One —" He laughed. "Not only are you frustrating, you're sneaky. However, if you need to hear it, yes, you're far more than a one-night stand. Well, on my side anyway. I hope the scalpel cuts both ways."

"Rest assured, it does. I missed you when I went to bed last night and when I woke up this morning. The bed seemed so big and lonely." Throwing caution to the wind, I lunged through the opening he'd given me. "What about tonight? Will I see you? Am I invited for a sleepover?"

David hesitated. "I'll have to get back to you on that. I want the answer to be yes, but I have a patient who is critical. I may spend the night at the hospital. If I miss you tonight though, I'll make it up to you later — I promise."

"Picture me disappointed, but understanding. Don't expect this treatment every time though. I'm a demanding woman, and I'm demanding you."

He laughed. "Don't forget frustrating. Look, I'd love to talk to you all day, but I really need to run. Before I go though, did your trip to Boca last night work out the way you wanted?"

"Better than you can imagine."

"Damn. There goes my beeper. I'll call you later."

"You'd better." I wanted to blow a kiss into the phone. When your heart sings like a teenager's, why not act like one? Before I could follow through, there was a click in my ear.

I sat for a moment, savoring his words. The future was indistinct as it always is, but I felt good about it. "David Rasmussen. What a wonderful name. Ms. Elizabeth Angeline Bowman-Rasmussen. Yeah, that has the right ring to it."

My coffee cup was past empty so I floated

to the pot for a refill. After plopping at my breakfast table with a fresh brew, I called Bob, but heard his canned voice mail message. At the beep, I said, "It's Beth. Call me when you get a moment. Otherwise, I'm headed your way." It didn't concern me that he didn't answer. I figured he was working his corner and didn't want potential customers to know he carried a cell phone. Probably had it set on mute or, maybe, vibrate.

I checked the kitty clock and saw eight forty five — that was seven forty five in Wisconsin. Time to call Mom at my brother's. She should be up by now. I sipped, then topped up the cup. I needed fortification.

"Dolores, it's Beth." Dolores was Harve's wife and mother to his children, a fact Mom reminded me of far too often. We exchanged pleasantries, then I asked, "Is Mom available?"

A couple of ticks later, I heard, "Are you all right? I had a dream last night. When I called, you didn't answer. Where were you?"

"Uh . . . Mom." I thought fast and came up with the only response I thought would force her off the subject. "There are some things a daughter *does not* tell her mother. There are some nights when phone calls are not appreciated."

There was a pause on the line before she said, "Is this the man you mentioned the other day? What's he do for a living?" That was my mom. Occupation first, then whether he was a serial killer or worse. "He's a doctor."

"General practitioner or specialist? Specialists make more, you know."

"Mom. Be nice now. He's a wonderful person who treats me like a princess."

"Uh-huh. You have a ring yet?"

She had me. I had successfully switched the subject. Now I was stuck with it. If my mother had one interest beyond her premonitions about my getting hurt, it was marrying me off again. "No, we haven't gotten that far. But I have hopes."

"You just remember, men don't buy what they can get for free."

I laughed. "Free samples help close the deal. You told me that once."

Now it was her laughter that came through the line. "Maybe I did, but I never remarried, did I? Probably gave away too many samples."

"That wasn't it," I said. "You had plenty of offers. Even a couple of doctors."

"Okay, I give up. You just be careful. Don't let him take advantage of you."

That was another thing about Mom. She had no confidence in my ability to manage my life. There was always something just around the corner ready to take advantage of me.

"Now, why did you call?" she said. "I'm sure it wasn't to tell me you slept with some man last night. And, in spite of what a mother might dream, it wasn't to tell me you're married."

If I hadn't been in such a great mood, I might have said something I'd rue later, but my success the previous night still had me on a high. "You can start packing. You should be able to go home in a few days. Things are looking up here."

"Good. I suspect Dolores would like the guest room back."

That took us into a conversation about Harve and Dolores, and their wonderful kids. At every opportunity, Mom slipped in jabs about my having given her no grandchildren. It didn't matter that she was my number one cheerleader when I told her I was dumping Sonny-the-Bunny. My lack of a husband and little ones to bounce on her lap trumped all. Most of my contributions to the conversation consisted of, "Yes, Mom."

Twenty minutes later, I hung up after telling Dolores how much I appreciated her putting up with Mom. I was sure I heard a tone of relief in Dolores' voice when I said Mom would be leaving soon.

FIFTY-TWO

The rest of the day was uneventful. I checked in at the bar and discovered that Bob and Dot were catching up on their sleep. Sounded like a good idea so I went home, crawled into bed, and did the same. After all, I needed to be fresh for David. I refused to consider he might have to spend the night at the hospital.

He didn't. His patient's condition improved, and I discovered a whole new level of highs. Compared to my previous experiences with men, I may as well have been a virgin. My last thought before falling asleep in David's arms was that I had to find some way to keep him. I knew he couldn't be as perfect as he seemed, but I was more than willing to take the chance on imperfections. Besides, Mom would love him. After all, he was a doctor.

I woke at five thirty a.m. when David's

alarm went off, and he got out of bed. "Don't go," I said. "It's such a big, lonely world without you."

He kissed me on the forehead. "Sorry, but the Hippocratic oath has to come first. I have hospital rounds, then a day filled with appointments. You stay out of trouble, don't get hurt, and be back here promptly at six p.m. I have special plans for this evening." He flipped back the covers. "Very special plans."

I watched him walk into the bathroom, then rolled over, smiling so wide I could feel new creases in my forehead. I don't remember his leaving the house.

I woke, a shudder flooding through me. I lay there, a feeling of déjà vu overwhelming me. Same as yesterday, same feeling, same everything. Then I remembered, different bed, different room, different world. David's bedroom, perfect bedroom, perfect world. I wanted to stretch and luxuriate, but an ominous dread drained me. Whatever snapped me awake was internal, something inside me. Not a noise, not an outside threat. What kind of kooky dreams could I be having that would hit me twice on successive days?

Although I told myself there was no danger, I went for Bruce's M9. I hadn't told

David I was packing, but it was now a fixture in my purse. My goal was to bolster my confidence. The Beretta had the effect I wanted. With the gun in hand, it was time to decipher the subconscious clue I had received.

As I concentrated, I released the magazine, then slammed it home. That felt good, so I did it again, and a third time. After beating the magazine up, I pulled back the slide until I saw brass, then let it go forward. So reassuring. Thanks, Bruce, I thought. Nice gun.

That's when I realized what woke me. Bruce. No, not the physical Bruce, but a mental image of him that formed while I slept. He had appeared to me in a dream, a dream important or fearful enough to snap me into wakefulness. What had it been?

I needed mental clarity so I headed for the kitchen, dangling the Beretta in my right hand. I didn't realize it was there until I opened the cabinet door. The weapon felt as natural as a trip to my hairdresser. David had brewed a pot of coffee, and it was still hot. There was also a note. I smiled as I read it.

If this is what a one-night stand feels like, I should have started a long time ago. Feels more like a one-lifetime stand. The day will be loooooong before I'm with you again.

My emotions surged and tears came to my eyes. What a precious man. How had I gotten so lucky? But I had to steel myself, set aside my feelings, and return to my Beth-the-Avenger status. The bums who framed me were still out there. And my at-sleep mind had tried to tell me something. I couldn't allow anything to interrupt my brain-dump.

After pouring a cup of coffee, I sat at the table and concentrated, searching for the dream. It had to be something I already knew. I didn't believe in premonitions. Those I left to Mom.

It came to me, at first in dribs and drabs, then in a rush. Tomasco said he had Bruce following his courier, Benjamin Jacobs. What was it Tomasco said? Something like *the best way to keep people honest is watch them.* He also told me Bruce's job was to make sure Jacobs kept his appointment. Then he accused me of being responsible for Jacobs' death and the loss of the brief-case because I came between Bruce and Jacobs.

I rummaged in the kitchen drawers until I found a pad of paper and a pen, then sat down and began to make notes. Once I caught up with my thoughts, I let my pen drift. Three stick figures appeared, one with a briefcase, followed by one in a skirt, followed by one holding a gun. Bruce following me while I followed Jacobs.

That was it. If Bruce was watching both Jacobs and me, he had to see me enter that hotel room and, contrary to what he said, know what happened next. That's what my dream had told me — my newfound friend Bruce might not have shared everything he knew. Then I remembered I cut off that part of his story, told him to concentrate on Tomasco.

I slapped my forehead. What an idiot. So now one of my questions was, had Bruce cooperated with me to divert Tomasco from tracking the diamonds? Was it to divert me while he monopolized the chase? Of course it was. Not only that, but the son of a bitch was probably hot on the trail of the briefcase right now.

I shook my head. The bastard snookered his boss by using me. And in so doing, he snookered me. However, Mom always said, she who snookers last, snookers best. And I planned to snooker Bruce last.

My coffee cup was empty, so I refilled it and settled at the table, mulling over my newfound memory. David's kitchen clock read eight a.m. Time to hit the shower, then get moving. Bruce had no idea what was about to hit him. I would turn him every way but loose until I squeezed every morsel of information from him. He'd think twice before he held out on the next woman.

I spent half a moment considering whether to bring Dot in for her own enjoyment, then trashed the idea. He was mine, all mine.

After showering, dressing, making the bed, and leaving a love note on David's pillow, I headed for home to get ready for the day. The clothes I'd worn out with David the previous evening were not what I had in mind for nailing Bruce to the proverbial wall.

Once I changed into my usual jeans, casual shirt, and sneakers, I dug Bruce's business card out of my purse. No address, only a phone number. I dialed and listened to a recording tell me I'd reached Langston Security Services and, if I left a brief reason for my call, someone would get back to me. Reassuring, but misleading. I figured if Bruce didn't like what he heard, he would ignore it. What a great idea though. I might copy it to keep from talking to the nuts who called my number. It was no pleasure hearing their disappointment when I told them I didn't pursue lost iguanas.

"Bruce. It's Beth Bowman. Something hot has come up. I need to meet with you. Phone me." I hesitated, then added as if an afterthought, "There's money to be made — for both of us." If I had figured Bruce right, that should earn me a call as soon as he heard the message.

FIFTY-THREE

I wanted Bruce on my team again, but I wasn't about to put all my eggs in that leaky basket. I figured even ostrich eggs could tumble through those holes. I'd track Bob and fill him in. If I was going up against Bruce, Gerald, and Lodo, I needed an edge. Bob and his homeless contacts might be able to provide it.

As I walked to the car, I considered whether to let the police in on my suspicions. Common sense said I should. They were the authorities, and I was onto multiple violations of the law. However, they'd pretty well told me to dig a dry hole in the beach. Every lead I gave them met with derision. Was it worth my while to bother them? I decided not — well, not until I had incontrovertible evidence to lay on them.

In case things did not go well though, I needed to let someone in on my suspicions, someone whose word would be trusted.

While I believed Bob and his friends to be honest, I was probably number one on a very short list of so-called reputable people who trusted them. If it came down to their word against Bruce and company, Bruce would win.

I knew one man who fit my needs — Sylvester Bergstrom, my dear lawyer-friend-boss. Flipping open my cell phone, I called his office and asked Donna to grant me a few minutes. She was ever the loyal secretary who protected her boss like a pit bull, especially when he'd given absolute instructions for no interruptions. Even my high standing with her and Sly almost didn't carry the day. I had to add the promise of a box of chocolates before she forgot his orders.

"Sly, it's Beth. I need to talk with you."

"Didn't Donna tell you I was not to be disturbed? You can be a real pain in the ass, you know that?"

"Of course. But you still think I'm cute. And this cute chick needs to come in and steal some of your time."

"I'm preparing for an important court appearance. Can't it wait a few days?"

"It can't wait a few hours. Even minutes are important. There are things you need to know in case I disappear. There are some really nasty people who don't find me as fascinating as you do."

Sly sighed, and I knew I'd won. He was a great trial lawyer, but putty in the hands of a whining woman.

"Okay. How soon can you get here? The clock starts the moment you walk through my door. Fifteen minutes maximum. Then you're out of here, and I get back to work."

"See you in ten minutes. And, in case I forget to use any of my precious time to tell you, you're a doll."

"Oh, shut up, and get in here."

Sly and I sat at his conference table, each nursing a soft drink. "That's about it," I said after catching him up on everything that had happened over the past several days. Everything except the details of what I did to Tomasco. Didn't want to watch Sly squirm. Men are so sensitive about their private parts. The proof of that is the paucity of Lorena Bobbit jokes originated by men. Of course, women will keep her alive forever.

I hadn't kept an eye on my watch, but figured I'd used about twenty of the fifteen minutes he promised me. "Those are the players. Bruce Langston and his goons, Tomasco, and the homeless folks who helped me. I'm convinced that Langston knows who conked me on the head, killed Jacobs, and stole the diamonds. Until I find the gems and bring the killers to justice, I won't rest. I suspect Langston is on their trail, ready to take the diamonds for his own. That's the only explanation I can come up with for why he cooperated and helped me."

Sly gave me a skeptical look. "How about the torture session you put him through?"

"That's what I thought at first. But it doesn't add up. He could have told me anything, even the truth, and I'd have quit. He didn't have to neutralize Tomasco's guards and alarms. He didn't have to switch sides. No, he had a reason other than my charming personality. And that has to be the jewels. His motive was to have me get Tomasco out of the picture. He probably thought I'd kill him." I hesitated, thinking through what I'd said. "That's my summation. You're the jury. What do you think?"

"Woman, you're impossible. You're up to your pretty little neck in trouble and still digging. What you say might make sense, but it doesn't matter. You're just Jane Citizen. That PI badge gives you no special privileges in something like this. What can I say to convince you to turn this over to the police?"

"What police?" I said. "Whose jurisdiction? And who's going to believe me? I have no proof, no credible witnesses to bring forward. Do you really think the authorities will mobilize because I ask them to? Do you think they'll even bother to interview Bob, Dot, and the other homeless people? I think not. I just wanted you to know in case things don't work out. That's my only objective in coming here." I pushed back from the table and stood. "Thanks for listening to me. I know you're busy, so I'll get out of here." It wasn't fair, but Sly's comment about the police irritated me. They had done nothing, and I had no hopes they would.

"Hold it." Sly rubbed his hand over his face. "Let me give this some thought. So much for spending my afternoon in trial preparation. This is not easy, you know."

"Sly, you're all I've got. If you don't —"

"Dammit, you act like I don't care. I do, but you made your decision, and you won't change your mind. Thus, I'm stuck with it." He hesitated and mixed in a sigh. "Before you go, I'd like you to tell your story to Donna so she can record and transcribe it. I don't know what will happen, but at least we'll have something to give to the cops who discover your body."

357

He smiled, but it appeared forced, then rose and came around the table. "The hell of it is I respect your opinions. You're a strong-willed woman who cuts her own path. I suspect you'll pull it off. In a few days or a few weeks, you'll walk in here with a shit-eating grin on your face and say, 'It's over.' And I'll say, 'Glad you made it, now let's get back to work.' " He hugged me, then stepped away. "From what you say, this Langston is tough. Be careful. Don't let your ego lead you in over your head. I'd hate to have to send a wreath to your funeral."

FIFTY-FOUR

After dictating my story to Donna, I left Sly's building wondering if I was headed down a route I shouldn't travel. Common sense sided with Sly — turn everything over to the police. But that went against my grain, against my *get-the-bastards* mentality. They had hurt and embarrassed me, and I didn't like the feeling. Sly was wrong. I was right. Besides, the authorities had accomplished nothing and, worse, treated me like a naïve rookie.

Of course, that meant finding Bruce. Not only finding him but somehow gaining his cooperation. That was the quickest way I could think of to locate the bums who framed me. I dialed Bruce's number again, got the same recording, and left another voice mail. I had no idea how often he checked his messages but hoped it would be soon. I was ready for the next step.

In the meantime, I sat in my car with the

air conditioner running, nothing but time on my hands. David was at work, Bob didn't need me involving him any deeper, and if I went home, Mom might call. Sounded like the perfect time to go shopping.

I headed for the Coral Lakes Mall. It had several anchor stores, Penney's being one of them. If I couldn't find anything interesting on sale there, I could hit Sears, Macy's, and Dillard's. And, if the big chains had nothing that caught my eye, there were about a hundred other places where I could kill time. I couldn't remember ever returning to my car empty-handed. There was always something I convinced myself I had to have.

I parked near a Penncy's entrance and headed toward the door. My cell phone played its ditty before I'd taken ten steps. Flipping it open, I saw an unfamiliar number from an unknown area code.

"Hello." I waited, hoping it was Bruce, but fearing it was another telemarketer.

"Beth. You called and mentioned one of my favorite words. Tell me about the money."

It was Bruce. My teaser worked. "We need to meet. I have an idea that will pay off for both of us."

"Tell me about it."

"Uh-uh. Not something I want to spread

across the air waves. Face to face. That's the only way it's happening." I held my breath, hoping greed won the day.

The line stayed wordless, but I could hear his breathing on the other end. I figured he was doing what I'd be doing — evaluating, sniffing for trickery, trying to find the trap in my words. "Where are you?"

"Coral Lakes Mall. Is it important?"

"Perhaps. You've got ten minutes. I'll meet you at El Toro's. Take a sidewalk table, sit facing the street, order a beer for me, and wait until I decide to show myself. I'll have a Dos Equis dark. If I see any of your friends in the area, I won't be there, and you can have my beer. Understand?"

"I would if I knew where the restaurant is. Want to give me a hint?"

Bruce chuckled. "I thought you knew everything. Just over the line in Palm Beach County on four-forty-one. Find it." He clicked off.

I headed for my vehicle at a quick pace, knowing his ten-minute deadline would be tough to meet. Bruce did what I hoped I would do were the situation reversed. He gave me a tight schedule, knowing I wouldn't have time to rally anyone to provide surveillance. What he didn't know was it made no difference. Bob was not in my plans at this time. Maybe later, but not now.

Traffic lights were my nemesis, one at almost every intersection. I nudged a few reds, but knew I risked a ticket. The state had recently authorized cameras to cut down on the number of accidents caused by crashers. Of course, the *anti*-crowd whined that it was only to produce revenue. I didn't care. I felt safer. Yellows — no problem. Everyone knew they were invitations to drive on.

In ten minutes, I parked in front of El Toro's. During the twelfth minute, I took a seat at an outside table — or that's the way I clocked it. All I could do now was see if my timeliness pleased Bruce. While waiting, I studied the area. There were few diners outside. I didn't blame them. If I were there for lunch, I'd be inside with the air conditioning. However, Bruce's instructions were explicit. Take an outside table and wait. The sun was brutal, but the umbrella provided a modicum of shade.

A waitress approached with the line used everywhere. "Hi, my name is Monica. I'll be taking care of you today. Can I get you something to drink?" Her voice and tone told me she'd used it so many times, she had no idea the words she spoke. Her poised pen said she was ready for an order.

"Two Dos Equis darks and two waters. I'm waiting for someone."

She gave me a look that said she'd like to change places with me. Her take must have been that I was waiting for a handsome man who was my afternoon delight. Handsome? Yes. Afternoon delight? No. David was the only *delight* that interested me.

The beers arrived with frosted glasses and a promise of the waters to follow. I poured mine and took small sips. Bruce's glass melted away, creating a small puddle beside his beer. He had either seen something, or he chose to keep me waiting. To hell with him, I decided. The next time Monica ventured from the air conditioning, I flagged her over and asked for a taco platter. Breakfast at my house had been a Rice Krispies bar.

When I ordered, she gave me her deep-sympathy look. She obviously thought my man had stood me up. I could only hope she was wrong. While sipping and waiting, I began to think of other ways to track Bruce. Maybe if I spent enough time on the Internet, I'd find him. After all, privacy in our country was a thing of the past. In today's world, everybody knew everybody's business and posted it.

I was far enough into my beer to wonder if I should order another when I felt a presence behind me.

"My glass is defrosted," Bruce said. "Forget the marriage proposal. Any woman who doesn't take care of a man's beer can't be a wife of mine."

"Oh, my heart is broken," I said. "Where the hell have you been?"

"Watching you." He took out his cell phone. "Before we go any farther, there's something you need to hear." He dialed. "Gerald, are you in position?" He waited, then said, "Okay, tell her." He handed the phone to me.

"Yes," I said.

"Ms. Bowman? This is Gerald. I want you to know I really like that necklace you're wearing. That's a B in the center of the pendant, isn't it? It makes a perfect aiming point. Head shots are risky. The wind gusts, or the target turns to speak to someone, and it's a miss. Chest shots are better. They don't move around so much. I hope I don't have to shoot you. Now give the phone to Bruce."

FIFTY-FIVE

A cold chill ripped through me, leaving goose bumps wherever it traveled. It could have re-frosted Bruce's glass with enough left over for a case of beer. My head snapped around like it was on a mission of its own, carrying my vision along for the ride. I saw nothing although I knew Gerald must be out there with binoculars — or a sniper scope. Otherwise, how could he read my pendant?

I handed the phone to Bruce. "He wants to talk to you." I hoped my voice was steadier than I felt. I couldn't let Bruce know the effectiveness of his ploy — damned effective.

"Okay, Gerald. From the look in her eyes, she got the message. Hopefully, this is on the up and up, and we won't have to leave a corpse for the police. Is Lodo in position?"

He went quiet, leaving me to assume Gerald was briefing him on Lodo. That sent another series of chills around my body. All I could do was wait until Bruce's melodrama played out. He had control — total control — for now. But worms had turned before. It could happen again.

"Excellent," he said. "Remember, if any of those homeless types show up, take them out. Nobody'll miss them. Cops'll give us a medal." He flipped the phone shut and looked at me. "I hope you understand how hopeless your situation is."

I swallowed, attempting to find my courage. I had to counter or the rest of the meeting would be his to manipulate. As I pondered, Monica came to my rescue, delivering my platter. The way she gave Bruce the once over, she thought I had scored big. I was tempted to ask if she would like to spend the afternoon with him. Hey, it was the best I could think of. His play with Gerald had left me befuddled.

"I'll bring you another beer and a fresh glass," she purred.

I looked up, but wasn't surprised to see that her remarks were not for me.

"Thank you, miss," Bruce said, all charm. He leaned close to her chest. "Monica. That's a beautiful name. Maybe you could bring me a taco platter also and a fresh beer for my, uh, for the lady."

I wanted to puke as she melted into his words.

"Oh, yes sir. I'll get the beers right now and tell them to expedite the platter."

She breezed away like she was on a mission for the president.

"Attractive young lady," Bruce said.

"Yeah, if you admire skinny and artificially enhanced." The moment it left my mouth, I realized what a petty thing that was to say. I was allowing Bruce to turn me into a sniveling, whiny female, rather than the rough-tough PI I had planned to be. That had to stop — and stop that moment.

I rolled my shoulders, which had tightened since his arrival. "Before we move on, a couple of facts. That was a great ploy you used with Gerald and Lodo. However, I'm not impressed. Yes, you can leave me here with a bullet through the heart, but the authorities will be on the three of you before you can have a celebratory drink. On the drive over, I left word with lots of people where I was going and who I was meeting. Among them is one of the most successful attorneys in South Florida. So you see, we're in stalemate."

He smiled and tipped his head. "Well said. But you'd still be dead."

Damn. He had scored again. It was certainly not an entertaining thought. "Enough of the bullshit. We need to talk."

He gave me a strange look. "You seem worried. Are you expecting reinforcements?"

"I don't need any. This is a straight business deal. Are you ready to talk, or are we going to play games all afternoon?"

Bruce looked at his watch. "You're right. We need to move on. What's on your mind?"

Before I could reply, he added, "But first, tell me about Tomasco? Should I expect him to arrive at any moment?"

I wasn't sure how to answer that. For all I knew, Tomasco had contacted Bruce and was the reason he agreed to the meet. On the other hand, my threats might have worked, causing Tomasco to disappear, and Bruce didn't know why. I opted for the safe way out. "If he or anyone representing him shows up, it won't be because of me. When I left him, he was physically healthy." That was true. His emotional state was another matter.

Bruce stared at me. I got the feeling he was trying to dig behind my eyes. It wasn't a pleasant state, but I returned the stare. We stayed locked together until he blinked.

"So, if I call him now," he said, "he won't have any knowledge of my helping you. Is that right?"

"Your name never crossed my lips. If he knows you were there, it's because one of the gang members talked, not me or any of my people."

Again, he gave me a pensive look. I was certain he was debating whether to believe me. There was nothing to do but sit and wait.

FIFTY-SIX

The sun pounded down like a physical presence, cocooning Bruce and me. Sweat trickled in rivulets from under my armpits, down my back, and between my breasts. I suppose it wasn't all temperature. Bruce's telephone stunt might have had something to do with it. I feigned nonchalance, pretending to be more interested in my beer than in Bruce's thought processes. It was a struggle. I'd have preferred to pace the area — or grab Bruce by the throat and choke agreement into him.

After what seemed like forever, he said, "Okay. What's this meeting about?"

Before I could respond, Monica, our waitress, was back, and I do mean back. I was afraid she'd have an orgasm while serving Bruce's food. That woman needed a man, and Bruce was her choice for the deed. I waited for her to quit gushing over him while vowing to keep David away from the restaurant.

Finally, she finished setting his platter in *exactly* the right spot, pouring his beer into a fresh frosted glass, smiling until it made *my* face hurt, and left the table. She gave him a *call-me-later* look as she walked away.

"If you've finished with your conquest," I said, "can we get down to business?"

He tore his eyes away from her swaying hips. "Sure. You called the meeting." He said this while dumping salsa into one of his tacos.

His actions said he found the waitress and his food more interesting than what I might have to say. To hell with it. I plowed on. "I want the guys who laid a frame on me. I suspect they believe they eliminated the link I had to them, their female accomplice. If so, that proves they don't know about you and me."

He crunched the taco. "What's my connection to them?" He looked at me, chewing all the while.

"Oh, come on, Bruce. How stupid do you think I am? You were following the diamonds, and I got in the way. So I'm supposed to believe you disconnected and went home? Not very damn likely."

"Better eat while your food is hot."

"Yeah, like it's going to cool off in this

371

ninety-plus heat." He was right though, and I was hungry. I prepared my taco and took a bite. Excellent. After taking my time chewing and swallowing, I said, "What do you say? Can we work together to find the diamonds?"

He ate a forkful of refried beans, then sipped his beer. "If, as you believe, I know something about where the diamonds are and who has them, why should I cut you in? I'm confident Gerald and Lodo are more than enough to help me."

I leaned forward to put more punch in my words. "All I want are the guys who set me up to take a fall. I want them to pay for Jacobs' death and, at the same time, remove any suspicion from over my head. What happens beyond that is no concern of mine."

He polished off the last of his taco and pushed his chair back. Looking around, he said, "I could use another beer. Ah, what luck, here she comes."

He was right. Monica must have been waiting for him to glance in her direction because she came racing to the table. Well, maybe not racing, but hot to trot described her movement. And I do mean it with its sexual connotations.

Bruce ordered another Dos Equis, and I asked about my water, which had not appeared. She promised both and, with another flip of her hair, headed inside.

"If you can quit watching her ass, I'd like to return to our discussion," I said.

He pulled his eyes back to me. "Discussion? I don't remember such. You were making some wild guesses about what I might know. Do you have more?"

I sighed. This was not going as I hoped. Why the hell was he being so obtuse? Time to take it back to the top. "Let me try again, Bruce. I'm not interested in the diamonds. They're yours for the taking. I'll even help you load them into your car. I want the bastards who set me up. I know you're on their trail, and I'm here to help. That's it. That's all. End of report."

He propped his elbows on the table and steepled his fingers over his lips. His gaze told me he was deep in thought. I hoped it meant he was considering what I'd said and not Monica's unspoken promises.

Damn. I shouldn't have thought of her. She showed up again.

Staring at him in adoration, Monica said, "Here's your beer and a fresh glass." She leaned over, giving him a full view of her cleavage, and slowly poured.

His eyes never wavered, drinking in the glory of her offerings.

I waited, wondering how much lower she could go without one or both flopping out. Her top didn't cover much even when she was in an upright position. I hated the games women and men played — especially when they played on my time. David popped into my mind. The games he and I played didn't count. They were different.

By the time she left us alone again, Bruce's mind had abandoned the decision track I wanted him on. Also, I still had no water.

"Well?" I said. "Can we work together?"

"Sorry. I have to get out of here before she drags me behind the dumpster. An invitation is nice but overkill is too much." He threw two twenties on the table. "Don't leave this table for five minutes. Gerald will be watching. I'll be in touch." He raised his hand and a moment later, the Mercury came speeding up.

"Before you rush off," I said. "Take this with you. If I don't hear from you in the next twenty-four hours, I'll have a long talk with the authorities. I feel sure they will take an interest in Langston Security. Even if they don't arrest you, you'll be out of business. Are you ready to abandon this area?"

He hesitated. "You know, Beth, you're cute. A pain in the ass, but cute. Keep your phone nearby. If I don't contact you, you'll need it to call the police."

The grin he gave me was not reassuring. A moment later, I watched him and Lodo drive away, realizing all I'd accomplished was learning Bruce had standards pertaining to the battle of the sexes. Or maybe he planned to come back later to collect on Monica's promises. In the meantime, I had gained nothing. On the other hand, I hadn't lost anything. The bad guys were still there, and Bruce had not said no.

Pushing away from the table, I stood and looked around. "Five minutes, my ass. Pull the trigger, Gerald. I don't think you're that stupid."

I took a couple of tentative steps and when no bullet slammed into me, picked up the pace. I didn't know where I was going, but I'd had enough of El Toro's.

My car had heated to bread-baking temperature so after starting the engine, I kicked on the air conditioner and lowered the windows, hoping to blow the hottest of the hot out. The vent blasted into my face and soon it felt good as it dried my sweat.

FIFTY-SEVEN

A few minutes later, I raised the windows and pulled out of the parking lot of El Toro's. While cooling down to a living temperature, I had decided Bruce was still my best, probably only, bet. And, since I wasn't content with moving at his pace, I wanted to know about him — much more about him. The Internet was a possibility, so I headed for home and my computer.

As I crossed into Coral Lakes, my phone rang. I hit the UConnect button. "Hello."

"Beth, it's Donna, Mr. Bergstrom's secretary."

"Yes, I recognize your voice. What can I do for you?"

"I finished transcribing your information and gave it to him. He called me in to talk a few minutes later. We're worried about you. He said you'd never listen to a man and asked me to call."

I chuckled. "He's not precisely correct,

but close enough for horseshoes. What's on your mind?"

"Mr. Bergstrom said you won't involve the local police, which is what you should do. But have you considered the Florida Department of Law Enforcement?"

"FDLE? Why them?"

"Your problems cross jurisdictional boundaries. They're statewide, perhaps nationwide. FDLE has the contacts to follow wherever the bad people go. Plus, Mr. Bergstrom knows someone he thinks he could interest in your situation."

I hesitated, my mind spinning around what Donna said. FDLE was a distinct possibility, one I liked. I had never worked with them, but word among those I knew was they were a competent and honest organization. However, I couldn't get a handle on what bringing them in might accomplish. I had no evidence, only what I surmised from my ambush and from what Bruce had told me. There was nothing I could produce to prove there was a briefcase full of diamonds that led to Jacobs' death. There was nothing tangible I could show to verify that Tomasco's import-export business was a front for illegal activities. And if my invasion of Tomasco's enclave became known, I could end up in jail.

"Beth? You still there?" Donna asked.

"Sorry. I was thinking through what you said. I think bringing in FDLE is a great idea, but not right now. Tell Sly, uh, Mr. Bergstrom, to keep his lifeline open. I'll let him know when I have something tangible to pass on."

"So, your answer is, not now."

"Yes. That's what it has to be. As he knows, I just don't have what I need yet. But when I get it — and I will — I love the idea of dumping it on FDLE."

"And that's your final answer? Think about it a moment. Mr. Bergstrom knows lots of people."

"I know you have my best interests at heart, but it has to be this way."

"I understand. That's the position he said you'd most likely take. I'll pass the word. Good luck."

Before I could express my appreciation, Donna disappeared. I knew because UConnect said, "Your call is complete." Donna must have learned her telephone etiquette from Sly.

I had closed another door that might have led me out of my problems. No one had ever accused me of being smart — hardheaded, yes, but smart, never. That left Bruce as my best bet. If I couldn't convince him to work with me, it was going to be a long, cold winter — figuratively speaking, of course. It's never cold in paradise.

Pushing Bruce to the back of my mind, I thought of Bob. He had been my rock before. Maybe he had another magic lamp he could rub. Decision time. Go home and research Bruce on the Internet — assuming I could find him — or talk to Bob. The Internet was cold and impersonal and would always be there. I needed to talk to someone. I drove north toward Boca Raton.

FIFTY-EIGHT

Bob wasn't on his corner. Bridge was. I edged up to him and asked, "Where's Bob?"

"Bar. Worried about you. Go there."

With that said, he turned his back and returned to hawking papers. Guess Dot was right. He was a man of few words. Either that or he found me boring.

I edged away from his position and, when the light changed, worked my way to the right so I could turn into the Bobby's Bar parking lot. Only received one horn toot so I figured I crossed the three lanes without insulting anyone. As on my previous trips, there were a few cars in the lot. Thinking about it, I decided there always seemed to be more cars than patrons in the bar. I resolved to ask Bob about it. Maybe he was selling park and ride spaces. If so, I needed to congratulate him. It kept cars off I-95. That meant fewer accidents bringing traffic to a halt and saved a few lives along the way.

Too bad there weren't more park and ride lots. I parked and walked into the bar.

Judy was on duty and gave me a wave and a smile. "Hi, ma'am. If you'll just have a seat, I'll get Bob. He told me to watch for you."

There was that damn ma'am bit again. However, I opted to let it go. Judy's parents had obviously taught her to respect her elders.

I went to the booth Bob called his office and settled in on the side facing the door. I had enough irons in the fire — the police, Tomasco, and Bruce. I wanted to be the first to see who entered the place. I was so busy covering that angle I didn't see Bob until he came from the rear and tapped me on the shoulder. So much for my super surveillance powers.

"Glad to see you in one piece," Bob said. "When you didn't contact me yesterday, I was afraid you might have gotten into more trouble."

"No. I thought you might need a day off."

"When you're a homeless bum, every day is off." His smile told me he was pulling my leg. "Anything new happen?"

I thought through the previous day and decided there was little worth sharing. "I did check in on you. Judy said you and Dot were asleep so I left you alone. Nothing happened."

He gave me a look. "Since you look so much more refreshed than you did the last time I saw you, I assume you and the doctor had a chance to renew acquaintances."

I smiled, couldn't help myself. "There are some things a lady does not discuss."

He gave me a knowing look, then said, "So, why are you here?"

My intent had been to tell him my suspicions about Bruce and my conversation with him, but my cell phone stymied that. It rang. The number brought a feeling of accomplishment.

"Hello, Bruce. Have you come to your senses about our little talk?" I said as I punched the speaker on so Bob could hear.

"Maybe. But first, what did you do with Tomasco?"

"I don't know what you're talking about. Like I told you, the last time I saw him he was a picture of health — a little confused maybe, but healthy." Remembering Tomasco's stagger into the bathroom, I couldn't help but smile.

Bob's grin said Dot had briefed him on our time with Tomasco.

"Uh-huh," Bruce said. "I'll believe that when he shows up and tells me himself. Did he mention any traveling plans?"

"No. He wasn't all that talkative while I was with him. Mostly just mumbled. Now, why don't you quit playing games and tell me what's up? Together, we might get somewhere. Separately, we'll just keep jabbing at one another."

Bruce's sigh came through the phone. "Tomasco has disappeared. The cell number I had for him is out of service, abandoned. I had Lodo cruise past his place, then knock on the door. The house appeared empty so Lodo took a quick look on the inside. Place looks abandoned . . . and abandoned in a big hurry. Clothes strewn around, dresser drawers hanging open, but not like someone was searching. Like someone was packing and didn't much care what he threw in the bag. As far as I know, you were the last to be with him. What did you do?"

"Maybe he went to visit his mother."

"Knock off the bullshit." Bruce's voice showed strain. "If you wasted him, fine. He's no friend of mine. But I don't want him popping up at a bad time."

"You mean, like when you have his briefcase filled with diamonds in your hands?"

There was a moment of silence. "Yeah, something like that. If you want my cooperation, you'll tell me what you did to him."

I pondered a moment, wondering just what had happened to Tomasco. Had I scared him so badly he dashed for a safer clime? Knowing how Sonny-the-Bunny worshiped himself, I figured it was a possibility. If someone had threatened to neuter him by bullet, he'd still be running. "Okay, Bruce. I'll just say I put the fear of God in him — or more accurately, the fear of Beth. It's quite possible he hit the road, never to be seen in these parts again."

There was heavy breathing into the phone, and I pictured Bruce engaged in argument with himself. Was I really so ferocious I could cause a scumbag like Tomasco to bolt? Or was I blowing smoke, trying to take advantage of Bruce's nervousness and lack of information? The former must have won.

"I'll pick you up at your house at eleven-thirty tonight," Bruce said. "Come alone and dress sexy — no jeans and T-shirt. A short skirt, the shorter the better, and a top that shows lots of cleavage. If your legs are full of cellulite and varicose veins, wear panty hose. And fix your hair. You have to look sexy enough to get through a door without the man questioning his good luck. Understand?"

I definitely understood, but didn't like it. "Suppose I don't choose to fit the hooker profile?"

"Then we have no deal. I grab the diamonds, get the hell out of town, and leave you to worry about the nasty people who want you dead. And after I rip them off, they'll be more pissed off than ever. Remember, you came to me for help. Not the other way around. I can hire a dozen women on a moment's notice to get the door open. It's your call."

I hesitated long enough to figure out Bruce was still my only option. But he needed me, too. Probably because whoever had the diamonds knew him by sight. Somewhere along the way, that would play to my advantage. "Okay, but I'll meet you and follow you to the destination. I want my car with me."

"You heard my deal. Take it or leave it."

"I bet you pulled the wings off butterflies when you were a kid. Okay, I'll play your game. My place. Eleven-thirty."

Bruce's next words filled me with dread. "No funny stuff. I want those diamonds. Whether you live or die means nothing to me." The phone went dead.

Fifty-Nine

I closed my phone, feeling the frown that covered my face.

"Interesting conversation," Bob said. "I gather you and Bruce aren't as good friends as when I last saw you together."

"You might say that." I caught him up on my meeting with Bruce earlier in the day. "He's an opportunist. My feeling is he saw me as a way to cause Tomasco to look the other way while he grabbed the diamonds. This call," I pointed at my phone, "tells me the thieves might recognize him. That could end up in a shoot-out with the bad people having the advantage. He thinks they'll open the door to a slut, and he'll be able to charge in while they're admiring my . . . uh, packaging."

"Works for me," Bob said through a chuckle.

I glared at him.

"Hey, it wasn't my idea," he said. "But,

seriously, it has worked for thousands of years. Why not again tonight? Man has always disengaged his brain when confronted with a woman's . . . uh, packaging. But the bigger question is what happens after that. Will Bruce be content to leave you and the others as witnesses to his theft? And will the others simply give up their treasure trove? Sounds like an intense situation to me."

"Damn. I bet you pulled wings off butterflies, too." I ran my fingers through my hair. "You're probably right though. Guess I'll just have to come up with a plan to bring down the thieves while keeping myself alive. No big deal. Should be a snap." I forced a smile, while attempting to snap my fingers. They didn't cooperate.

"Want my help?"

"Yes . . . and no. I've put you and your friends in enough danger. I choose to ride this one out alone."

"Be sure. And don't give our futures much thought. Remember, most of my friends have none. They live from handout to handout. Helping you has given them something to be proud of, to look forward to."

"Thanks. I truly appreciate everything, but, to throw your words back at you, it could get intense. If bullets start flying, I don't want any innocent people caught in the crossfire."

Bob sat for a moment, his mouth opening then closing. Finally, he said, "Okay. It's your decision. Sure hope you'll be around for a beer tomorrow."

Dinner with David that evening did not live up to my expectations of earlier in the day. He was not thrilled we could not have a sleepover at his place. That was the positive. The negative was he told me how stupid beyond stupid I was to meet with Bruce.

His exact words were, "Beth, for one so beautiful, so desirable, and so smart, you have to be the dumbest woman ever born. Are you sure you're not a blond? I've heard dumb blond jokes with subjects smarter than you're acting. You —"

I'm not sure how long he would have gone on, but didn't want to find out. I cut in on his diatribe. "David, please trust me. There are things here you can't possibly understand. If I don't track these men down, I'll never be able to live with myself. Every time I look in the mirror, I'll see a quitter. Would you hire a quitter to investigate a problem for you?"

He opened his mouth, but closed it when I charged on. "No. I don't think you would.

That means I'd have to turn in my PI license — and that would hurt as bad as anything I've ever done. I love being a PI. I love the feeling of helping people — even if it's only to help a spouse trap a two-timing partner. It means a lot to me, David. Can't you accept that? Can't you trust that I'm doing what I must?"

I stopped talking and squeezed his hand between mine. I'd done all I could. The future of our relationship dangled precariously in the next few moments.

He lifted his hand and kissed my knuckles. "I suppose there have been things in my life that consumed me the way your lifestyle does you. But then again, maybe not. In any case, I'll try to understand. You've become very important to me."

I returned his gesture by kissing his fingers through a smile. "Thank you, David. I knew I'd picked a winner the moment you first felt the lump on my head. I mean, a man with a touch as gentle as yours has to be a keeper." If we hadn't been in a public place, I'd have done more than caress his fingers — far, far more.

He took my hands in his. "I'm on call tonight, but that can be from anywhere. All I need is my cell phone. I'll go with you."

I hoped his words meant I was as special

to him as he was to me. But it didn't matter. He couldn't go. No way. I'd have enough on my mind without worrying about him. "That's sweet of you, David, but this isn't your kind of operation. If blood spills, it won't be because a doctor used his scalpel to save a life. It'll be bad people ripping at one another. I know how to take care of myself. And the first rule is to concentrate on me and me only. With you there, I'd be concerned about you, and that could get both of us dead."

He frowned. "So you think I'm a wuss, a softie who can't take care of himself? That's certainly reassuring. Anything else I need to know before we start picking names for the children?"

"No. That's not what I meant. You're more than enough man for me." I ran my index finger across his palm. "But going face to face with criminals is not your bag. Your bag contains medical instruments and prescriptions. Mine holds weapons and handcuffs."

David concentrated on his meal, his eyes locked on his steak. It was obvious I had hurt his feelings, but that was better than getting him killed. I'd make it up to him later, if there was a later.

His goodnight kiss — on the wrong side of my front door again — was dry, lips only.

SIXTY

I watched David drive away, a feeling of loss overwhelming me. What a stew I had brewed myself into. My desire to be the kind of woman David wanted and my insatiable drive to solve the case put me in a dilemma, but there was only one path I could follow. Someone had tried to frame me, and that someone had to pay. I didn't want to consider one of the payers might be me — if I lost David. The proverb *Pride goeth before a fall* came to mind. Damn, I hoped it was wrong. Failure was not an option. Not when I had so much riding on success.

David turned the corner and his taillights disappeared. I opened my door in time for the phone to catch me with its ringing, jerking me back into the moment. I rushed to it and picked up without glancing at the caller ID.

"Hello, Beth Bowman here."

"Are you okay? Is everything alright? I fell

asleep on the couch and had a horrible dream. We were walking along the beach. And you were being pigheaded like always. I told you not to go in the water, but you insisted. Then a big wave came along and washed you out to sea. I tried to run, but couldn't get to you. My feet sunk into the sand up to my ankles. Each step was like wading through a pool of molasses. You —"

"Mom," I said. "Slow down. Everything is fine. It was only a dream. I'm nowhere near the beach."

"Thank God," she said. "It's just that . . . that it was so real."

"All your dreams seem real. And everyone of them are about bad things happening to me. Maybe you should write a book. You could call it *Dreams of a Frantic Mom.* I bet it would sell a million copies."

"Quit making fun of me. You know how I worry about you. You took that horrible job and moved to South Florida, the crime capital of the world. I watch the news. I see what happens there. Shoot-outs and car chases and dead bodies everywhere. Plus, people driving into canals, and . . . and alligators eating people. I have every reason to worry. Why can't you lead a normal life as a wife and mother? You know I want grandchildren."

I sighed. Things had returned to normal. Every one of her lectures ended with my failure to give her grandchildren — like they were something I could purchase at Penney's and put under her Christmas tree. Her next question caught me off-balance.

"Why are you home at this hour? You should be out enjoying yourself. Is your special doctor with you?"

"Uh, no. He has patient visits in the morning," I said with my fingers crossed. "He dropped me off and headed home to get some sleep. We had dinner at a delightful restaurant. I'm going to turn in early."

"Is that all you have planned for tonight — sleep, I mean? You sure you're not going to the beach — or some other place else you can get hurt? You don't fool me with your paper-pushing stories about your job. I bet you're always involved in a fracas, putting murderers in jail, getting involved with the dregs of society. Doing things I never taught you to do."

Dregs of society, I thought. Many label the homeless with that tag. Mom's premonitions weren't so far off-base.

"Wrong, Mom," I countered, "although some of the paper cuts make it look like I've been in a knife fight. Tonight, I'm going to read in bed. It's been a tiring day. Bet

I'm asleep ten minutes after my head hits the pillow." It wasn't entirely a lie. I did plan to read to kill the time — after I decided on an appropriate slut outfit.

"So if I call later tonight, you'll be there to answer? My dream had the beach scene occurring about midnight. You won't mind if a worried mother wakes you, will you?"

Damn. If she called and I wasn't home, I'd really have to come up with a whopper. Should I piss her off now or tell her a huge lie later? Irritation was better than lying, or so I equivocated. "Yes, I will mind. Please don't call. I promise I'll be sound asleep. I may even take a sleep aid. I need my rest." Once again, I crossed my fingers behind me. I was a firm believer that crossed fingers erased lies told to mothers. After all, I read it in a book — somewhere.

"Go to bed, Beth. I'll try not to bother you any more with my mother's love."

The phone clicked in my ear. I suspected she was not thrilled with me. It's not easy being the only daughter of a woman who dotes on you and believes she has special sight. And, as much as I hated to admit it, she was too often right. A slight tremor circled around my spine. Tonight, I had to make her wrong.

SIXTY-ONE

At eleven fifteen, I stood in front of my mirror, wondering who was glaring back at me. I'd gone through my entire wardrobe, especially to the end I seldom viewed, to find the clothes I had on. A push-up bra that Sonny-the-Bunny gave me years ago. And I have to add he liked them *really* pushed up. The peasant blouse rode off the shoulder, well down on my arms, leaving little doubt what was being pushed up. The skirt was normal by design, above the knee, but a few rolls of the waistband brought it up to peek-a-boo land. The heels were three-inch stilettos. I didn't remember why I had them. I only had to hope I didn't fall off them. But, in spite of what Bruce said, I refused to wear pantyhose. Damn things were invented by a sadistic male. No woman would have dreamed them up. If the diamond thieves didn't like my cellulite, to hell with them.

All in all, I was pleased with my image. I could still turn myself into a sexy babe. Of course, if it weren't for Bruce's demands, I wouldn't be caught dead in the getup. Unless . . . I pirouetted, wondering what reaction I'd get from David dressed that way.

The phone rang. When I answered, a familiar voice said, "We'll be there in ten minutes. Go easy on the mascara, eye shadow, and other goop. I want you crying when you ring the doorbell, but I don't want black trails down your cheeks. It'll make you look like a Wiccan. Be ready when we get there. I'll call again when we get out front."

The phone clicked off, leaving me with a feeling of depression. I had expected the call from Bruce, but hoped the ring might be David. That seemed to be my recent history — hoping David would phone. I sighed, knowing it was best he hadn't. I might have caved and begged him to come with me.

Then I remembered I was one up on Bruce. I wasn't wearing mascara, eye shadow, or any other *goop,* as he called it. It took a really special occasion to get me into full camouflage, and Bruce's evening didn't qualify. Besides, I didn't intend to cry — not for Bruce or any man.

After selecting a shoulder purse and loading it with my paraphernalia, including the Beretta Bruce gave me, I walked into the living room, a bit of apprehension creeping up my spine. I didn't want to doubt my decision, but knew I'd feel better if Bob and his homeless contacts were with me — or even David. Well, only sixty-forty on David. I meant it when I told him this was not his world. He was too gentle, too compassionate. But at that moment, I'd have accepted him by my side, even if it meant I'd have to protect him. But decisions said are decisions made, and we had to live with them. Second chances only occur on the golf course when the friendly competition grants you a mulligan.

My cell phone chimed, and the little window said it was Bruce's number. I flipped it open.

"We're outside. Move it."

"I'm coming out. And a good evening to you, too." I hung up. No need prolonging things. Not like we were headed for an evening of dining and dancing.

Leaving my house, I looked left, then right. Subconsciously, or maybe consciously, I hoped to see a familiar vehicle or a head peeking around a bush. None in sight. The back door of Bruce's Mercury opened.

"Get in," Bruce said. "And you can quit

looking. We scoured the neighborhood. None of your heroes are here." He chuckled. "I hope that means you followed instructions?"

"Of course." Climbing in, I scanned the area one last time. Looked like Bruce was right. And, in this instance, he should be. None of my friends should have their lives on the line for me tonight. It was my party. I wrote the rules, and it was time to adhere to them.

I settled into the back seat beside Bruce. "Yes, your instructions just as you gave them. Where do our friends live?" Checking the front, I saw Lodo behind the wheel, and Gerald in the suicide seat. Hail, hail, the gang's all here, I thought and smiled at my jocularity. Then I realized it was gallows humor, fueled by my nervousness.

"Let's go, Lodo," Bruce said. "Stay within the speed limit and drive around a bit. I need time to bring Beth up to speed."

"Works for me," he said. "I don't need another ticket."

Bruce turned his attention to me, especially my cleavage. "You look good," he said to my chest. "You may have a future other than the PI racket. I can see where elderly guys might find you sexy as hell. You could do Viagra commercials."

I chose to ignore the remark. No need stirring a pot that was already bubbling. Plus, I didn't want him finding me too sexy. He was a man accustomed to getting what he wanted, either through guile or force.

We backed out of my driveway and headed north. Lodo made several turns and even doubled back on his route. My guess was Bruce didn't trust me.

"Okay, here's the deal," Bruce said after spending the first five minutes staring through the back window. "The people who stole the diamonds and popped Jacobs are two men named James and Jamison. Yes, the names are real. They went to ground in a dingy bungalow in Pembrook Acres. We scouted the area pretty good. It looks like a typical low-rent residential neighborhood. Probably why they chose it. Lodo will drop Gerald and me off a couple of houses down, and we'll work our way to the front door on foot. You'll stay with Lodo in the car until Gerald and I are in position. When I give the signal, you go rushing to the front door. Muss your hair before you leave the car and turn on the tears. You're in distress, scared out of your wits.

"Bang on the door and lean on the doorbell, sobbing your baby blues out. When one of them opens the door — it'll probably be on a chain — give them a sob story about some guy chasing you. Make sure you're shoving your tits in his face. Beg him to let you use his phone." He ogled my chest again. "If he's not blind, he'll open the door to let you in. Gerald and —"

"It's okay to look me in the eyes," I said without apologizing for interrupting him. "You've seen enough for tonight. Don't want to raise your blood pressure too high. You might have a heart attack. Now, about those men in the house. Won't they find it strange I don't have a cell phone. Everyone over the age of three has one today."

"Good point," he said, lifting his gaze. "Glad you brought it up. If he says anything, your battery died. Anything else you need to ask?"

"Continue," I said. "You're paying for the gas."

"Once he starts to swing the door open, get the hell out of the way. Gerald and I will be on him before he can get his eyes off your boobs."

"And if he doesn't buy my story? If he doesn't open the door?"

Bruce frowned. "That, my dear, will be your loss. I'd hate to waste you and him in the doorway, but I won't hesitate to pull the trigger. Sometime in the next hour, those diamonds will be mine. I much prefer not to leave bodies behind, but I will if that's the most efficient way to accomplish things. I suggest you crank up your acting talent. It may save your life."

My body wanted to shudder, but sheer willpower stopped it. "I'm glad you prefer not to kill me. So reassuring. Suppose I can't act?"

Bruce laughed. "You can. You're a woman. It comes with the territory. Just pretend you're faking an orgasm, but convert the energy into your sob story."

He had me there. Remember what I said about Sonny-the-Bunny? With his speed, acting was the most I'd had.

I stayed quiet for a moment, wondering how Bruce intended to leave the scene. The feeling of uncertainty was growing. Would he live up to his end of the bargain? That shuddery feeling rose again, but I forced it back down. "After you get the diamonds, I get James and Jamison alive. Right?"

"Of course. Isn't that what we agreed? You don't doubt me, do you?"

I wanted to say something cute, but decided to let it ride. No need giving him any excuse to change his mind.

"Questions?" he asked.

"I'm ready," I said. Let's get to it."

"Okay, Lodo. Point it toward Pembrook Acres."

SIXTY-TWO

Most of the lights were out on the street Bruce identified as the hideout for James and Jamison. One streetlight in the middle of the block burned, but it put out only a dull glow. Looking around, I surmised the lack of illumination might not be an accident. It was not the kind of neighborhood working people wanted well lighted. By working people, I mean drug dealers, prostitutes, and those seeking funds to buy drugs. If I lived there, I'd probably just leave the front door open and my valuables near it. It would save the trouble of replacing locks and broken windows and having people search through the house.

We cruised slowly up the street and circled the block. Bruce pointed at the house we were going to hit. I noted the absence of people on the sidewalks, but did notice one thing that made me feel better. A white Toyota Avalon rested against the curb. I couldn't read the license plate, but knew that wouldn't matter. They probably had a trunk full of plates they'd stolen so they could switch at their leisure.

"Lonely area," I said.

Bruce chuckled. "It'll be teeming with people later. The girls and the dealers with the little white bags are in the more affluent neighborhoods now. They move here when business slows down. This is kind of the last stop, the last chance to turn a few bucks — or whatever. From here, they go to bed and rest up for the next night. Besides, if anyone sees anything happening on this street, you can believe they'll see nothing. Get my drift?"

I did. Another of society's failures. Another group who believed cooperating with the police was more dangerous than tolerating the hoodlums. When would they ever learn?

"Okay, Lodo, head for the target. Drop us three doors away. After that, you know what to do. Are you ready, Beth?"

I gave him my cool look. "I was ready while you were still gelling your hair. Let's do it."

"Good. I assume you're packing. If this turns into a shooting exercise, you make damn sure you know where you're pointing your gun. We're the good guys. Try not to kill one of us."

"Then don't give me a reason," I said. "As you should remember, I hit what I aim at."

Bruce took out his pistol and checked the chamber. I noticed it was a Beretta like the one he gave me. I couldn't see if it still had its serial number.

Lodo quit circling the neighborhood. A moment later, he stopped along the curb, and Bruce and Gerald jumped out, quickly disappearing into the shrubbery.

I messed up my hair and pulled some of it into my face. So much for the time I wasted trying to duplicate a hooker's hairdo. By the time I finished, I figured it looked like it hadn't been combed in a week.

A small light blinked one short, two longs from in front of the target house.

"That's the signal," Lodo said. "I'll open your door."

"I can —" I started, but stopped when he climbed out. If he wanted to play gentleman, who was I to complain? From what I'd seen, he needed all the practice he could get. He circled the front of the car, then opened the back door and extended a hand. I took it and got out of the back.

"Nothing personal," he said and gave me a solid open-handed slap across my left cheek, hitting me hard enough to bounce me off the car.

My first impulse was to go for my gun and shoot the bastard, but calmer emotions won the day.

"Bruce says you gotta look like you been attacked. Is one enough or should I give you another? Maybe make both sides of your face look alike."

"Oh, I think one is quite sufficient," I said, rubbing my cheek. The surprise had worn off, leaving in its wake a burning sensation like someone had held my head against a burner on a stove. I felt sure it would be red enough to convince anyone I'd been hit. "But when this is over, remember that I owe you one. And I always pay my debts. Think about what I'll do."

He laughed. "I doubt you can hurt Lodo."

"Yeah? Well, don't blame me if you sing soprano after I'm through."

He laughed again. "It is time. Do what Bruce said."

I took off up the sidewalk, watching for broken pavement, moving as fast as I could on the three-inch stilts. When I arrived in front of the house, I cut across the lawn and climbed two steps onto the porch. The front light was on so I had no problem spotting the doorbell. Following Bruce's instructions, I pushed it and held it in while pounding on the door with my other fist. "Help me, please. Help me," I yelled in my best imitation of panic. With my cheek still burning, I had no trouble cranking out tears. "Help me."

It seemed like I kept the noise and the tears going so long I expected the neighbors to call nine-one-one. In reality, it was probably only a few seconds before the door swung inward a couple of inches, a security chain stopping it.

"Who the hell's out there?" a gruff man's voice said. "Quit beating on my door and leave my doorbell alone."

"Oh, thank goodness. My ex-husband is after me. I escaped, but he's right behind me. Please, let me in. Let me call the police. He said he'd kill me." I was sniffling and sobbing and flailing my hands around as if scared out of my wits. It was no accident that I banged under my boobs causing them to almost jump out of the push-up bra. The guy in the door did what any red-blooded male would do. He stared.

"I don't know," he said to my cleavage. "It's mighty late to be opening the door to a stranger."

"Please. I'll do anything if you just let me in. I need to hide. I need protection. You're a big, strong man. My ex would never bother you."

One of my pleas must have worked because he said, "Okay. But only to call the police. Then you gotta leave." He pushed the door closed, and I heard the chain rattle. A few seconds later, the door swung open.

Bruce tore by me, knocking me to the side as he shoved the man backward into the room. Gerald was hot on his heels and, like Bruce, held a gun in his right hand. I heard, then saw the man in the door stumble backwards, his rear end bouncing along the floor.

SIXTY-THREE

"Check the house, Gerald," Bruce said. "Find the other guy. Beth, get in here."

It appeared Bruce had done this before. I was impressed with his command presence.

Gerald moved fast and a moment later, brought a sleepy-looking man into the front room wearing only boxer shorts with a big hairy belly protruding above them. Not a pretty sight.

"He was in bed," Gerald said. "No one else here."

Bruce waved them to the sofa. "Have a seat, and we'll have a genteel conversation. I'll ask questions. You answer them."

"Go to hell," the door-opener said. "I got nothing to say to you."

Bruce slammed him alongside his face with the flat side of the pistol, sending him reeling backward onto the couch. Blood oozed from a tear in his cheek. "Wrong answer. How about you, Sleepy? You want to give me shit, too? Sit your ass down — now."

Sleepy complied.

Bruce turned on a lamp that sat on an end table. The closed blinds negated the danger of anyone seeing in. The two watched him, fear on their faces and question marks in their eyes.

"Okay, which one is James?" Bruce asked.

Sleepy said, "Me. Why do you want to know?"

Ignoring him, Bruce said, "So smartass here is Jamison."

"You mighta broke my jaw," Jamison said, wiping the blood off his face with his upper arm. "Who the hell are you?" He squinted. "Wait, I know you. You're that asshole who works for the smuggler, the guy who was following the courier. Shit, how'd you find us?"

"Not important," Bruce said. "But just so you know for the future — if you have one — you hide like the Abominable Snow Man at a tea party."

Gerald chuckled, and Bruce gave him a thumbs-up.

Bruce looked back at the two. "Since you know who I am, you can guess why I'm here. You have certain merchandise I was supposed to protect. You stole it. I want it back."

Jamison's eyes locked on me. "You look familiar, too. Are you some hooker I laid? Must not have been very good 'cause I don't remember much about you." He grinned.

I stood in the center of the room. I'd been watching the situation develop, admiring how professional Bruce and Gerald were. With Jamison's eyes boring into me, I unrolled my waistband, allowing the skirt to settle to its natural length, then pulled the peasant blouse up onto my shoulders, covering most of the cleavage I'd been advertising. He'd seen all the peep show I intended to give him. With that done, I pushed the hair off my face, locking it behind my ears as best I could.

"Wait. I remember now," he said. "That getup fooled me. Aren't you the broad we left with the courier's body? I thought the police would have you locked away by now."

"Your mistake, buster," I said. "You shouldn't try to do something you're not equipped to do."

"Huh? What you mean?"

"Think."

"Knock off the old home week crap," Bruce said. "I'm here for the diamonds.

Where are they?"

"Go to hell," Jamison said.

"Sorry, Mac, but I don't have time for games. Gerald, his thumb, if you please."

Gerald walked to Jamison and grabbed his left hand. With a twist, he dislocated the thumb, leaving it jutting out at an odd angle.

Jamison screamed, tears glistening.

"How about you?" Bruce said to James who was busy looking at everything except his partner's thumb.

"I . . . I don't know where they are. He hid them." He pointed at Jamison.

"You lying sack of shit," Jamison screamed, cradling his wounded hand in the other. "I ain't hid nothing."

"Ah, brotherly love," Bruce said. "Gerald, perhaps Jamison's pinky, then James' ring finger. Looks like they're both right-handed so keep it to the left for now."

Gerald didn't even bother to nod. He just followed orders, leaving both men writhing in pain.

Bruce pulled a straight-backed chair over so he faced them. "Gentlemen, let me explain the exercise. You've had a small taste of what the night holds for you. Gerald will keep breaking fingers until he runs out, then he'll address your hands. Since you probably never had much schooling, let me inform you there are twenty-seven bones in the hand. Gerald knows how to snap each of them individually. If you're still big brave men when he finishes with the hands, he'll switch to your feet, starting with the toes and work his way up. Incidentally, there are twenty-six bones in each foot." He paused and appeared to think. "Help me with my math here. Twenty-six times two equals fifty-two. Twenty-seven times two is fifty-four. Fifty-two plus fifty-four . . . Wow. That's a hundred and six bones in your feet and hands. And since there are two of you, that's two hundred and twelve bones. Imagine how much fun Gerald can have breaking each and every one of those. Of course, that many will take a while, meaning you'll have more time to suffer between breaks. When he's gotten that far, you'll probably never walk again and never hold a pencil, or more likely, a remote control. Your hands will be useless. But he won't be finished. He'll work his way up. Ankles, shins, knees, wrists, forearms, elbows. He's especially good with knees. In spite of the stress they can endure in normal activities, they are quite fragile. And Gerald knows how to get the most pain out of them."

I was fascinated with Bruce. His tone was that of a person talking about a shopping trip to the supermarket, or a boring professor giving a lecture. Nothing in his voice or inflection was sinister, but the content was almost debilitating. I shivered. From what I could see, James and Jamison were suffering the same effect.

"Somewhere along the way," Bruce continued, "you will tell me what I want to know. When you do, Gerald will quit breaking parts, we'll collect the diamonds, and leave you to your pain. Depending on when that is, you might still be able to seek medical attention. But if it's too late for you to use the phone, or walk, or call out to a passerby, you'll just lie here and die in agony." He looked at his watch. "I don't have time to waste. I'm waiting for your decision. Should I ask Gerald to continue?"

James and Jamison spent a moment looking from Bruce to Gerald to one another to their injured hands. With each switch of the eyeballs, their looks of fear increased. After a couple of revolutions, there was no doubt they believed Bruce.

"The briefcase is under the bed in the back bedroom," Jamison said. "We ain't tried to move the diamonds yet. They's all there."

"Gerald," Bruce said.

Gerald walked down the hallway.

"You wouldn't really break all our bones, would you?" James asked. "I mean, nobody's that cold."

"Of course not," Bruce said. "Not me. I don't like touching people, especially low-lifes like you. A gun is much faster and so much more sanitary. However, Gerald enjoys it so I allow him to entertain himself."

James appeared to shrink into the sofa — or try to.

Bruce stood and looked toward the back of the house. "I hope you didn't lie, Jamison. Gerald hates wild goose chases. They give him the urge to break something."

I had stood mute through the whole show, but now felt the need to remind Bruce I was there. "Hey, leave enough for me to turn over to the police. We have a deal, remember?"

"Not to worry. I won't cut out their tongues. They'll be able to bark like the dogs they are."

Gerald came into the room carrying a tan cowhide case. I recognized it as the one Jacobs, aka Garcia, carried — or its twin.

"Open it," Bruce said.

Gerald put it on a chair, flipped back the lid, then lifted a piece of thick green felt. Even in the dim light, the diamonds

416

gleamed, the most beautiful things I ever saw.

Without giving it a thought, I walked over and picked up a couple, then riffled my fingers through the others. I'm no expert, but I know perfection when I see it. They fit the definition. "My God," I said. "As Bogie said in *The Maltese Falcon,* 'The stuff that dreams are made of.' "

Bruce appeared at my elbow. "Yes. Aren't they? We've done a good night's work." He closed the lid. "Let's go, Gerald. Beth, they're all yours."

SIXTY-FOUR

The front door closed behind Bruce as he and Gerald exited, leaving me staring at its flat panel. I heard a sound and spun to see James coming at me.

"You'll pay for this, bitch," he shouted, his wounded hand hanging by his side, his healthy one reaching for me. "Get 'er," he yelled at Jamison.

There I stood, unarmed, the Beretta still in my purse. I swung my bag by its shoulder strap and felt a satisfying jar up my arm when it connected with James' head. His bad hand swung upward but never reached its destination before his face connected with the floor. One glance at him made me glad I hadn't taken the pistol out and had the foresight to bring a shoulder bag.

Jamison's plunge in my direction took him straight across James' body. "I got 'er," he screamed as he tripped.

I yanked open my purse, intent on mak-

418

ing sure there was no encore by either of them. I might not be so lucky next time.

A hand encircled my ankle, then my butt hit the floor hard. Sparks of pain rippled my spine as I watched my bag skitter under the couch. After an instant of confusion, I realized Jamison had recovered from his tumble and jerked me down. I rolled away and scrambled to my feet as he did the same.

We faced one another from a distance of about five feet. He held the advantage in height and weight and just plain orneriness. But he also had an injured hand. I hoped I was quicker and smarter.

He stomped toward me. "You gonna die. I ain't leavin' it up to the police this time." His attitude shouted his superiority. He thought I was fluff, cotton candy he could toss aside.

If I couldn't outwit that mental flyweight, I deserved to be taken out. I gave ground, keeping my distance, judging his step, watching his balance. He leaned forward, groping at me with his right hand, his left held out of danger's way. I stepped into him and slammed my head upward, connecting solidly with his chin, using the upper part of my forehead. I hit him so hard, I almost went down, but managed to stay on my feet as I watched him fall. His unnatural position on the floor told me he was unconscious. He'd never make it as a boxer — glass jaw.

I turned back to James and nudged him with my foot. No response. That brought a smile to my face. Blood trickled from his right ear. The sight didn't bother me at all. I figured we weren't even yet. He still owed me for an attempted frame for murder. I looked around, then remembered seeing my bag slide under the couch. Kneeling, I reached and snagged the strap. Once I had it back in my hands, I retrieved the Beretta, swearing to never let it out of my sight again.

Feeling weary as my adrenalin flow slowed, I plopped into the straight-backed chair Bruce had occupied. With the pistol secured in my right hand, sweeping it between my two adversaries, I took out my cell phone with my left. Time to call the police, and let them take these guys off my hands. This time, the police would have to believe me.

A series of gunshots sounded through the front wall. What the hell? I ran to the window and peered through the blinds. I saw shadows, but that was it. The darkness was almost complete. The front door slammed inward. Spinning, I saw a body crash through, gun in hand, no one I knew. His head swiveled around the room. When he saw me, his pistol started coming up in my direction, a snarl twisting his face.

Instinctively, I fired, and his motion stopped. He dropped like he'd been hit on the head with a rock. Blood spurted from his chest.

A second body came through hot on his heels. I pulled the trigger again. Nothing happened. I looked at the pistol. The slide had locked back. Oh shit. What could I do? Damn Bruce for giving me a defective street weapon.

There was a moment of silence as the second young man stared at the first lying on the floor. Then he raised his weapon and pointed it toward me, a sinister grin spreading over his face. I could see his finger tightening on the trigger. It was one of those slow-motion moments. One that would end with my death.

"Easy, Santos," a voice said, coming through the door. "You'll get to avenge Rivera, but not now." The new entry turned to me. "Well, Ms. Bowman, we meet again. Finding you here brings extra pleasure. Note that the circumstances are quite different. The pleasure will be all mine this time. You taught me an interesting game.

Perhaps we'll go some place and play it —
play until you have holes through both
breasts and worse. Of course, you may
remember I was naked when you entertained yourself. You'll be the same. Does
that sound like fun?"

I didn't want to believe what I saw — Tomasco standing in the living room. He and
the young punk who had preceded him both
held automatic pistols with the business
ends directed at me. My guess was their
weapons were more reliable than mine.

I lowered my worthless gun. "Good to see
you again. You seem to have recovered from
our last meeting. How's your sex life?" Yeah,
it might have been stupid baiting him, but I
figured I had nothing to lose. May as well
enjoy myself while I could.

Tomasco smiled and stroked his chin. "I
assure you my sex life is as strong as ever."
He glanced at his companion, then at James
and Jamison. "Are these the lowlifes who
stole my diamonds?"

"That's what I've been led to believe.
Bruce tracked them down for you." Bruce?
My spirits jumped. Maybe he'd rescue me.
Then I remembered the shots I heard before
the door burst open. Was that Tomasco and
his gang versus Bruce, Gerald, and Lodo? If
so, had they gotten away with the diamonds?

If not, what happened to them? Were they sprawled across the grass in the front yard?

"Ah, yes, Bruce," Tomasco said. "Your good friend. I hope you didn't have a romantic interest in him. He's permanently indisposed along with his two loyal companions." He nudged the punk beside him. "Santos here is an excellent marksman."

For the first time, I noticed he carried a tan briefcase in his left hand. So much for that avenue of rescue. I knew Bruce would not have given up the briefcase if he were still mobile. My last hope was neighbors who heard the shootout and called the police. If so, they should be here any moment. All I had to do was stall. Of course, in that neighborhood shootouts might be common enough that folks simply hunkered down and waited for the bullets to quit flying.

As if he read my mind, Tomasco said, "Don't expect the police to show up. The people who live in an area like this don't like cops and don't want them around. And they won't come in except with a SWAT team. It's that kind of place."

I believed him.

"Back to work," he said. "These two on the floor. Did you handle both of them — or did your boyfriend do it before he brought me my briefcase?"

Brought him the briefcase. Not likely. No way Bruce would have handed it over. But if he did, that meant he might be alive, which meant he could still ride to my rescue. Which meant I needed to stall as long as possible. "Yes. They're my handiwork. And it was a pleasure. Hopefully, you're next. Why don't you put down the gun and call off your gangbanger? We can see what happens one-on-one."

Tomasco laughed. "I see you continue to bluster no matter what the circumstances. Or you might be tougher than I thought. I'll have to keep that in mind. However, I do not intend to allow you to get the upper hand again. Santos, take care of those two."

The sinister grin returned to Santos' face as he stepped to where James lay. He held his pistol a few inches from the back of James' head and pulled the trigger. There was a sharp retort and what had been a head turned into mass of hair, skin, shattered bone and blood and brain. Then he repeated the act with Jamison. "They won't steal no more, Mr. T."

While I cringed, my stomach doing a complicated acrobatic routine, he giggled, leaving no doubt his sanity had disappeared long ago. "Can I do her now?"

"Well done," Tamasco said, then looked my way. "No, not just yet. We'll have some fun with her first. First, get those two out of here. They're stinking up the place."

Santos dragged Jamison from the room into the hallway, leaving a trail of gore along the way. Then he returned and did the same with James. My stomach wanted to add to the stench in the room, but I fought it and won.

"Now, Ms. Bowman, it's time for us to leave," Tomasco said. "Please take the lead position. And no tricks. I might not hold Santos off the next time." He walked to the front door and waved me through.

SIXTY-FIVE

A body slammed through the open door, banging into Tomasco, knocking him deeper into the living room. His gun flew from his hand and landed at my feet. I stooped and grabbed it, but before I could take out Santos, he fired and the person who crashed the party fell. I pulled the trigger of Tomasco's pistol, and Santos settled onto his knees, clutching his chest. Then he tumbled face first to the floor and lay still.

I turned back on Tomasco in time to see him in a crouch, ready to launch himself at me.

"Try it, and you're a dead man," I snarled. "And we both know it's not a game this time."

Tomasco relaxed, settling back on his haunches.

"Using your foot, push your buddy's gun over here," I said. "And please, please, try something stupid. I'd love to save the state the cost of executing you."

He stared at the pistol a moment, and I could almost see the gears turning in his head. Could he grab it and make a play for me? Would I really shoot him? Then he looked at Santos who no longer moved although blood continued to drain from his chest wound. Apparently, my nasty personality won out because Tomasco reached a foot toward the gun.

"Move slow," I said. "My hand is getting sweaty. My trigger finger might slip."

Proving he was a good listener, he followed orders, and the gun slid across the floor toward me. Without taking my eyes off him, I picked it up and slipped it into the front waistband of my skirt. "Now, get up and sit in that chair." I motioned toward the straight-backed chair that had been getting lots of use.

He followed my instruction, giving me the space I needed to get to the person who had crashed through the door, probably saving my life. As I rolled him over, I groaned. It was Bridge. How had he found me, and why had he risked his life to save me? I'd never know. I checked his carotid artery — he was dead.

I felt tears welling up, but forced them down. There would be time for mourning later. Right now, there were other things to do.

Someone jumped through the open door. I spun, my finger tightening on the trigger. The place was beginning to resemble a shopping mall on Black Friday.

"Whoa, deary. Don't shoot me," Dot said. She had stopped and held her hands high in the air, a broomstick dangling from her right one. "Remember me? I'm on your side."

I lowered my aim and turned back toward Tomasco, making sure he wasn't doing anything to increase my rage. "You see the man your thug shot," I said through clenched teeth. "One more reason I want to blow you away. He was one of the most gentle people you could have ever known. And you killed him. You might not have pulled the trigger, but you did it. You brought that animal here with you." I raised the pistol and pointed it at him. "You have no right to live."

All reason had left me. Bridge lay dead at my feet, and that picture was all I saw — well, not all. A grinning Tomasco was imposed in the middle of the image — the same Tomasco who had threatened to shoot my boobs off. My finger tightened on the trigger, squeezing on its own. I had no control.

Tomasco cowered. "No, please. I didn't tell him to do it. I don't want to die. I'll help you. I'll give you anything. Please." He rose to his knees. "Here. The diamonds. Take them. They're worth millions." He shoved the case toward me. "I'll get you more. You'll have more money than you ever dreamed of."

I didn't want his damn diamonds or his money. There wasn't enough in the world to stay me. I wanted his life. The bastard had to die. Rage had total control of me.

Dot grabbed my arm, pulling it down.

My first reaction was to hit her, knock her out of the way. But her diversion served its purpose. I reclaimed myself as reason reappeared.

"Hold it, deary," Dot said. "He ain't worth it. If you gun him down like this you'll spend the rest of your life in jail. You deserve better than that. You got that doc outside, and he's one hunk of man." Keeping a death grip on my arm, she let out one of her witch's cackles. "Besides, he's mine. I'll do him for you. I want him for Bridge."

Before I could react, she grabbed Santos' pistol from my waistband, spun, and pumped three slugs into Tomasco. His face went from pleading to surprise, and his hands reached upward. The look stayed there as he clutched his chest, then crumpled forward in slow motion. It was almost as if he continued to stare at me as his upper body hit the floor first, then his face. In that brief moment, he joined the others.

"Sorry, deary," Dot said. "I needed to do that. I really did. Hell, I ain't got no future no how. Bridge was all I had." She handed me the pistol, then knelt beside Bridge and cradled his head in her lap. "Guess you oughta be calling 9-1-1. Bob and the doc might need some help outside with them three shot dudes. I'll take care of my man. We won't need you."

Sixty-Six

Dot's words jerked me back to reality. Did she say David was outside? Yes, she had. I rushed through the open front door, leaving Dot inside with Bridge, tears streaming down her wizened face. In my last view of the room, she was stroking his cheek, her face inches from his. She cried as if her heart had imploded. And perhaps it had. Who can explain love? Certainly not I, but at that moment I knew I was witnessing it at its destructive worst. It has the ability to lift us to the heights or crush us into the depths. I hoped Dot and Bridge had shared the former because Dot suffered the latter now.

In the front yard, I found David and Bob tending to Bruce. I breathed a quick sigh of relief. Their postures said he was alive. Later, I would wonder why I cared whether he lived or died.

I expected another Valentine's Day Massacre, and there were elements of it. Gerald sprawled on the lawn, obviously dead, his pistol beside him. It was a stupid thought, but I wondered if he managed to get off a shot. Lodo's body was on the sidewalk, the pool of blood surrounding him all the proof I needed to know he was lifeless.

David knelt over Bruce's upper body and Bob beside his lower. Stepping closer, I saw that David held Bruce's hand on his chest while pushing down on it. Bob had strapped a belt around Bruce's upper thigh and held it tight with one hand, his other hand pressing what looked like a red handkerchief a couple of inches below the belt.

The sight irritated the hell out of me. While I was inside with four killers, fighting for my life, they were in the yard playing footsy with another killer. What the hell were they thinking?

"Excuse me, gentlemen," I said with as much sarcasm as I could muster. "Remember me, the damsel in distress — the one you're here to rescue?"

David looked up. "Thank God you're safe. Dot said she'd get you out of there. Do you have a baggie in your purse?"

"A what?"

"A baggie. A plastic bag. A candy wrapper. Anything I can use to close this hole."

I took another look and saw blood between Bruce's fingers and heard a hissing sound. My first aid training kicked in, and I knew what David was doing. He had to seal the wound or the lung would collapse. By applying pressure to Bruce's hand over the hole, David could get better weight distribution on the chest. But at best, that was a temporary fix. He needed something that would cover the hole on the inhale and allow air to escape on the exhale.

Kneeling, I dumped my purse on the ground. A Ziplock bag tumbled out with all the other paraphernalia. I used it for extra business cards.

David looked over. "Great. That's perfect. Dump that stuff and give it to me."

I did, and he grabbed it. When he lifted Bruce's hand, I saw an ugly hole in his chest and the hissing sound grew louder. David slapped the bag over the hole, then replaced Bruce's hand, and covered it with his own. "Where the hell are the EMTs? How long has it been, Bob?"

Bob looked up from his concentration on the thigh wound. "I don't know. Seems like forever. Probably only a few minutes."

"If they don't show quick, we're going to lose him. Beth, call nine-one-one again. We need that ambulance."

Remembering the carnage inside the house and the other bodies in the yard, I nodded. Not only did we need the ambulance, we needed about a platoon of cops.

I quickly dialed and explained to the operator how desperately we needed the medics. I also told her there were multiple shooting victims. Then I placed a second call.

"Sly," I said, after rousting him from bed. "I need you. And if you lined up a defense attorney, try to bring him along. I'm in deep shit, bodies everywhere with the cops on the way."

All he said was, "Where?"

I gave him the address.

"It'll take the better part of an hour to get there," he said. "In the meantime, keep your mouth shut — shut tight. Don't even open it to breathe. Do it through your nose only."

"Thanks, Sly." I closed the phone, then glanced toward the house. "Listen, you three," I said to David, Bob, and Bruce. I didn't know if Bruce could hear me, but I wanted him to know my words were meant for him also. "Dot was *not* here tonight. Do you understand? You have NOT seen her tonight."

David looked at me. "Why? What's the game? What happened in there?"

"Nothing you need to know," I said. "Bridge and several others are dead though, and Dot had nothing to do with any of them. But you know the cops will go after her if they learn she was present. Easiest way to solve a case. Blame it on a homeless person, especially one with a murder conviction on her record. She won't stand a chance."

When I switched my view to Bob, I saw something in his eyes I hadn't seen there before. Could it have been a new level of acceptance, maybe even admiration?

"I understand," he said. "I haven't seen her since she left the bar this morning."

"David?" I said.

He concentrated on Bruce. "I've been too busy to know who was here. But, offhand, I don't remember any woman other than you."

"What about Bruce?"

David shook his head. "I doubt he'll remember anything after the bullets tore into him."

"Good," I said. "Whoever shows up first, EMTs or cops, keep them out of the house until I signal you." I headed for the front door.

Dot sat as I had left her, Bridge's head in her lap. She was smoothing his hair from his face, stroking his face. Her tears had stopped, but only recently. Tracks of wetness on her cheeks reflected the light of the room.

I sat beside her. "Dot. I need you to listen. Can you hear me?"

Her head turned slowly in my direction, and she nodded, eyes glazed.

"You have to leave. I want you to leave by the back door. Do you understand?" I tapped her on the arm. "Concentrate, Dot. This is important. You have to get out of here."

"I can't," she said, a catch in her voice. "Bridge needs me."

"I'll take care of Bridge. He's my friend, too."

"And I have to tell the police about killing that man. What was his name again? Thomas? Something like that."

"Tomasco," I said. "And you didn't kill him. His partner did. His partner shot him three times. He wanted what's in the briefcase. They argued, then he shot Tomasco."

She went back to running her hand through Bridge's hair. "Poor Bridge. All he ever wanted was to be left alone — and to help me. And they killed him. What am I going to do without him? He was all I had."

I expected more tears, but she must have

been cried dry. Only a few sniffles punctuated her words.

"We can't help Bridge," I said. "But I know what he'd want. He'd —"

SIXTY-SEVEN

Sirens sounded in the night air, coming closer with each wail. I listened and recognized them as police cars. That didn't surprise me. If I were an EMT, I wouldn't want to be the first on scene in that neighborhood.

"Now, Dot, now. You have to leave — *now.*" I tugged at her arm. "Let Bridge rest. You know he'd agree with me. If the police find you, they'll clamp you in a cell faster than you can say Rumpelstiltskin. With your record, they'll be all over you. Quick. Out the back door." I rested my hand on hers and squeezed.

"I'll go if you want me to. But if the police arrest you, I'll be back. One of the things Bridge taught me was I have to be responsible for myself. I spent too many years letting others take care of me." She looked away, then returned to me, a new openness on her face. "You'd be surprised how many men I was a mistress to. They took care of me, and I gave them what they wanted until I got too old. Then the last one used me to support his business deals."

In spite of the urgency of the situation, her words stopped me. "How," I said, staring at her, really seeing her for the first time. Underneath the rough exterior, I saw remnants of beauty. Dot might have been a beautiful woman at one time.

Her eyes took on a faraway look. "I guess the short version is I entertained his clients, gave them what they wanted. They came in, and my job was to make sure they left satisfied. Most of the men just wanted sex. But there were others . . . Let's just say it was nasty. And it wasn't all men. There were women, too. Hard to say who hurt me the most, the males or the females. Women can be awful. And in between, the asshole I lived with used me as a punching bag. One night, I got tired of it and stuffed his balls down his throat."

She sighed. "When I got out of jail, I only knew how to do one thing, and I was too old for anybody to want it. I couldn't sell it, couldn't even give it away. That's when I hit the streets. I spent every day feeling sorry for myself, blaming society for my own weaknesses. Then I met Bridge." She stroked his forehead. "He said I was beautiful. He made me feel good about myself." She looked up at me. "I don't know what love is. I never had none when I was young, but I think Bridge loved me. And I think I love him."

A police car stopped in front, its siren dying with a last whoop.

"You have to leave now," I said. "I'll see you at the bar this afternoon. I'll take care of Bridge. I promise."

She squeezed my arm, then stood and moved toward the rear of the house. "Thank you, Beth. You're 'bout the best girlfriend I ever had." She started toward the kitchen, then turned back. "You'd better do something about your clothes. You don't want them cops to haul you in as a prostitute."

In all the excitement, I'd forgotten how I was dressed. I wondered if David or Bob had noticed. Hopefully, they were too busy with Bruce. It didn't matter. After earlier unrolling the waistband of my skirt and pulling the peasant blouse up on my shoulders, there was nothing more I could do. The push-up bra was what it was — an advertisement in any language. So be it.

When I heard the back door close behind Dot, I picked up the pistol she'd used on Tomasco and wiped it with my skirt. I

440

needed to erase or at least smudge Dot's fingerprints. Once I felt pretty sure they were gone — or as sure as I could be — I fumbled in my purse for a tissue. Holding the pistol by the barrel with the tissue, I placed it in Santos' hand and closed his fingers firmly around it. Then I let the hand fall back to the floor. His fingers relaxed and the gun lay on the palm of his out-stretched hand. Hopefully, the only prints the police would find would be Santos'.

I stood and looked around the room, studying the crime scene like I did when I was a cop in Dallas. James, Jamison, To-masco, and Bridge, no problem. They were killed with Santos' gun, which now bore only his prints — I hoped. The thug who had crashed through the door shot with my pistol? That could be a problem since it was a street gun. Nothing I could do about it though. After all, he was armed, and I suspected bullets from his gun would match some the authorities would find outside. The most they could nail me with was hav-ing an unregistered weapon. Santos was shot with Tomasco's pistol, which also car-ried my prints. Another case of self-defense. I took a deep breath. It was as good as I could make it with such short notice.

Show time with the cops. I walked into

the front yard and waited beside David.

The first police on scene were uniforms, and they were not thrilled with what they found. They seemed to think eight bodies and one seriously injured man was a bit much. Their initial actions toward Bob and me were aggressive, having us drop and spread, doing the whole ten yards.

David refused to move from his position hovering over Bruce. The police relaxed a bit after David showed his medical ID and told them that treating Bruce was more important than their procedures. His exact words were, "Get your hands off me. This man's dying and if you don't let me treat him, I'll see that you and the city are sued into bankruptcy." That seemed to have a soothing effect on them. After that, he vouched for Bob and me, and the cops said we could get up, but not leave the yard.

The uniforms secured the area, then started with the yellow tape. In the meantime, the EMTs arrived and assisted with Bruce's care. A few minutes later, they loaded him into the ambulance and roared away with David still hovering over him. That left Bob and me to face the authorities.

Next on the scene were my old buddies, Bannon and Sargent. The thought crossed my mind that they might be out of their jurisdiction, but I decided not to mention it. Even if they had no authority, my shaky position said I should keep my mouth shut. With all the bodies lying around, I didn't need them challenging me.

More plainclothes joined them, ones with local authority, and the fun really began. Since I was the only person left alive who knew what transpired inside the house, they were most interested in me. It was touch and go for a while as I stammered, stuttered, and stalled, not saying much except my attorney was en route. I believed it. Sly wouldn't let me down.

Thirty minutes after that, a man and a woman in jeans and T-shirts with pistols on their hips arrived and introduced themselves as FDLE agents. Sounded good to me. At that point, they looked like the cavalry. They told the locals Tomasco's crimes were statewide, then took over and walked me away from the group. I could see that Bannon and Sargent were not happy with the change and were deep in conversation on their cell phones.

I continued my stall, saying I was waiting for my lawyer and he advised me to say nothing until he arrived. They demanded to know who he was, so I gave them Sly's card.

After advising me they knew he handled civil cases, not criminal, the agents, Montee and Nichols, nodded and agreed to wait. I wanted to ask them why they were there, but decided to save it for Sly. It had to be his doing.

I glanced toward Bannon and Sargent and saw them leaning against their car, uglies all over their faces. I gathered the phone calls had not brought the results they wished.

After another ten to fifteen minutes, Sly's Mercedes arrived, and he and a man I'd only seen on TV emerged. Salvatore Bercini was one of the top defense lawyers in South Florida. I didn't want to guess what his hourly rate was, but I was sure thrilled to see him.

SIXTY-EIGHT

Bercini took charge, which wasn't difficult since every cop on the scene knew him and his reputation. Part of that reputation was he never attempted to make the police look bad. Without much effort, he backed the authorities off, even the FDLE agents, saying he needed to consult with me and hear my story. He said it in such a positive way even I believed it.

We sat in Sly's car, and I elaborated on the tale I told Dot I'd use. The first thug, Rivera, Tomasco had called him, burst through the door armed and tried to shoot me. I got off the first shot. Santos killed James and Jamison, following Tomasco's instructions. Then Santos and Tomasco argued about the diamonds, resulting in Tomasco's death. When Santos turned his gun on me, Bridge saved the day, only to be shot by Santos. His interruption allowed me an instant to pick up Tomasco's pistol, and I used it on Santos, leaving me the only person still standing. I emphasized that the real hero of the evening was Bridge. If he hadn't crashed through the door, I'd be dead, and Santos would be free and on his way to fencing a million dollars or so in diamonds. That was my story, no loose ends for anyone to pick at. I stuck to it through several iterations.

I'm not sure Bercini believed it, but he went along. People in his business always have clients who are *innocent.* I guess it helps them sleep at night.

I almost felt sorry for the police. They had dead bodies all over the place and no one alive to arrest. Bob and I went to the police station where I made a formal statement of the night's events — under the supervision of my attorney, of course. Later I learned that Bob did the same thing with Sly beside him without mentioning Dot. He could only talk about what happened outside. The inside story was all mine. After Bruce's condition stabilized, David joined us at the station house and corroborated Bob's version, with Sly standing by his side.

In this situation, a little perjury did no harm. My hope was the story would stick, and the police would close the case.

Finally, after what seemed days, but was

only a few hours, the police released David, Bob, and me with warnings they'd want to talk with us again. We crawled into David's car and headed for Boca Raton to deliver Bob. Dot was on her own to get back to her home turf, or wherever she chose to go to grieve.

My curiosity was at a fever pitch about how David, Bob, and the rest had made it to my rescue when I had no idea where Bruce was taking me. I'd watched Lodo scanning his rearview mirror and Bruce and Gerald checking behind us, looking for surveillance.

"Not too difficult," David said, smirking. "We just applied our PI skills and, *voilà,* there you were. What? You think —"

I smacked him on the arm. "If you don't tell me, I'll . . . I'll go to a different doctor the next time I bang my head." I laughed so he'd know it was a joke. The last thing I wanted was a different doctor feeling me up.

"What do you think, Bob? Does she deserve to know?"

"I suppose," he said. "Might teach her a whole new technique."

"All right you," I said. "I —"

David cut in. "After you sang me your version of *By Myself,* I —"

"What? I didn't sing to you."

"Sure you did," David said, chuckling. "You know, the lyric goes something like *I'll go my way by myself.* That's what you said, you'd do it alone and didn't need any help from anybody. With that reverberating in my ears, I called Bob. He agreed you'd be helpless without us. So he brought in Dot and Bridge, and I picked the three of them up. Then we hid out near your place. When you roared away with Bruce, we followed at a discreet distance.

"Bridge was behind the wheel. He said he used to drive for some *guys,* so I gave him the keys. Since I'd seen Bruce and his henchmen operate, I expected they'd be watching behind them. It was tricky because they kept doubling back and running around the thumb to get to the elbow. There were times when I doubted we would keep him in sight. Fortunately, he had that big white Mercury and traffic was light. It was easy to find you each time we got lost — until the last time.

"We'd have been there sooner, but he shook us off at the last minute. If it hadn't been for the gunfire in the front yard, we might not have found you again. Bridge was circling in the area where we last saw you when we heard the shootout. Anyway, we rolled up to find Bruce wounded and the other two dead. You know the rest. Bridge headed inside, and Bob, Dot, and I tried to save lives. When we saw Gerald and Lodo were beyond help, Dot took off for the house. Her loyalty to you is admirable." He smiled. "And that's the secret of our success. Now it's your turn. What happened inside the house?"

Before answering, I reflected on Dot. It wasn't me she swore loyalty to, but the man she loved. And that's how it should be. But she was tough. She'd led a life of having to be tough. She'd survive.

After a moment, I gave them the police-approved version, ending as we pulled into the parking lot of Bobby's Bar. At that point in the investigation, I didn't want anyone to know the full story. Even Dot only knew the last part. Everyone except Tomasco was already dead when she burst into the room. The less they knew, the less they could perjure themselves.

After saying our goodnights to Bob, David and I headed for Coral Lakes. My adrenalin flow had backed down to almost zero, and I was in full letdown mode. But I had no desire to spend the night alone. Even if there had been no David, I didn't want to sleep with the dreams I expected to have.

"Are you okay?" he said. "Want to stop for a nightcap or something?"

"No. Alcohol is not the high I need now. The *or something* sounds much better. Are you taking me home . . ." I asked, hoping the answer was not yes.

"I should," he said. "Everything my dad ever taught me says you'll spend your life rushing from catastrophe to chaos to self-destruction until you are no more. I can see many sleepless nights in my future, wondering if you're all right or lying somewhere bleeding out." He squeezed my hand. "However, I feel like a moth attracted to a bright light. I don't want to turn away. Ms. Bowman, I fear you've squirmed and squiggled your way behind my clown's façade."

He smiled and lay his hand on my thigh. "Besides, my medical training says you should have a full body examination. After what you've been through tonight, there may be wounds or injuries you're not aware of. If not found, multiple problems can occur. Only an experienced doctor can spot and diagnose such things. Thus, we shall go to my place where I can properly scrutinize every inch of your gorgeous body and give you the tender loving care you deserve."

He waggled his eyebrows.

ABOUT THE AUTHOR

Randy Rawls is a retired US Army officer and Department of Defense civilian. He is the multi-published author of the Ace Edwards, Dallas PI series, as well as of short stories in various anthologies and *Thorns on Roses,* a South Florida thriller. Living in South Florida, where fact and fiction run together, gives him a rich environment in which to harvest plots. He smiles because life is fun.